Enfilade

*En-fil-*āde

*Noun: a discharge of firearms that sweeps a line or position
from end to end;*

a number of things arranged as if threaded on a string.

ISBN: 978-0-9934330-0-9

This book is a work of fiction. Names, characters, businesses
and events, other than the particular places and WW1 battles
described, are used fictitiously. Any resemblance to actual
persons, living or dead, is entirely co-incidental.

Typeset by alain.grint@sfr.fr

Printed and bound in Great Britain by
Clays Ltd, St Ives plc

Front Cover: Original photograph, taken by
WP Collier of Bellingham, of farm horses
from the North Tyne Valley in Bellingham, 1915.
From the collection of the late V. Blankenburgs
in Northumberland Archives.

Back Cover: Mill Road CWGC cemetery
near Thiepval,taken by the author in June 2015.

Cover graphics by Slim Palmer

ERGO PRESS
Hexham
United Kingdom

FOREWORD

Enfilade came into being because of two photographs, both taken during the Great War. The first is of a group of women standing in the street, anxiously waiting for letters from the front. Some of them would no doubt eventually receive Army Form B104 … notification of the death of a loved one. The other photograph, which became the front cover, was of farm horses of the North Tyne valley, requisitioned for service, lined up before being led to the station for the first leg of their journey south to war. Both of these moved me beyond telling, and were a revelation: I realised that I had at last found the motivation to write my first novel.

"The pity of war", Wilfred Owen's telling phrase, embraces not only the appalling suffering of men in battle, but also the effects on their families, including the miserable fear and loneliness that resulted from their absence. Some families never recovered, even when the menfolk returned home, apparently unscathed. It was a brutal time, one that brought out the best and the worst in people, as do all wars of course. My characters are caught up in the Great War, but also in a personal battle: the pity of love.

ACKNOWLEDGEMENTS

Writing is a solitary occupation, but while I was writing Enfilade I was fortunate in being surrounded by friends and colleagues who encouraged and cajoled me. They trusted me to finish what I started.

Enfilade takes place in the Great War, and I have my husband, Alan Grint, to thank for his enduring support, and for his help in making sure that the novel is historically accurate; for taking me to walk the battlefields so that I could better describe them. He also typeset the book for publication, a painstaking task, for which I am hugely grateful.

My thanks to Ruth Sadler, Helen Speakman, Andrew Bowden and James Vance, my readers; they convinced me that Enfilade was taking shape ... that it was complete. Thanks also to Tracy Stewart, my editor, whose red pen was light but incisive.

Slim Palmer, my friend, another writer and a graphics wizard, created exactly the cover I wanted. He's done this many times for Ergo Press, and deserves a medal.

* * * *

Enfilade is dedicated to the men of the Territorial Battalions of the Northumberland Fusiliers who died in the Great War, and to the women they left behind.

ONE

Jim

They began the move forward just after midnight, treading steadily behind their guide in the moleskin darkness. The route to the front was new to Jim, although the rhythmic drumming of 'C' Company's boots on the hard-packed floor of the communication trenches was oddly reassuring and familiar. It took a couple of hours; their movement was interrupted every few minutes by shells landing, some close by. There was no direct hit, but the hideous din prevented any communication. Occasionally they could hear sniper fire from a distant part of the line as flares glowed briefly, malign fireflies in the night sky. Earlier that evening his sergeant had been humming Onward Christian Soldiers as he cleaned his rifle, maybe ironically; the tune was fixed in his own mind now, a vexing mental accompaniment to the march.

Zero hour was six twenty. The men weren't daft: they knew they were going from one rotten position to another even worse, and they were sobered by their own imaginations. When they arrived and spread along the line, some of them hunkered down, eyes closed; others just stood, exchanging the odd word, smoking. They were waiting for the rum to arrive, then dawn, so they could get it over with. Jim made his way through the company, checking kit and trying to temper the mood, but the response was merely respectful; there was none of the usual warmth or humour. One of his lieutenants pushed his way through the line to find him.

'It's a right bugger, Sir. I suppose we couldn't hold back a bit; let the London lads do the business first? Before we go over?'

Jim grimaced in the darkness, wryly amused at the very suggestion of postponement. The man might be joking, but he wasn't wrong ... not if they hoped to make it past the wood ahead on their right, now unseen in the darkness, to reach the enemy trenches beyond. They needed the division on their right – the 47th Londons – to move forward alongside them, cutting a deadly path through the trees, clearing out the enemy. As it stood, there was a dog-leg in the line leaving his lot out in front and vulnerable. They would be in clear view of the machine guns to the east in High Wood when they advanced in the morning, exposed to bullets hammering the length of their forward line.

'We've been trying to shell the bastards out for weeks ... *months*; it'll not be easy for the Londons, whenever the whistle blows.'

'They're hoping to have the wood cleared by seven, Sir. They're going in with some of the land ships. That should set the Hun running if nothing else does.'

'Surely. All we need to do is to get round the back of the wood ... cut the bastards off from behind.' *All we need to do.*

'True enough. We'll be there in time for a late breakfast, Sir.'

What he wouldn't give for some proper Northumbrian bacon and eggs. Still-warm bread and butter to mop up. Tea with fresh milk.

Jim left the lieutenant and moved along the trench; he wanted to be alone for a while. Further on there was an old dugout caved in by a shell, comfortably rounded. He leaned against the crumbling recess and lit a cigarette. There'd been no time since yesterday to weigh up his unexpected meeting with Ivan, but in his gut he knew that whatever he'd said, today he wished he hadn't said it. He was glad he'd run into him, and not just because of the photograph. He pulled Ivan's envelope from his pocket and slipped the photo out. It was too dark to see, but he knew the image so well that it was enough just to hold it.

Ivan was right: he should never have left it behind, whatever she'd done. He'd left it at home deliberately, to hurt her, and he'd had no right to do that, however angry he'd been; she was part of him … had been ever since he met her, from the first minute, from the second he'd looked up and seen her and been lost. Only Ivan had understood. And they'd been such good friends, the three of them, larking about like bairns. Was it there from the beginning? Surely he'd have known. He pushed the photograph back into the envelope and slid it into his tunic pocket. There had to be some sort of future for them. If this bloody war had taught him anything, it was that it was weak not to forgive; he had to release himself from all the damned pain and give to her what he most needed himself.

Nearly time.

He walked back to his men, making sure every soldier was ready. In the pall of first light he could make out their faces, dull with fear and fatigue. Few, if any, had slept at all. This was the worst time, just before zero hour. He looked back along the trench; the company was standing-to, each soldier gripping his rifle stock, hands sweating in spite of the cool air. How many of them were praying? And where the hell was the rum?

As if he'd heard, the runner arrived, breathless, the heavy

clay jar bouncing by his side. Jim began the routine walk along the line with his sergeant, greeting every man by name and doling out a generous ration – well beyond the regulation slug. As he'd hoped, it brought a smile to nearly every face, the rum ration. Sometimes he wondered whether there'd be any fighting at all without it.

He looked at his watch, synchronized with others across the eight mile front line. *Six nineteen.*

'Over the top in one minute, lads.' His voice was steady. He felt calm and impassive, as a man is when the worst has already happened.

They'd been warned to expect a new kind of barrage, to be tried out with this push. When they went over the top their own artillery would be firing over their heads at the enemy as they moved forward: the gunners would be adjusting the sights and shelling, yard by yard, in front of them, clearing any Hun sheltering there, giving them a straight passage over no-man's land. He'd practised the pace: fifty yards a minute. Sounds good, if it works. *We'll see.*

At six twenty – zero hour – he led his men up the ladder and over the parapet, heading straight for their first objective, a trench a couple of hundred yards ahead. The din was hellish as their own guns delivered the promised barrage over their heads and onto the ground in front of them, pounding the earth where it had already been battered for weeks on end. Dust rose in wild, turbid clouds, choking the air. Even without that it was hard walking at a measured pace; the terrain was pitted and cluttered with debris. At least the recent sunshine had dried it out so they weren't wading through mud. *Keep the pace steady … good lads.* No point in running even if they could: they'd be killed by their own artillery. At fifty yards a minute he kept the lead; only a few minutes to Hook Trench, with little to stop them. The Hun must be firing back, surely, but nothing much seemed to be getting through. Maybe the bastards had already retreated. *Maybe they weren't even out there.* He'd expected far worse, but the guns behind them had done a lot of damage, and they took their section of the trench without too much trouble. No casualties. *Onward Christian Soldiers ...*

His company was digging in when it started: machine gun bullets began to zing over them as they hunched in the trench: enfilading fire from the north-west corner of High Wood. *Oh Christ ...* the 47th Londons must be held up. What about those bloody great fighting machines? Where were they?

He blew the dust from his watch face. Six minutes before the next advance.

Zero. Same again: keeping the pace, their own artillery barrage whining over their heads, a mind-numbing metal umbrella that smashed the earth in front of them as they advanced. He was steady and his men were steady, but bullets were zipping at them from machine guns ratatatting in the concrete placement at the corner of the wood. His men were being scythed with hot metal ... he turned to urge them on. *Come on, lads, not far to go now ...*

Then he fell, his heart broken for the second time, but this time the pain eased after only a few seconds.

TWO

Elsie

Elsie was sick to death of men dying. She flipped back the lace curtain to see what was going on across the square. As she expected, the women were already there, grouped in tense silence. Their bodies were stiff with the strain of waiting, and even with their thick shawls they looked cold, facing a wolfish north wind that tore at their skirts and chased the fallen leaves in restless circles. It happened most days now: as the postman cycled away, job done, some wife or mother would bow her head, crushed by the first few seconds of a broken life. The others would share her pain; they'd help her home and close the curtains so the neighbours would know. Then they'd stoke the fire and put the kettle on, keeping their voices low, knowing that no amount of tea could wash away the words: 'It is my painful duty to inform you ...'

There was grime in the corner of the glass pane. Elsie scraped at it with her thumbnail. It wouldn't have been there when Jim's mother kept house; it was all gleaming brass and polished wood in her day, but now the place seemed determined to get its own way. Mind you, it was still better than if the old bitch had lived. True enough, if his mother hadn't died Jim would have bought them a house of their own ... but she would still have been in the same town, with her

6

mouth like a terrier's arse.

The flimsy curtain fell back into place as she slipped off her perch at the parlour window. Every day she came and watched, half wanting to be out there, taking part in the ritual. Why not? She knew why not, but before the thought could hold her back she walked briskly to the hall, grabbed her coat and opened the heavy front door. She stood on the top step, pushing her thin arms into the sleeves and fastening the leather buttons, uncertain now that she felt the cold air on her cheeks. The unexpected movement caused a ripple of interest in the huddle of women across the square; there was nudging and one or two words exchanged. Head up, she strode purposefully across the cobbles and stood slightly apart and behind, but making herself one of the group nonetheless.

'Wey, look what the wind's blown ower!'

The speaker hadn't turned to face Elsie; her gaze remained fixed on the road and she was addressing everyone and no-one in particular. Elsie thought for a second that she'd misheard, but then another of the women turned completely round, her narrow face twisted, sneering.

'What's brought ye out, Mrs Errington, with yer fancy coat?'

She knew the woman. Not well, but her daughter had been in Elsie's class at school; they'd been kind when her mother died, but there wasn't even a hint of it now. Another of the women joined her, leaning forward to jab her finger in Elsie's face.

'Ye've no place oot here with the likes of us. Why divven't yer gan back in and sit with yer bliddy feet up like, 'til yer fancy husband comes haem safe from his shop?'

'I just thought …'

'What? What d'yer think? Howay, lasses … Mrs Errington's gannen to tell us poor folk what she thinks!' The woman was

7

putting on a high pitched voice and simpering smile, her pale eyelashes fluttering comically. In spite of everything, most of the women smiled, glad enough to relieve some of their tension at Elsie's expense.

'Gan on – git thesel away. Y'er not wanted heor.'

One of the woman shoved her; not hard, but hard enough to make Elsie stagger backwards and fall, her heels slipping on the damp cobbles. They ignored her now, turning back towards the empty street. Without a word, Elsie clambered back to her feet. Not waiting even to brush the muck and leaves from her coat, she walked carefully across the square back to the house, head and eyes down, struggling not to run as the boldest of the women turned and called her name, hoping for a bit more fun. She opened the front door and slammed it behind her.

Who cares what they think? *Who bloody cares?*

Back in the kitchen, she shovelled more coal into the range and made a half-hearted attempt to clean up the dust, lips pressed hard together to stave off the tears that threatened to make the humiliation even worse. The rejection made her livid – at the women, at their misunderstanding of her and at every bit of running this damned house. She didn't have enough help really, just a girl, but she refused to have any more servants when by rights she should be one herself. It was embarrassing enough having Agnes … no wonder the women didn't want her with them.

Another thing, the endless meals. She glanced at the grandfather clock in the hall: less than an hour to make dinner. How many to feed? Jim, Lily and her, probably Ivan if he can get away, and Agnes in the scullery. Four then; five if she was going to eat, which she supposed she'd have to.

She nipped back through to the parlour and shifted the curtain again to see what was happening. She watched as Dorothy Charlton sank to her knees in the road with the official letter pressed against her eyes like a starched handkerchief. Postie was pedalling off down the street, head over the handlebars. Dorothy's friends were huddling around her, groping for her hands. Elsie could imagine how they'd feel: *Not my Jimmy, not my George, thank God.* Anyone could see it: you shared the sorrow but you hid the relief ... a bit of time off until you stood there on the draughty corner again, waiting your turn.

Poor soul. God help you. She doubted it even as she thought it.

She stepped briskly back along the passage to the scullery, found the pan of potatoes Agnes had peeled and put them on to boil. They were grown in their own back garden, planted in spring by the men, dug up and cooked by the women. Well, by *her*, because 'I'm needed in the shop' Lily never lifted a finger once she'd walked into the house and tossed her hat onto the hall stand, always with that sideways look at herself in the narrow mirror. She wondered if Lily realised how easy it was to read her thoughts. She might as well just say it: *why keep a dog and bark yourself? If Jim wants his shabby little wife to run the place then let her, but don't expect any help from me.* Even after four years it was no better. She smiled to herself. It really did offend her sister in law to live in the same house as her. Well, tough. She laid the table and carried the joint through from the pantry.

* * * *

'It was Fred Charlton. Today, I mean.' They were sitting at the kitchen table. Agnes had brought the vegetables through then retreated to the scullery for her own lunch.

Elsie helped herself and glanced round to see if they'd understood. Of course they had, but no-one paused; heavy spoons still clattered on china serving dishes. When the war began, if one of them brought news of a death they used to put down their knives and forks in a kind of awkward respect. But that had been months ago, and too many men had died since then to keep it up.

'Poor bugger; his mam'll be past herself. He'd no brothers and sisters, and he was the money in the house: his pa died years ago.'

She knew Ivan's feelings about Fred's death had to be stronger than his words: the young men of the small town had been to school together; they drank together, played football together on a Sunday; they'd won the local league. He glanced towards the scullery.

'We should tell Agnes; they live in the same row, and her brother's Fred's best mate. Was.'

'No, better *not* tell Agnes, least not until it's time for her to go home; she'll get nothing done all afternoon for crying'. Lily helped herself to more potatoes.

'You're all heart, Lil; let's not allow the lass's feelings to get in the way of the cleaning up, eh?'

They ate in silence. Another local lad dead ... underground for ever without a Davy lamp, just when he thought he'd escaped. Fred had been one of the first of the local miners to volunteer; he'd been in the shop, chattering as he bought his Woodbines and chocolate for the journey. His grinning face had shown not a glimmer of fear: all he had to do was scrawl his signature and take the King's shilling – his ticket out – just like that. Freedom. Elsie and Jim had walked down to the market place to see him and the others off, and there was quite a turnout ... the vicar was there, shouting a blessing, his robes billowing. You could pick out the mothers, gripping the hands of their bewildered younger children, standing back and trying not to fuss as their sons joined the jostling crowd. Flinging haversacks over their thin shoulders, they were setting off to walk to Newcastle to sign up: impatient and patriotic, itching at the prospect of sunshine and smouldering French girls: 'You should see the pictures in them magazines'; they'd been dreaming about women with tight bodies and loose morals for weeks. Elsie and Jim had stayed alongside the mothers and wives, waving as the colliery band led the lads on their way. They were playing one of the jaunty songs they usually played at the Miners' Gala, boys marching behind proud fathers playing tubas and trumpets, hollering out the chorus ... *Oh! me lads, ye shud a' seen w'us gannin* ... their voices, some barely broken, could still be heard as they crossed the bridge over the Tyne.

Elsie began to stack the plates as Jim lit a cigarette and reached over to pluck the local paper from the sideboard. Ivan pushed his chair back to leave the table. He rolled his sleeves up and carried the plates out to the scullery for Agnes to wash. Already irritated with her, he tried to shame Lily into helping:

'Are you going to get your fat bottom off that chair and give us a hand, sister mine?'

Lily gave a corrosive little smile but made no attempt to help; instead, she pushed her pudding bowl towards Elsie and stood up. As she was leaving the room she half turned, as if she'd just had a thought.

'It's strange there's no word for it.'

'For what?'

'For a woman whose son's been killed. Or a daughter for that matter. There's "widow" if your husband dies, but nothing for the likes of Dorothy Charlton ... for if you lose a child. Of course there's "barren" for women who can't even get started with one, but that's different. Don't you think so, Elsie?' All of this was in a sweet voice, like a school teacher

11

talking to a class of seven year olds.

Before Elsie could respond, Ivan did:

'You'll need to bridle that nasty tongue of yours, our Lily. Unless your Frank's a mouse who won't bite back.'

'Dear me, Ivan, I'm just showing some sympathy for sad Mrs Charlton. She *nobody's* mother now ... but she's not the only one, of course.'

'Sympathy? You'll be calling round to hold the poor woman's hand, then?'

'She has other women for that: friends with their own boys away.'

'Just as well. She doesn't have to rely on your tender heart, then.'

'Ivan, don't. Leave it be.'

He turned to her – *what?* – he didn't want to give way, but she shook her head at him and picked up Lily's bowl, placing it carefully with the others as if it were fragile and valuable.

'You see? Elsie understands what I mean.' Lily had her arms folded; she was leaning against the door jamb, enjoying the moment.

'I'm sure she did. We all do.' Ivan was looking directly at Lily, but he was talking to his brother, waiting for him to throw his newspaper down, to bridle Lily for once. Nothing. Lily smirked and left the room. Ivan looked from her to Jim, then back to her, eyebrows raised, as they listened to Lily's heavy tread on the stairs. Elsie felt shamed. It was *all* shameful, even the things she couldn't help.

'Will you manage, Elsie?'

'Of course. You go ... but maybe through the back?' She nipped along the passage and came back with his jacket and cap. She didn't want him meeting Lily in the passage if she came back down and started again.

'You're soft.'

12

'You mean daft?'

'No, just soft.' He took his cap and jacket, then left by the scullery door. She followed him out and stood at the window, watching as he leaned over to fasten the back gate behind him. Back in the kitchen she lifted Jim's Hexham Courant to wipe underneath it. Without taking his eyes off the page he smiled and grabbed her hand and kissed her warm, damp fingers. She leaned over and brushed her lips on his cheek.

'Come here, sweetheart.'

He pulled her onto his knee; took the cloth from her hand and tossed it onto the table. She rested her head against his chest as he reached down and put his hand on her ankle below the hem of her skirt, playing his fingers up and down her leg.

'You mustn't mind her.'

'I don't. Not all the time anyway.'

She leaned back as his fingers reached the bare flesh above her stocking, smoothing, trying to restore her.

'Ivan's like a cockerel; he just keeps coming back. He always did. It was the same when we were bairns. She's best ignored, then she'll stop.'

But Lily's footsteps in the hall made them both start, and she slithered off his knee and reached for her cloth again. Lily was pinning her hat in place as she opened the kitchen door.

'I'm going back along; I've things to do before Frank arrives.'

Jim nodded as he reached for his cigarettes. 'I'll follow you; just give me an hour.'

'An hour? But Jim, Frank's coming ...'

'I can be longer if you like?' He went back to his newspaper.

THREE

Jim

With Lily gone, Jim lit a cigarette and took another ten minutes with the paper. His eyes flickered over reports of local fat-stock prices and church fundraising, homing in on articles about recruitment and the war effort. There were more names of the local dead, all younger than him: the Births, Marriages and Deaths section was all out of kilter. So many weeks and so many names had driven him down to Hexham to sign the damned register. They could call him up now, if they needed him. The whole thing had made him angry: wasting a whole morning, standing in a queue with beardless boys as anxious to enlist as he was not to. He'd had enough of messing about with guns when he was a lad in the OTC at school. These days he'd shoot the occasional rabbit, a pigeon now and then, but this? The thing was, he had nothing against the Germans and had no interest in trying to kill them unless they crossed the channel ... and even then he'd hang back until they reached the Tyne. The longer this war went on the worse it sounded and the less he wanted any part in it. Too late now, though: he'd arranged to have a word with Archie and he'd know soon enough.

He needed to think who was going to take his place in the business if he went; someone who would make sure the shop kept its end up. People relied on them: it was unthinkable just to close the door and wait for peace. Ivan could do it; he was a worker – no doubt about that. But he had his smithy to run, and even if he hadn't, he'd do anything rather than be a grocer … often said as much. Worse still, another few months and he could well be called up to fight, unless things changed. They'd used up all the regular soldiers, all the volunteers; before long there'd be no choice at all.

Lily? She knew the business backwards and forwards but she needed a lot of help; she was too idle to run it without someone strong beside her. And she'd taken up with that smarmy salesman – if Frank Liddle asked her she'd probably marry him and go off to Newcastle. She hadn't had any better offers, and she was no spring chicken.

Elsie was sorting cutlery, placing it neatly in the drawer. He put his paper down, watching as she moved from one task to another. He wondered again whether she should have started work in the shop after they were married, instead of keeping house. At the time she'd seemed happy enough to take on the running of the place, but maybe that was just because it was what she was used to; she'd kept house for her father when her mother died. Either way, they'd agreed there was no point in her learning the job because before long she'd have children to look after, and she'd be at home all day anyway. That was four years ago. Elsie working in Erringtons? It would infuriate Lily, but it would be in her own interest: Elsie would work hard, take some of the responsibility. Lily would hate the idea but she'd enjoy the benefits. Mind you, if Elsie was in the shop all day, shouldn't Lily do her fair share at home? Fat chance. He let the newspaper drop to his lap.

'Elsie, are you all right, lass?'

He tossed the paper aside and went over to where she was stacking crockery on the dresser. He put his hands on her shoulders and gently turned her round so that she could lean against him, her head resting against his waistcoat. She looked up with a wry smile. He knew that look.

'Not very exciting, is it? You must be bored rigid. Do you mind it?'

'What are you asking now for? I've been here with Agnes and that other daft lass before her, day in day out for over four years, and I don't remember you asking me if I minded before. Not once.'

'I know … but it wasn't meant to be for this long. You know, you'd have had more help, if things had been different.'

'I don't need any more help. They already think I'm setting myself up, trying to be something I'm not.'

'Who? Who does?'

'Lily does. And other people. Women.'

'Elsie, which women?'

'Nobody that matters.'

'Who, then?'

'Nobody … it's probably just me.'

'Sweetheart, I'm asking you how you feel now because I'm going over to see Archie Pumphrey this afternoon, about officer training. I may have to go down south … to learn the job. There's only so many willing men can die before they're going to want to make soldiers of us all. Even me. Which means there'd be a place for you in the business.'

She pulled away and looked hard into his eyes.

'When did you decide to do that? You don't want to go, surely? You're needed here – loads of people depend on you. They know that, don't they? Don't they?'

'I know that's how it was when it all started. Not now.'

'Why now?'

'Elsie, I don't want to go, I don't want to fight, and I certainly don't want to kill anyone. But I think it may be my turn. That's why now.'

16

She was tense, standing apart from him, looking away. He'd promised always to look after her … hated the thought of causing her any distress. But this wasn't his choice.

'People need you.' Her voice was small, an almost whisper.

'It's not me really, it's the business people depend on, isn't it? I mean, if you and Lily were up to scratch you could keep things going until it's all over, surely? What about coming in and having a go? Learn the ropes? It won't be for long, I'm sure of that.' He scanned her face to see the reaction.

'Lily won't have it. She'd die sooner than work with me.'

He wasn't surprised to see her grimace at the thought of Lily's reaction to the idea; even when she just called in at the shop Lily ignored her, unless it was to put on a show in front of the customers. He gripped the top of her arms and held her firmly in front of him.

'Lily will just have to do as I say. We'll find some way of making it work, even if it means one of you out in front with the customers and the other doing the rest … the books and suchlike.'

'I think I'd like to if she would … if she'd let me.'

'Let you? She'll let you. She'll have no choice. And it'll mean you'll have plenty to do when I'm away; keep you out of mischief!'

Elsie nodded her acceptance and stood on tiptoe to put her arms round his neck. He kissed her smooth forehead. Just the smell of her made him want to stay at home all afternoon. He cupped his hands round her bottom, lifting her body against his.

'Right, I'm off to work before I lose control. I'll be home late, after I've seen the Major.'

He strode back to the shop, light-headed with the relief of having finally told her. He'd spent dismal hours – worse than dismal – awake in the night, longing to rouse her to talk

17

about it, knowing that if he did her concern would feed his own reservations. He couldn't do it if he wasn't sure. As it was, he'd wavered for months, until a wormlike doubt had slithered up on him. Yes, married men weren't required to fight, yet, but legal obligation and moral obligation weren't the same thing. They weren't even equals. His conscience had been reminding him daily that if it weren't for Elsie he'd have signed up over a year ago.

The other thing hadn't helped. If they'd had a child it would be even harder for him ... but easier for her. They'd both just assumed it would happen: why wouldn't they? But it didn't; her time had come, month after month after month. Every few weeks she became edgy and anxious, then utterly miserable for a few days ... more like grief than disappointment. It'd started to affect the way she responded to him. Recently she'd started to turn away in bed, avoiding him. She was affectionate – always that – but sometimes she kept him at arms' length, and he hated it.

It had taken him a long time, years, to share his anxiety with Ivan, and in the end it was one of Lily's nasty jibes over supper that had forced him to talk about it. He'd retreated to the bench in the back garden for a smoke and waited for Ivan to join him. They'd sat there together, bent forward with their elbows on their knees, cigarette smoke curling into the night air. It was Ivan who'd raised the subject.

'What's our Lily mean when she says Elsie's "too thin for her own good?"' He'd mimicked her sharp voice. 'What's that about? Just 'cause she's got an arse like a carthorse doesn't mean Elsie should!'

'She means she's not pregnant yet.'

'What's that got to do with her? Anyway, it's early days.' He'd drawn on his cigarette; it was more a question than a statement.

'Not really. We've been married years now.'

'And you've been at it like rabbits.' Ivan had grinned at him, nudged his arm. It was hard to be discreet when they lived in the same house, even one with solid walls.

'Until recently.'

Ivan had raised an eyebrow, exhaled a long, slow line of smoke.

'Things slowed down have they? Maybe she's not in the mood. It happens.'

'It's not that she doesn't want to. You know what I mean? It's something else. I think she feels that if we can't make a bairn then somehow it's … wrong.'

'Wrong? Let's get this straight. You say she's liked it up to now, but because she's not pregnant she doesn't want it any more?'

'That's about it, yes.' He pinched his cigarette out, heeling the stub into the soft ground. Talking about it had made things sound worse, not better as he'd hoped.

'Well, you need to get it sorted. For one thing, you're going to be chewing your arm off if you can't make love to your own wife.'

'You're not wrong there.'

'And for another, she won't have any chance of getting pregnant if she doesn't … I know that's stating the obvious, but she needs to think on it.'

It was stating the obvious … but as he'd said, you try telling that to Elsie when she's curled up, back rigid, silent tears draining onto the bolster. To make things worse, all their married friends had had babies, often within the year. In the early days Elsie was excited every time, visiting with offers of help, baking pies, knitting little jackets. But after a year or two she stopped the visiting. Now she would wait until she met the mother in the street, but even looking into a pram picked open a wound as large as her womb should be. So, maybe getting out of the house more would help her, even if it meant spending long hours with his sister ... He'd need to tell Lily what he was planning when he'd talked to Archie. Now, there's something to look forward to.

The walk back to Erringtons was short ... not far enough to relieve his restlessness. In a different year he'd be feeling good about the business: Erringtons was doing better than ever; it would take worse than a war to interfere with the way of life in Northumberland. There wasn't even any problem with supplies yet; goods that came in by ship, then train, then cart, were still getting through exactly as before. You wouldn't know there was a war on. It was only the missing sons, the daily list of dead and wounded, that made the difference, followed by the sale of black dye to sad women with swollen eyes. They'd stopped charging for the dismal little tins; he'd put them in a box on the counter where they'd be easier to pick up without having to ask for them.

When he got there Kit Jobson was leaning against the wall outside the shop: one of the local lads home from the front 'unfit for service'. How old was he? Twenty? Jim stopped and chatted for a while. The lad seemed cheerful enough waiting there, his sticks put to one side, but there was an unsettling blankness behind his eyes. Kit's mother had been wrecked by his suffering: she'd started muttering, repeating herself, tittering nervously. Jim held the door open for her, and he could see Kit gritting his teeth with irritation as she came out, gripping her heavy basket in front of her with both hands. He knew the story from Ivan; he'd been in The Crown when beer had loosened Kit up enough to talk about it. Both of his legs below the knees had been shattered when a shell landed beside him as he advanced over no man's land near Ypres ... they'd gone over the top at dawn so he'd lain where he'd fallen for hours. Thank God he'd been numb at first, but the midday sun saw hot shafts of pain looping through his body. He'd hardly dared look down; shards of bone gleamed white through his shredded trousers and he could sense the blood seeping warm into the mud; the earth around him was oily with it. Mind, he'd been 'dead lucky'; in the darkness some lads from his company had crawled out to find him; they'd given him morphine and lugged him back to safety with his legs dangling like joints of mutton in the butcher's. He'd had a few days in casualty clearing where they'd patched him up, then on to a field hospital where a cheerful Scottish surgeon saved his life by swift amputation. He'd remained there until he was fit for the journey back to England and yet another hospital, this time for several months of good food and healthy fresh air. He'd learned to walk again on artificial legs, but above all, there was peace; June days sitting outside in the sunshine, playing cards with some of the other lads. Then home to Northumberland, and being 'fucking useless' and dependent on his daft bloody mam.

Jim stayed where he was and watched as Kit made his way down the street with his lurching gait and flapping trouser legs. His tired little mother hurried after him, weighed down by the groceries. Jim pushed through into the back of the shop and leaned against the edge of the sink in the cool larder, nauseous with … what was it? He was glad he'd arranged to see Archie.

The afternoon was busy as usual, with news of Fred's death spreading in whispers across the counter. Then, late in the afternoon, there was talk of horses being requisitioned, and people began to hover to share any news. Jim was aware of it all but he was too preoccupied to listen to the details. Before closing time, he made an excuse and set off for Fairstead Hall, an impressive stone-built house in its own grounds a couple

21

of miles east of Bellingham. He could have taken the train, but he preferred to walk over the open hillside and across the Rede. The Pumphrey family owned several hundred acres of fertile land, all tenanted since Edith Pumphrey had produced only daughters, much to Archie's disappointment. 'Lovely girls of course, but it's not like having a son, is it?'

A daughter would do us fine, actually.

He was ushered through to the large sitting room which overlooked first the garden, then a sweep of Northumberland hillside towards the North Tyne below. There was the smell of tobacco and dogs; two foxhounds lumbered over to greet him then flopped back down on the rug in front of the fireplace where logs were burning red, throwing out a gentle heat against the autumn chill. Archie poured two large measures of single malt, indicating to Jim to sit in one of the padded leather armchairs.

'I've been waiting for you to make a move, truth be known.' The Major took a long, satisfying mouthful, then picked up the paraphernalia to light his pipe. Jim felt his pocket … he could do with a cigarette.

'May I?'

'By all means, light up if you wish, Jim; Edith's partial to an evening cigarette, so you'll be at home.'

Good old Edith. They sat in silence for a minute while Archie lit one match after another and finally, with a lot of tamping down and extravagant sucking, achieved a good pipe.

'Archie, I was in my school OTC. You know that. Father was keen for me to join, and it was good fun. Hard at times, but I enjoyed it.'

'Go on …?'

'Well, I think it's time for me to volunteer. I'm on the register, but before my name gets to the top of some list and

I'm obliged to go, I think it's time I put myself forward as an officer. Up to now I've felt all right about it, what with the business, and being married ...' He tailed off, wondering whether his reasons would seem like craven excuses to the Major.

'But the war's moved on, and you feel the need to serve King and country rather than your customers, is that it?' Archie smiled at his own joke.

'Yes, I suppose that's exactly it. But I'm hoping it won't be for long.'

'Well done, Jim. Good man. We need officers; men with common sense and courage. Needs to be someone the men will respect and follow, don't you know. I feel quite sure you fit the bill in every respect. Are you sure?'

He wasn't. Not really.

'That's why I've come to see you. It's ten years since I left the OTC, so how would I know? And how do I convince them I'm still officer material?'

'You leave that to me. I may be an old buffer but I'm an old buffer with clout. Let me make a few calls, write a few letters. I'll trot over when I hear anything, tell you what's what. Here, let me top you up.'

'King and Country!'

'King and Country!'

Jim downed it in one before placing his tumbler carefully on a table and shaking Archie's hand. As he made his way up the long drive he could hear voices in the paddock next to the garden: the Major's groom, head bent, was deep in conversation with Edith Pumphrey, still wearing her gardening gloves. He couldn't hear what was being said, but he could guess what they were talking about.

He needed to get home, to see Ivan.

FOUR

Ivan

Ivan made his way out of the town centre and up the hill to the forge. His studded boots clattered a complicated rhythm on the cobbles; he'd walked this route and back again, twice daily, almost every day since he was thirteen. He could do it in his sleep. Nothing much had changed over the years, except that he was in charge now: being indentured didn't last for ever, and he'd been ready to take over when the time came. He couldn't imagine doing anything else. He greeted everyone he met on the way, but he was thinking about Isabel. He wanted to see her, no – he *needed* to see her. He'd sent her a message with Alfie, his lad; they lived in the same row.

A few days earlier she'd come up just as he was starting to close down for the day. Alfie had just gone – she must have been watching – and he was busy hanging up his tools, checking that the fire was low enough to leave. He'd looked up as she came to the door, glad to see her even if he wasn't expecting a visit. They'd been walking out since August, *weeks now, must be a record*, but the nights closing in had made it harder for them to meet up.

'Well, this is a treat. Come on and give us a kiss, then!'

'That's what I've come for. Couldn't wait 'til Sunday.'

She'd grinned up at him, pushed the door closed behind her and leaned back against it in case anyone tried to come in. You could tell she was up to mischief by the look in her

24

eyes. He'd wiped his hands and face and walked round the forge towards her, brushing the damp hair from his forehead. She was hot and out of breath from the steep walk and they'd kissed in a way they hadn't before, urgently, tongues touching in a way that made him so stiff it was painful. Within a few seconds, still breathless, she'd helped him undo the buttons on her blouse so he could see her and feel her warm skin against him. He'd fondled her breasts, bent to kiss them. They were just as he'd imagined: soft and full. And it was Isabel who'd taken hold of his right hand in hers and pushed it down over her belly and between her thighs, pressing it against her. It hadn't lasted long enough. Whether she'd taken fright, or perhaps there'd been footsteps outside, he didn't know, but she'd pushed him away suddenly, and begun to fasten her blouse. With a quick kiss on the lips she'd slipped away. *God, she was just what he needed. Howay, Isabel, I'll be waiting.*

Alfie saw him coming up the hill and was already firing up for the afternoon as he reached the door. They had a batch of shoes to make for the pit ponies as well as a few bits of mending; nothing requiring too much thought unless someone stopped by with a horse that'd thrown a shoe. The hours passed quickly and he was about ready to pack in for the day when he heard the clatter of clogs. Isabel? *No, bugger it … too heavy.* It was John Richardson that barged into the smithy, breathless, clutching a piece of paper. He thrust it towards him. Ivan had worked on John's horses for years but he'd never seen him without a smile on his face until now.

'What's up, John?'

'Have ye seen this, man? Has anyone else had one d'ye na?' He pulled his cap off and dragged a shaking hand through his hair.

Ivan chucked his hammer down and took the official piece of paper over to the open door where he could read it, then read it again. *God in heaven, no.* He looked at John and shook his head.

'When did this come?'

'Today. Now. The lass brought it down to the field with me tea.'

Ivan handed back the letter and patted his friend on the arm. What could he say to make it any better? Once John had left he sent Alfie home, damped down the fire and went through all the familiar tasks of wiping and hanging up his gear, then he locked the door and set off down to the town. He called in at The Crown for a pint, but it was gloomy in the public bar: nearly everyone there knew someone who'd had the same letter; desolation seemed to hang in the air, making it hard to breathe. When he'd heard all he needed to know he carried on home, down the back lane and through the garden to the scullery door. His boots scraped on the tiles as he made straight for the sink to wash his hands and face. Elsie looked up as he came into the kitchen, ready to smile a welcome, but his expression stopped her. He leaned wearily against the door jamb, eyes closed, his hands cupped over his face. Elsie stood, uncertain for a moment, then hurried over to him. She touched him, and his arms dropped dead at his sides. He turned to her and he could hear his voice cracking as he talked; *hell, he was going to cry like a bairn in a minute.*

'It's the horses.'

'What is?'

'They're taking the horses, Elsie.' He could see her trying to work out what was wrong, so maybe she hadn't heard about it.

'Who? Who's taking the horses? Which horses, Ivan?'

She stood, her hand stroking his arm; her eyes were searching his for some clue as to what was going on.

'This *bloody* war. They've sent requisition orders out, the

26

bastards.' He thumped his fist against the wall. 'As if it's not enough to expect people to give up their sons, they have to turn over their horses as well. Poor bloody animals'll be pulling guns instead of harrows.' He gave a hollow laugh. 'What's that it says in the bible, about turning swords into ploughs? Fuck it!'

She was shushing him like a child, holding him against her and smoothing his face. She must have grasped what he was talking about. Everyone knew the army was losing thousands of horses on the battlefield and they'd been buying up new stocks in the south to replace them ever since the war began. Now they'd come north. They'd been in the area earlier in the year and done a kind of census, but it hadn't seemed too much of a threat at the time.

'They won't take them *all*, surely?'

'No … they can't. You can't work the fields without them unless you've got a tractor, and there's precious few of them around here. But they're taking as many as they can get away with. You'll see … there's a dozen I can think of straight away. George Graham's going to have to send Prince – you know? He *bred* him, for God's sake, and his dam before him.'

Elsie did know; of course she did. Yes, horses were Ivan's livelihood, but his anguish wasn't about that. It was the part they played as trusted workers. Friends and family even.

'When?'

'Next Friday. A week today. They have to bring them in; meet in front of the town hall, then they'll be taken to the train and away. I tell you what, if I had a horse and they wanted him, I'd be off by now. They'd have to catch me first.'

'I'd come with you.'

'No, I'm serious …'

'So'm I.'

She was blushing … what was she up to? It was months

27

since they'd agreed to keep a safe distance. There'd been weeks and weeks of avoiding each other unless the others were there.

'Don't do this today, Elsie … it's not fair.'

He closed his eyes … she was clinging onto him as they cantered across the moors. They'd find somewhere safe to stay, alone. He looked at her, as what she'd said sunk in.

'Would you? *Really*, would you?' He gripped her shoulders.

'You wouldn't want me to; I'm useless on a horse. I'd slow you down, or fall off more likely – they'd catch us in no time!'

Don't do that … don't pretend you were joking.

'Elsie, would you come?'

He said the words slowly, as if she were deaf or ill. He wasn't in the mood for playing around. She looked away from him; he knew she would, she always did in the end. He gently turned her face back towards him and before she could stop him, without even asking with his eyes, he kissed her firmly, holding her so that she couldn't pull away. She went rigid, and when he freed her she stepped back, shivering. He reached out and stroked the hair from her forehead.

'I'm sorry. No, I'm not sorry. Are *you* sorry? Oh, come here.' He wrapped his arms round her. That way he couldn't see the look on her face.

'D'you know what this feels like?' She was whispering as if the walls of the kitchen might be eavesdropping.

'I know what it feels like for me, if that's what you mean. It feels like coming home after a long, long journey. I've been away, now I'm back.' He squeezed her … *you know what I mean*.

'I was going to say that it feels like putting out to sea in a little boat. No paddles … nothing. That's the opposite of how you feel, isn't it?'

She drew herself away.

'Ivan? Isn't it?'

He didn't want to do this … discuss it again. She knew very well how he felt. Nothing had changed.

'Lily and Jim'll be back very soon. I'd best get the table laid.'

She was right: a bit of ordinary stuff would be best after the last few minutes, but even so …

'Where do we go from here, then?' He wasn't going to let her ignore it this time.

'Well, not across the hills to Rothbury on horseback, that's for sure.'

She opened the drawer and took out four knives, four forks, four spoons; Agnes went home before supper. He prised them from her hands and walked through to the gloomy dining room, then began to lay the table, finding the cruet set, the napkins, setting everything in its place as if it were going to be a normal supper, except of course it wasn't. Elsie came through and watched him but she said nothing, so he kept going. Once he was satisfied with the table, he went over to the mantel shelf and lifted the Maling vase down from where it always sat, always empty.

'Wait there.'

He was surprised when she did as she was told. He left her leaning against the door, glancing at the hall clock. He hoped the others would be late, so there would be time to have it out with her. He went outside and picked some late blooms in the back garden – asters mainly, with some ivy to set off the colours – to fill the colourful vase. He placed it in the centre of the table, a statement.

'For you.' Elsie just looked at him. 'Mind, they're nowhere near as beautiful as you are.'

He couldn't decide whether it was the flowers or Elsie that most transformed the room. He went over and kissed her again, softly, his hands on her waist.

29

They both noticed Lily in the hall at the same time. At some point the front door had opened and she'd come in. On a normal day Jim would have followed her, blocking the light as he stood in the doorway looking along the hall for Elsie. But today he wasn't there. Ivan was relieved; later would be better. But how long had Lily been in the house? Elsie backed away from him and walked along the passage towards Lily; to distance herself from him.

'Evening, Elsie. Is Ivan here?' Lily was taking off her gloves. Her voice carried to where he'd stepped back, out of sight.

'Yes, he's in the dining room. He's ... upset.'

'Yes, I'm sure he is.'

He could just make out Elsie hesitating at the kitchen door; he wanted to go to her, but he stayed where he was. What did Lily mean, 'I'm sure he is'? Had she seen something? She couldn't have. But then, why make the comment? As usual she went straight into the parlour to 'take the weight off her feet'; she'd be pouring herself a glass of Harvey's. Elsie walked along and he followed behind her quietly, listening from the shadow of the doorway. Lily was already in an armchair, a large glass of sherry on the round table beside her. *Christ, she was so like their mother.*

'What did you mean, when you said that about Ivan?'

Elsie's voice was firmer than he'd expected. He could picture Lily's expression; she'd be affronted that Elsie was standing there, disturbing her, asking questions.

'I meant that half the nags in the valley are going on a jaunt. They'll be hauling guns in France instead of agricultural machinery in Northumberland. They've had their notices today. Why, what did you think I meant?'

At this, he shifted so he could see Lily. He watched as she took a sip of her drink then rested her head back and closed

30

her eyes: dismissal. Elsie caught his eye and shook her head, gesturing towards the kitchen.

He stepped back quietly.

* * * *

He was outside in the back garden when Jim arrived home from Archie's. He'd been double digging the plot where they'd taken up potatoes for storing. He'd dug hard and deep, without a second's break, working out his anger. Job done, he'd cleaned the spade and was sitting on the bench, smoking, glad to be alone in the dusk. From where he sat he could watch Elsie busy in the scullery, crossing over to the sink, then back to the table. He'd finished his cigarette when Jim appeared, pecking Elsie on the cheek as he came through from the kitchen looking for him. Elsie gestured to the garden and Jim came straight out and put a hand on his shoulder.

'It's a right bugger.'

Jim joined him on the bench. 'It'll make a big difference to you. And the farmers. We've had one or two in today: it breaks your heart.'

'D'ye know what makes it so terrible? It's that they have no choice. Not the farmers, and certainly not the horses. The lads that've gone and died ... at least they *chose* to go. It makes me feel desperate! I know they're not human, but that almost makes it worse. They'll feel it, but they won't understand what the hell's going on.'

'Ivan, you do know that this *choice* thing isn't going to last much longer? For us, I mean? The word is that the volunteer registers haven't been enough so there'll be conscription by early next year. That's why I've been to see Archie Pumphrey.

'You've already signed the damned register. What's the Major got to do with it?'

31

'I've been thinking. If I have to go, I'd rather go as an officer – Northumberland Fusiliers if they'll have me. It's Archie's old regiment, so he'll know who talk to. I've already trained once. He's going to let me know if he can find an OTC that'll take me.'

It was Jim's turn to study the ground. Ivan rested his arm loosely round his brother's shoulders and they sat together for another few minutes as the evening closed in. He was cold now; the warmth from the digging had worn off.

'You'll make a good officer. If that's really what you want.'

'I'm not scared to go, you know. I don't bloody want to, but it's not because I'm some pansy coward.'

'I didn't think you were. No-one thinks that.'

'It's Elsie. If it weren't for Elsie I would've gone by now.'

He nodded his head, accepting the truth of what Jim was saying. He felt exactly the same way.

As if she'd been listening, Elsie appeared to call them in for supper. He could see her silhouetted in the kitchen door, her hands untying her pinny as she stood, gauging their mood. Jim stood up immediately and walked down the path towards her, giving her an affectionate kiss as he entered the house. She looked over at him, still sitting on the bench.

'Are you coming?'

'Yes, bonny lass, I'm coming. You go in.'

As they sat down together, Lily commented on the vase and flowers. It looked … what? Outrageous; wantonly colourful.

'What's all this in aid of? Are we celebrating something? Mother would have a fit, *you* using that vase; it was a present from Uncle Arthur.'

She began to help herself to vegetables, not expecting any response but clearly assuming that Elsie had picked and arranged the flowers. Elsie flushed, not knowing how to react without incriminating either herself or him.

'I've never heard anything so daft as *not* using a vase to put flowers in. And don't you start on Elsie, it was me that did it.'
Why can't she just mind her own fucking business?

'Good grief, my little brother picking flowers? He must be in love! Who's the lucky girl?'

'Just shut up, Lily, will you.'

His tone was light enough, but even she could sense when it was time to stop. She put on her offended, *what did I do wrong?* face, but she was sullen and quiet for the rest of the meal as he and Jim discussed how many horses there would be in the square on Friday afternoon, and if there would be soldiers in case of any trouble. He could sense Elsie looking at them as they talked and wondered whether she was comparing them: she always said their features gave them away as brothers, apart from their eyes; Jim's were brown. But he wasn't quite as tall or as broad as his older brother, in spite of all the manual work. At one point she caught his eye and gave him the briefest of smiles; apart from that he could have imagined the whole thing. *Where do we go from here, then?* He had no idea.

FIVE

Elsie

Everything was as it had been before, because it had to be. There was nothing to ease the urge to touch Ivan and be touched, so she was avoiding being alone with him, even though the sound of his footsteps in the passage was enough to make her feel sick with apprehension. One smile, and the day had some meaning to it.

His words chipped hard as hail in her mind. He'd said she was beautiful, but he'd often said so, when she wore a new frock or tied her hair differently. He'd kissed her and said he wasn't sorry. But, why should he be? He often kissed her: he was her brother in law, for God's sake. He'd needed comfort and she was there to give it, that's all. She was Jim's wife, not his. Hot tears blurring, this would take her thoughts along another track until they came back to Ivan as she clashed the oven door shut.

The following Friday, the last in October, was cool and clear. Before the low autumn sun had reached the front of the house she lay awake, taut, Jim sleeping bearlike beside her. She listened to every small sound as Ivan rose even earlier than usual and left the house before anyone else was up and moving. He'd been quiet at supper the night before, but before he left the table he'd mentioned that he was going to be on top of his work by early afternoon in order to be away from his forge later on – to be down in the town when the

34

horses came in for four o'clock. He wanted to see them off.
A photographer was coming – there was going to be a record
of the day and of the horses.

Lily and Jim came home for lunch earlier than usual
because the shop was quiet, but Ivan didn't appear. After
they'd eaten, Jim was reading The Times when something
caught his attention. She turned as he groaned and threw the
paper onto the table.

'What is it?'

'You know the battle where Fred Charlton was killed?'

'What about it?'

'I'm just reading the report. Would you believe it was in
a mining area? Remember how the lads went off crowing
about leaving the coal seams behind? Well, if I read this right
it's all pit villages and slag heaps where they went.'

'Well, at least they'll have felt at home.' Lily rose from the
table; it was nearly time to go back to the shop. 'I think I'll
get along; we'll be busy this afternoon, what with the horses
going. It's an ill wind ...'

Jim's eyes met hers as his sister left the kitchen.

'Can you imagine even thinking that, never mind saying
it?'

'Which? About Fred ... or the horses?'

'Both.'

'Only Lily.'

Ivan would be leaving the forge just after three thirty; his
lad would stay and keep an eye on things. She could think
of nothing else; if she closed her eyes she could picture him
making his way down the hill, hands deep in his pockets. She
left the house early to meet Jim in the market place, and they
found a space at the edge of the crowd where they could look
out for him, try to pick him out in the press of local families.
At last she caught sight of him, hunched and solitary, moving

35

intently towards the square. She blinked back tears as he approached; she felt wrung out with sorrow ... for him, for the horses, for their owners. Just before the hour, a hush fell on the milling crowd as people gradually became conscious of the faint clatter of hooves carrying towards them on the wind. Fathers held their children's hands, still and quiet, as the din grew louder: the great horses were being led from all directions to the centre of the town. It was the saddest silence she'd ever heard.

They stood, grim and wordless, as the minutes ticked by. She gazed at Ivan as he moved from horse to horse, smoothing his farrier's hand over their flanks, his fingers touching goodbye as he exchanged a few words with their owners, all of them friends. They'd used clean ropes, bought new to lead their animals in; pride she supposed. Or love. Ivan stood apart from the horses now, head bowed, arms folded; he'd forged and fixed the shoes for every one of them. As the town hall clock struck four, the photographer declared himself ready:

'Can we have you in a line please, across the square?'

His voice carried, and people began to shift. He shouted directions, gesticulating to the onlookers to make their way behind him, out of the picture, while the farmers with their horses formed an orderly row in front. The requisitioning officer joined them, standing alongside in uniform; nobody seemed to bear him any ill will: the man was just doing his job, after all. In fact, old John Dinsdale handed his mare Dora over to him for the photograph, then left the square. Elsie watched him as he hobbled off. It was a dignified withdrawal: he obviously couldn't bear it any longer. It took a while, but eventually the photograph was taken. The crowd began to shuffle away as the horses were led the short walk down to the siding at the mart to be loaded into trucks. Jim took her hand and they followed behind, silent. By the time the train pulled away it was growing dark, which helped a little as the last few owners watched, hands clenched, resisting the urge to wave. With hardly a word they turned away for the long walk home, the new ropes coiled and shoved deep into their jacket pockets, out of sight.

Elsie walked home, hoping that Ivan might call in on his way back, but she suspected he'd gone straight up to the smithy. Knowing him he'd be hammering the pain out of his system. She wandered from room to room wishing that she had something strenuous and exhausting to do, to block out thoughts of Ivan, or of the cattle trucks thundering towards Dover. She moped into the dining room and touched the flowers he'd placed there, still in the centre of the table. They were already well past their best, but she couldn't bear to throw them on the compost heap because the fading petals were all she had to remember the kiss. Actually, that's exactly why she needed to throw them away. She grabbed the vase and strode out through the kitchen and into the back garden, her chin quivering as she held it upside down and watched the blooms drift down into a tangled bouquet on top of the grass clippings. She would dearly love to throw Nancy's precious vase at the dry stone wall – the noise of shattering china might help her mood – but she thought better of it, if only because she'd have to explain to Lily how it happened. Instead, she carried it into the scullery and washed it, then dried it carefully and restored it to its place on the dreary marble shelf. She'd go down to the shop and help Jim close up; if he wanted her to work there it was time she got started.

The mood in Erringtons was as she expected; it was as if another local man had died. Just before closing time the telephone rang; Lily picked up the receiver, answering with her telephone voice.

'Erringtons. Miss Errington speaking.' After a few seconds she beckoned to Jim.

'It's Archie Pumphrey. He'd like a word with you.'

Jim turned his back towards her as he greeted the Major. She could hear nothing, but she saw him reach for a pad and pencil and make a few notes. After a few minutes he slowly replaced the receiver, wiping his face with his hands in a gesture she knew well. He turned to face her, straightening up with a forced smile. It seemed that Archie'd had a word, pulled a few strings: there was a place for him in one of the officer training units at Cambridge University.

'At the University?'

'Trinity College: he called it his alma mater. A fine CO and the food should be passable. Trust Archie to mention dinner. I'll need to get kitted out as soon as possible … they'll be sending me lists and a cheque. He says the best place for my uniform is Pope and Bradley in Bond Street.'

'Bond Street? London Bond Street you mean?'

'London Bond Street. The Hexham and Newcastle tailors aren't posh enough, unless you just want something ordinary.' Jim smiled ruefully. 'How did he put it? … "The men at Trinity will soon pick out a fellow with an ill cut jacket."'

She smiled at Jim's attempt at Archie's voice and accent, but she could see that Lily was anything but amused.

'And what is it that's going to be an honour?'

'That was another thing – he said not to worry about a pistol. He still has his and he says he'll be proud to let me use it. He said it took him through Modder River and the girls have no use for it, thank the Lord.'

'So what did you say?'

'Well …I said it's a very kind offer, and I'll be proud to use it. He's going to get his man to check it over for me.'

'How long?'

38

She could barely speak. The idea of Jim even holding a gun, never mind aiming at someone … using it to try and kill … it was horrible. Unthinkable. He came over and hugged her, perhaps to avoid looking into her eyes, and spoke gently, so that only she could hear.

'We've got a few weeks before I go, if it all goes through.'

'So, how long have you been hatching this?'

Lily's question, from the other side of the shop, was hostile; it was difficult to tell what she was feeling, but there was no warmth in her tone. Elsie felt him stiffen, then he turned to look at his sister, still holding her tightly pressed against him, as if to shield her.

'Well, Lil, things are going to have to change around here.'

At this Lily came straight over to them, her curiosity fully roused. Elsie shrugged his arms from her shoulders and moved away; she hadn't wanted to be part of this conversation. Jim crossed over to the door and turned the sign to 'closed', pulling the bolts across. He stood with his back to the fading light, looking first at Elsie, then at Lily.

'I'm going to war.'

His tone of voice made it obvious that this was no joke, and at last Lily began to respond.

'I knew this would happen eventually. Damn this war! When are you going? And who's going to help me in here? Will's too young to do much more than he's doing now. Shall we advertise, or what?'

'We don't need to. Elsie says she'll take over from me, just while I'm away.'

As he spoke he beckoned Elsie over and held her again, his watch fob digging painfully into her cheek. Then he faced Lily, his arm still around her, keeping her by his side. She knew he'd been putting it off for days, but now was the time; she kept still, waiting for Lily's reaction. Lily slowly folded her arms across her chest and stood there, her lips in a line, shaking her head.

'Over my dead body she is! I'm not going to say very much because she is your wife after all, but she's just not the sort of person we want in here.'

Jim shifted her away and strode over to Lily. His arms were rigid at his sides, his fists clenched against his legs rather than raised against his sister. Elsie was more hurt than angry, but she headed Jim off and put her hand on his arm in an attempt to calm him. She stood between brother and sister with her hands on her hips and her head up, looking Lily directly in the eye. Lily took a step back. Was she blushing? Good!

'Not the sort of person you want in here?'

'Well you're not ... you know nothing about business, you've never been used to dealing with the public, you don't even know how to ...'

Lily was tripping over her words and Jim cut her off midsentence.

'Nor will she, unless she has the opportunity. I should have done this long ago. Elsie's coming in with me tomorrow, and you will be helpful, polite and sensitive to her needs. Do I make myself clear?'

'But, I ...'

'Do I make myself clear, Lily?'

He was calm ... implacable. He wasn't easily roused, which made it far more intimidating when it happened. He wasn't going to back down, and she could tell that Lily knew it; she wasn't going to argue with him as he loomed over her. It was a relief. Instead, Lily turned away and began to finish off the day's work, tight-lipped and brittle with frustration.

Supper that night was difficult for all four of them. Although he'd missed lunch, Ivan ate very little and left the table immediately, not even stopping to help clear.

'Sorry Elsie, it was grand ... very tasty, but I'm off out. I'll be late in.'

She glanced up, hoping for some sign – a look, a smile – but he left the room quickly, without looking back.

'What's up with him?' Lily gestured towards Ivan's back. It was the first thing she'd said all evening.

'The horses went today, and his brother's going off to train as an officer. I think he has the right to be a bit upset, don't you?'

'Upset again, is he? Well, at least he's not having his business turned upside down, taking on riff raff to work in it!'

Jim started to rise but Elsie held his arm.

'I'm sorry you still think I'm riff-raff, Lily. You've known me for five years or more, we've lived in the same house for four, and I've done my best to look after us ...you. If Jim wants me to work in Erringtons, then I will.'

'He's no business going off and leaving me to run the place.'

'He doesn't want to leave, and I hate the very idea of him going away and – hand on heart – I don't really want to spend all day with you, either. Everyone'll have to learn to put up with it.'

'Have you finished?' Lily's voice was toneless. 'Because everyone's not me.'

'Yes, I think so. Actually, no, I haven't. If I'm going to be working in the shop all day, then we're both going to be in the same boat. So I'm going to do less around the house, and you'll have to do more. Cook occasionally, for example, and help to clear away. Agnes can't do everything.'

She continued to look Lily straight in the eye across the table, and Lily returned her gaze, unblinking. She sensed that Jim had risen to his feet, but she didn't allow herself to look

41

anywhere other than at Lily's impassive face. Today was the first time she'd been a turned worm, and she wasn't going to back off. Nothing had changed but everything had, just like that.

Jim leaned over to rest both hands flat on the table among the tea cups and pudding dishes, closing his eyes as he thought about what he wanted to say.

'Look, I am going to be fighting in France in a few months' time; leading men into battle. God knows I don't want to, but it'll make me feel a lot happier about it if I know that my wife and my sister are working together, not fighting their own war against each other. We need to keep the business going.'

He straightened up and looked from one to the other. As he registered the look on Lily's face he gave a wry smile.

'You know, it may be easier fighting the Hun than dealing with you. Grow up a bit, will you Lily?' He turned to her. 'Come on, sweetheart, we've got a lot to talk about.'

He took her hand and helped her to her feet. As they left the table, Lily swept her hand across the cloth, brushing her pastry crumbs onto the carpet. She had no intention of sweeping them up.

To get out of the house they went for a stroll, as they often did, through the gloomy streets down to the bridge over the Tyne where they'd spent their first hours alone together on a glorious June afternoon. She'd worn her Sunday best, pretty and floral, her shawl over her arm as she waited, leaning against the stone parapet of the bridge. Her hair, longer then, had been tied back with ribbon, but some curls had already escaped, framing her face. Unlike this damp October evening, on that day there'd been several other couples strolling across the bridge as well as a few fishermen with their rods and baskets along the banks of the river. He'd taken off

42

his hat as he approached and held out his hand as if to shake hers, but instead he'd taken her fingers and put them gently to his lips. She'd made no attempt to pull her hand away … just smiled up at him. He'd offered his arm, suggested a walk along the river.

It was late afternoon before they'd dawdled their way back across the bridge towards the town. Anyone watching them in that golden hour before sunset would have noticed how his eyes rarely left her face as she chattered on. He'd leaned towards her so that he could hear and see her; adapted his stride – normally long and purposeful – to her shorter steps. Her hand was still tucked through his arm, now in shirt sleeves, his jacket over his shoulder. She'd never felt so happy and relaxed. Every now and then she would look up, her eyes gleaming with laughter, waiting for an answer to a question he hadn't heard. He'd told her later that he hadn't been able to concentrate because all he could think about was that he wanted to kiss her, there and then, in the street. They'd reached the end of the row of miners' cottages too soon.

Tonight it was too chilly to walk far, so after a while they turned back towards the town. Anyway, it would soon be too dark to see where they were walking. At home, the dining room was exactly as they'd left it, other than that Lily's chair, now empty, stood apart, pushed back from the cluttered table. They cleared up together, then Elsie went to bed leaving Jim in the parlour with a glass of whisky and the newspaper beside his chair.

She slept through him coming to bed but woke in the small hours, anxious about the day ahead. What should she wear? Would Lily have a spare apron of the sort they wore at the counter, or should she take her own? Yes, she'd do that. But it would be different from Lily's; would that matter? Jim had better stick with her at first, show her exactly what to do.

43

Of course she knew where lots of the stuff was kept – she'd been in the shop with Jim many a time over the years when Lily was out or ill, helping a bit. She turned over towards the window, her face away from Jim's heavy breathing. If it had been summer she'd have got up, maybe wandered downstairs, into the garden. But it was too cold. What would she make for lunch tomorrow if she was out all morning? Or should she make a stand, now she knew she could – suggest that Lily leave early and cook, for once? Where had Ivan gone that evening? It was nearly time to get up when she finally dozed off again.

Tired as she was, her first morning turned out to be easier than either she or Jim had hoped for. Lily behaved well, in the sense that she kept herself busy in the back office, only coming out when necessary. And she could tell that Jim was pleased that virtually every customer greeted her warmly, sympathetically even, recognizing – or having already heard from within the small community – the reason why she was behind the counter.

'We all have to do our bit, hinny. Our Dorothy's away to Newcastle, working in a factory down at Elswick.'

And it was true: many of the younger local women were off doing jobs that would have been unthinkable before the war. There were girls ploughing, bagging coal, working in munitions factories down on the Tyne. The older women were spending the evening knitting socks for the troops. Some turned out once a week to wrap bandages in the library. It was surprising, how rapidly the women had plugged the gap left by their menfolk, and how willingly.

She was quick to learn and it was a treat to be out of the house; she hadn't realised how dreary her days had been. Jim took it slowly, explaining the different systems and processes, so that by lunch time she'd mastered the use of the scales and learned how to use the meat slicer. She'd made notes: Mrs Jameson - bacon very thin. She chattered away on the walk home for lunch, firing questions and passing comments about prices, packaging … anything she wasn't sure about. By mid-afternoon she'd begun to suggest how they might improve the layout of the goods, and by evening she'd already started to change things.

'It makes the place brighter, don't you think? And we could do with the shelves being longer: reaching right along that wall, to the window. Can we do that?'

'You can do whatever you want, my love.'

As the last customer left the shop Jim drew the bolts and turned the sign round, then carried the takings drawer through to Lily in the back, blowing a kiss to Elsie as he went. She was giving the counter a final wipe when she heard a tap on the window and looked up. Ivan was standing outside in the dark street, his face pressed to the glass, pointing at the door.

SIX

Ivan

He left the house by the scullery door. The air was chilly on his face as he followed the pale flagstones of the garden path in the dark and nipped through the gate into the back lane. Buttoning his jacket and turning up the collar, he set off towards the Crown, hoping that there'd be a good crowd in: it was Friday night, so maybe one or two of his mates from the football would be there. He couldn't stand being in the same room as Elsie a minute longer, not even with Lily and Jim there as chaperones. After the daft way he'd carried on last week he'd decided to avoid being on his own with her ... perhaps even find somewhere else to live. But it was so fucking hard! The smell of her, the way her hands played with her hair, everything about her was a temptation. What if he did move out? He couldn't now, anyway; Jim had already started piling on the responsibilities: make sure the doors are locked last thing; keep a check on the coal left in the cellar; pay Agnes. But what about Elsie? He could hardly stop himself from grabbing her as she walked past. Damn, damn, damn! As he pushed open the battered door of the public bar he was relieved to see that there was a fair number of men standing in a warm haze of cigarette smoke, beers in hands and a few whiskies already lined up on the bar.

'Ah, here comes the smith ... we're all here now. Give him a pint, George.'

'Thanks, John. Expecting me, then?'

'Aye, knew you'd be here. Drink up … here's to a safe return for man and beast alike!'

A chorus of voices repeated the words: farmers' sons, a groom and a few lads from the pit, all together. Several of them had enlisted and were waiting for their papers; all of them had already seen at least one friend killed or missing. One had lost his brother at Loos alongside Fred Charlton, another a cousin on Gallipoli; there were families in the valley with dead branches on their family trees. It was only a matter of time before they'd all have joined up, and the mood was too dark for a Friday night; someone needed to change it.

'Howay lads, let's get the darts oot.'

It was the suggestion they'd been waiting for, and almost immediately there was jostling for position. They larked about as they ordered more beers, lining up in front of the board, the gravity of war shrugged off for the moment. Ivan leaned against the bar as the game got underway, wishing he was at home, glad he wasn't. By last orders they'd had a riotous last round and were back at the bar, maudlin from too much ale. As the sentimental stories began Ivan lit up and said his goodnights before leaving the bar. The air outside was fresh and cold after the fug inside. He pulled on his cap and set off home, trusting that everyone would be in bed.

There was a lamp burning in the parlour. He hesitated, one foot on the bottom stair. He really didn't want to see anyone – that's why he went out, for God's sake. With a sigh he stepped back down and went along and looked round the door. Jim was sitting in front of a glowing fire, a half empty bottle of whisky and a full glass on the table beside him.

'Thought you'd be in bed.'

'I should be, really, but I didn't feel ready for sleep. And anyway, I want a word with you. You sober?'

47

'Sober as I want to be.'

He fetched a glass from the cupboard and pulled up a chair opposite his brother, reaching for the bottle as he sat down.

'I'll be down south, training for a few months, then over to France. You know that.'

'Aye … yes I know. Will you get home between training and joining your battalion, d'ye know?'

'I think so. Once I'm commissioned I'll have a bit of leave. Only a few days mind, probably.'

Jim took a swig of his drink and rested his head back against the antimacassar. His eyes were red-rimmed.

'I can't bear the thought of leaving her, Ivan. I don't want to go. It'll be like dying.'

Ivan sipped at his drink and waited for Jim to go on. There was nothing he could think of that would make it any easier. He would, he did, feel the same way.

'The gutters need cleaning out.'

Jim's eyes were closed, the words delivered in a monotone; it was as if he were talking in his sleep.

'What?'

'The gutters; I was going to ask Will Davidson to come up and sort them out before winter, but I might not get round to it.'

'Jim, for God's sake, I ll sort the gutters, and the coal and the bills. Write a list, man, but don't worry about home. I'll take care of everything.'

'And Elsie?'

Jim was looking directly at him. For one heart-stopping moment Ivan thought he must know. Had Elsie told him, is that why he'd waited up? No, she wouldn't. What then?

'What about her?'

'Look after her for me. Don't let Lily push her around. Give her as much help as you can … please.'

It was almost more than Ivan could take. Look after Elsie? The nearer he got the more he knew he should keep away from her, the more he wanted to be near her. It was cruel … unreasonable … to be asked to 'look after her'.

'Course I will. You know I will.'

'Bless you, Brother.'

Jim heaved himself out of his seat and drained his glass.

'I'm going up now. Good night. Don't forget the lamp.'

He turned back as he reached the door.

'And Ivan …'

'Yes?'

'Thank you.'

He left the parlour, closing the door behind him.

Ivan was left sitting alone as Jim had been. He imagined his brother entering the bedroom, taking off his clothes, lifting the blankets. Elsie would be lying there, her nightdress maybe rucked up around her thighs. Jim would curl up against her, his arm round her waist, slim as a girl's. Would she wake up as she felt his body cold against hers? Or would she mutter and pull away? She might turn towards him, put her arms around him … Ivan could feel himself flushing at the image in his mind. It was grotesque to feel this way, especially now. He shook his head to throw off the thought of Elsie's body, but he couldn't help it, wanting to be there instead of his brother, pushing the soft material up so that her nipples would show dark on her small, pale breasts. Ivan swigged the rest of his drink then poured another. He wanted to delay going upstairs until there was no possibility of hearing anything from their bedroom.

* * * *

Early the following morning, after only a few hours of restless sleep, he was up and out as usual, grabbing some bait from the pantry so that he wouldn't need to come back for lunch. He had a backlog of mending work as well as a few pit ponies to shoe, so the day would be full. It was better that way: the harder he worked, the less he had time to think about her. Even so, he knew she was spending her first full day in the shop, and his mind went back to her over and over again, whenever there was nothing else to hold his attention fully. At six thirty he strode back down the hill; he was going to call in, see how things had gone. He stood at the window for a few seconds, watching as she busied herself behind the counter, then knocked to be let in.

'How's it been?' He grinned; she looked so happy and proud to be there.

'It's been ... I don't know ... wonderful. You see so many different people, and everyone's been really patient with me. I'm a bit slow at weighing stuff out, but I'll quicken up.'

'You will. I bet they love seeing you here. You just wait: there'll be a queue of men wanting to do the shopping all of a sudden!'

'Don't be daft!' But she was blushing.

He folded his arms and looked around.

'It seems different in here; have you been moving things round, you minx?'

'Just a bit. Are you all right?'

She was looking up at his face, trying to gauge his mood. He knew he looked rough.

'Not really, I drank too much last night.'

'Why?'

She began wiping the counter again, as if there was a mark that only she could see.

'You know why.'

He leaned over the counter and spoke in an urgent whisper, one hand resting on hers to stop the compulsive wiping.

'Do you know what I did last night? Eh? I promised Jim to look after you when he goes. But he doesn't know how I want to look after you. I'm being tortured, Elsie; it hurts when I don't see you.'

She left her hand where it was. Jim was in the next room, talking with Lily; he could hear their muffled voices. He took the cloth away and put her hand to his mouth. Watching her eyes all the while, he gently covered her palm in tiny kisses. She closed her eyes, but she didn't pull away. He kissed her pale wrist.

'I love Jim, you know.'

Her words were barely audible; she was swaying against the counter.

'Of course you do. So do I; he's the best brother anyone could have. And he loves you more than he loves me and Lily and everyone else put together. So why am I standing here wanting to kiss your lips so much it's making me feel ill?' It was true. He was shivering at being so close to her.

'Because you know I want you to.'

Was it a statement of fact, or an invitation? As he studied her face, the door behind her began to open. He jerked his hand away and stood apart as Jim came through lugging some boxes from the storeroom; he set them heavily onto the counter, then wrapped his arm round Elsie's waist and squeezed her to him.

'Ivan, this lass is a natural! She's been a little wonder today.' He kissed her cheek. 'We'll have her trained up and ready to take over in no time. In fact I'm a bit worried that by the time the war's over I'll be out of a job!'

'A new broom sweeping clean.'

Ivan looked round again and raised his eyebrows.

'Lily seen this yet? She's not one for fresh ideas, our Lil, even if it's improvement. She's like Mother ... you know? "I don't approve of change for change's sake"'.

He mimicked Nancy's whine so well that they were all laughing when Lily emerged from the office, coat and hat in hand. She looked from her brothers to Elsie, then regarded the shop, making a point of twirling right round, gazing at every quarter. The changes were subtle but she missed nothing.

'I see you've already started interfering. Well, I suppose it's a bit of a novelty for you ... like leaving the hovel you were brought up in. Or like having a bairn would be. No offence intended.'

She was fastening her coat as she spoke, and she gave a tiny smile as she walked towards the door. Ivan looked across at Jim ...wasn't he going to say anything? No? Well he bloody was.

'No offence? You nasty, jealous bitch! Have you been working on that one all afternoon? Have you?'

He was normally impossible to rouse, but before he could stop himself he'd grabbed Lily by the arm and dragged her back. Lily yanked her arm away from his grasp and pinned her hat carefully into place, staring blankly ahead.

'Look at me when I'm talking to you!' He grabbed hold of both arms now and shook her. He wanted to slap her smug face.

Lily wrenched herself away and smoothed the sleeves of her coat, then turned to face them.

'I'm having supper with the Taylors, so I'll bid you all goodnight now.' She left the shop, leaving the door slightly ajar.

Ivan looked at Jim. He hadn't moved ... hadn't said a word.

'Were you going to let her get away with that?' He couldn't understand it; surely he ought to be defending Elsie, not just

52

standing there.

'So help me, if I once took hold of her I'd strangle her, sister or not.'

'You'd need to wait your turn.'

He kicked the door shut behind Lily and looked over to where Elsie stood, numbed by Lily's spite. Her face was miserable, all pleasure in her day wiped out – exactly as Lily had hoped, no doubt. She was brushing her hand up and down her pinny, embarrassed ... or was she unconsciously wiping away his kisses? He fetched their coats as Jim made the last few checks and turned out the lamps. He helped Elsie into hers, resisting the urge to fasten the buttons for her as she stood, silent and still in the darkened room. They left the shop together to walk back home. Jim stepped to the outside of the pavement, as he always did when he was with Elsie, and she linked her arm through his.

'Ivan, you go on the other side; she can be our rose between two thorns.'

He did as he was asked, taking her hand, the one he'd kissed, and tucking it through his arm. They stepped out, all three of them linked together, threaded on a string of love. He supposed it was the best he should hope for.

SEVEN

Jim

The list, when it arrived, was daunting. He wasn't short of a bob or two, but all the same he was glad it came with a cheque for fifty pounds from the officers' account in London. After a bit of thought he'd decided to have his uniform made by Isaac Walton in Newcastle. It wasn't about the cost – the difference between Pope and Bradley and Walton's was significant but not unaffordable – no, it was that he'd need to travel down to London for fittings; wait around for days … a week even. He didn't have the time, but even if he did he wasn't going to lose precious days at home just to ensure the right lapels, as if that would change anything. He scanned the list and left it lying on the kitchen table for later. There were items on it he'd need to order from London, but he'd be down in Newcastle for measuring up so he'd take Elsie and they'd make a day of it, maybe even stay the night.

He'd been given a date to report of Monday 13th November, so he had just over two weeks. He expected to be training for several months, and although he'd volunteered, the very idea of it made him wretched; all that marching, gun drill and so on: the grinding need to conform after being his own man for so long. At least he could already ride a horse; he'd read about a Reservist from London who'd been more terrified about being on the back of a horse than he was about facing the Hun! He smiled to himself; being a country lad had its uses.

Elsie'd opened up an attic bedroom for his packing, rather than have their own room disturbed with what would be a constant reminder of his leaving. On the bed there were already piles of clothing: underwear, socks, warm shirts. He'd added writing paper and pens; some books to read. After their trip to Newcastle there would be more, of course. He needed to talk about that with Lily: which days would suit her best? When he raised the subject after church, Lily was unusually helpful. He'd found her in the parlour, where she was sitting with her feet up. She didn't mention it, but she was clearly subdued by Ivan's anger of the night before.

'When do you want to go? Why don't you leave early on Tuesday morning, have a night in a hotel and come home late on Wednesday? That'll take advantage of half day closing. I'll manage. Will can come in on Tuesday if we're very busy. And Ann's always saying she's there if we need her. I'll sort it all out tomorrow.'

He was surprised and relieved; he'd expected a whining list of obstacles, not simple, sisterly help ... not like her at all. Maybe they should have tackled her earlier. Or perhaps she was just glad they were going, so she'd have the place to herself. That seemed more likely.

'Right, we'll do that. Thank you. We'll try to get as many orders as possible sorted out tomorrow so you don't need to worry for the next few days.'

He used 'we' deliberately, wanting Lily to be clear that Elsie would be back in Erringtons the following day, then later in the week. He left Lily and returned to the kitchen where Elsie was sitting with a cup of tea, scrutinising his officers' kit list. She made a face as he sat down beside her.

'You do know you need a sword? What use is a sword going to be if you're in a trench somewhere?'

'You tell me! Ceremonial, I expect it is. Goes with the

55

dressing-up gear for Mess. Lord, what a palaver.'

'You'll look wonderful.'

'No I won't; I'll look like a Northumbrian grocer wearing a sword.'

'And that's what you'll be. It's what you've decided you want to be. Isn't it?'

She gazed at his face. She was wanting to find out how he really felt, but he wasn't sure himself. He wished he felt motivated, compelled to go, like the thousands of men that signed up as soon as ever the war began: he'd seen the local lads, and there were photographs in The Times, and they all looked cheerful. As if going to war were just another jaunt. Why couldn't he feel a bit like that?

'Maybe I should have just gone in as a private, like the rest of them. Trouble is, I went to public school, and I've been through OTC. And I'm my own boss here. It's difficult: I don't feel much like an officer. But I'm even less like the other ranks, really. Anyway, it's too late now.'

'Is it? You volunteered, remember. Can't you just say you've changed your mind?'

She took one of his hands in both of hers and held it to her face. He traced her nose and lips with his fingers; kissed her.

'You know I can't.' If only I could. Anyway, it's only a matter of time before they start forcing people to go; I'm jumping before I'm pushed, that's all.'

They'd had many conversations like this over the last couple of weeks. He knew she was puzzled, hurt even, by his decision to sign up early. And given his previous reluctance it wasn't surprising really. It was fear that drove him, or fear of being afraid. Or maybe ... just fear of being judged for being afraid, for not doing his duty? How could she hope to understand if he didn't? Mind you, as Ivan had pointed out, she had a 'lasses view' of the whole thing. There were a few women in the town with sons or husbands on the Front Line, starting to pass comments in the street at men who could be in uniform but weren't. It made Elsie furious.

'If their menfolk have gone willingly, before they even had to, that's their choice. Probably glad to get away from them!'

He knew that if anyone said anything about him or Ivan she'd be at them like a mother hen. He loved her for being so protective; for such a small lass she could be ferocious.

'So, we're off to the big city this week: just you and me!'

'Well … me, you and a very long shopping list, actually.'

She screwed her nose at the sheet of paper, but he could see she was excited at the thought of a night away. They sat together and went through the list, marking things to take from home or the shop, from Newcastle, and others that would have to be bought later in London, such as the sword and the Sam Browne belt.

* * * *

They had their two days in Newcastle, and they managed to stay strangely light hearted. In Isaac Walton's the elderly tailor complimented him on his broad shoulders and long legs. Elsie waited outside the cubicle while the tape measure flicked up and down, but as soon as they'd left the shop she was helpless with giggles; she twisted her face into a fair copy of the tailor's, and nodded sagely:

'A fine back, Mr Errington, a fine back!'

'You've picked up this mimicry lark from Ivan, the bugger; I'll have to have a word.'

'"Which side do you dress, Sir?" What's that mean?'

'You know fine well what it means.'

'No I don't. Tell me!'

They browsed around Bainbridge's Department Store, choosing new shaving gear, braces, a medicine chest, some

57

good binoculars. The compass they found in a special army supply store. Towards the end of the afternoon he took Elsie's arm and headed up Grey Street to Northern Goldsmiths. He thought she might be difficult about it and he was right; she stood, resistant, at the doorway, standing firm against his hand on her back.

'Come on, in you go.'

'But I don't need anything. When will I wear it?'

'You've been waiting around all day for me, now it's your turn. Anyway, if I choose to buy jewellery for my beautiful wife, that's my decision. You can wear it all the time! I'm an officer – well, nearly – so you'll do as you're told.'

She gave him a mock salute and allowed herself to be ushered into the elegant store. They emerged half an hour later, a small parcel tucked into Jim's coat pocket. He smiled down at her; it was like courting all over again. Better, even.

As they ticked items off the list they used taxis to ferry their parcels down to their hotel – the Royal Station, chosen by Elsie because it was where they'd spent their first night together, before going on to Tynemouth for their honeymoon. Best of all, they ambled up Grey Street, past the Theatre Royal and found interesting places for lunch, for afternoon tea. Supper they ate at the hotel; Elsie was worn out by the day's walking and Jim was content to take her into the restaurant on his arm. She was wearing a dress she'd made herself in the new style; long, fitted and high-waisted, which showed off her slender figure. Around her neck she was wearing the gold locket they'd chosen earlier in the day. As the maître d'hôtel showed them to their table Jim bent over and whispered to her:

'There's not a man in the room can keep his eyes off you.'

'Don't be daft.'

There were several soldiers in the room, including four

officers dining together; they all followed Elsie with their eyes. One of them even raised his glass to Jim as they passed. For the first time he wished he was already in uniform; his civilian self wasn't worthy of her.

Later, in their room, she sat on the bed to take her shoes off.

'No, wait!'

He took her hands and pulled her gently to her feet, then knelt in front of her. He eased off her shoes, placing them neatly to one side, then he carefully unfastened and rolled each stocking down her legs, kissing her knees, the arches of her feet, her toes. Without looking at her face, he gathered up her dress around her waist and undid her drawers, easing them down and onto the floor. She put her hands on his shoulders to balance as he undressed her; he could feel her fingers grasping him tightly as she felt the cool air on her skin. Without removing the dress, he pushed her gently back onto the bed and then bent down to kiss between her thighs. He stood up to unbutton his flies. Unlike their first lovemaking – in a room just along the corridor – this time he didn't need to ask whether she was ready for him: her arms were lying wide on the bed beyond her head; her hips in their silk corset were raised to meet him.

Their return to Bellingham the following afternoon was dispiriting. As Jim tipped the porter he remembered their home-coming from honeymoon four years ago; it caused a sharp stab of pain in his chest. He took Elsie's hand and they walked the same route through the town, although today the road was slick with rain water; she held tightly onto his arm as they walked across the square towards the house.

By the following weekend the piles of clothing and equipment were ready for packing, apart from the tailoring which was due to arrive by post in the next few days. With a lot of banging about, he and Ivan managed to lug his old school trunk down from the loft. Ivan unscrewed the lock which had been broken years before, to mend or replace. He gave the trunk a lick of varnish, printed his name in white paint. It stood in the spare room, lid open, ready. He hated it now in a way he'd never done as a boy: a new term at St Bees had been something to look forward to.

On Sunday morning Elsie lit a fire in the grate, wanting to make the afternoon's packing comfortable in at least one way. It smoked at first having been unused for years, but it wasn't long before the coals were glowing and flames were dancing, mirrored in the brass fender. After lunch she went up and knelt on a cushion beside the open trunk, list in hand. She began to place everything carefully inside, checking as she went. Jim passed the items from the bed as she named them. He loved to see her so serious, so efficient. She frowned now and then as she riffled through the piles of clothes.

'If you don't have enough of anything I suppose you can always buy some when you're home. Or in Cambridge.'

He took her arm and lifted her from the floor, pulling her onto the bed. His books scattered onto the wooden boards.

'I know exactly what I won't have enough of, and I certainly won't be able to buy it in Cambridge!' He leaned over and kissed her. He wanted to keep on kissing her until the last second, until the end of the world.

Well before dark he walked over to Fairstead Hall. He'd been invited to collect the promised pistol, thoroughly cleaned and overhauled by Archie's gamekeeper, an ex-serviceman himself. At Archie's insistence the man came in to shake Jim's hand and gave a demonstration, there in the drawing room. The parts moved and clicked, solid and elegant ... such precision ... no wonder men grew to love their weapons. Later, over a large brandy, he mentioned the sword. He had a day in London; where should he go to buy one?

'Good Lord, why didn't I think of that? Damn and blast! Just leave it with me. I have two. I know it sounds a bit extravagant, but one was bought for me by my father, the other was presented by the regiment when I got my DSO. I dare say you won't mind a second-hand blade? Good!'

Archie topped up his glass then left the room, reappearing ten minutes later with the sword and its fittings carefully wrapped up in cloth and tied with string.

'Here you are, old chap. Don't open it out now; take it home – let that clever brother of yours take a look at it. It's yours if you want it.'

Jim took it reverentially from Archie's outstretched hands.

'I feel that I should pay you for these, Archie. They're expensive things.'

'Heaven forbid, I wouldn't sell these. But they're yours to use while you need them. All I ask is that you bring them back safely.'

Archie patted him on the arm, then turned away, reaching for his pipe. It wasn't only the gun and sword he wanted back in one piece. Jim knew that. When he set off back down the hill to Bellingham he had a Webley Mark IV revolver in his pocket and the officer's sword with its tackle bundled over his shoulder.

Four days left.

EIGHT

Elsie

She returned Jim's kiss, but her mind was in the kitchen where Ivan would be sitting at the table, fettling the lock. Eyes closed, she could see his hands, busy with a screwdriver, deftly turning and re-turning the key to check the motion. When Jim left for Archie's she stayed upstairs, packing and repacking the trunk, guilt making her blot out everything except her husband and the journey he'd be making. Bellingham to London: three trains; if he starts with the milk churns he'll do it in a day. She felt nervous and edgy at the thought of him being so far away.

When Jim arrived back from Archie's they gathered round as he unpacked the weapons and placed them on the kitchen table. They looked sinister alongside the china cups, and the milk jug with its delicate beaded cover. Ivan was intrigued by the sword. Apparently he'd thought once or twice of making one, but it was a specialist job.

'Just look at this blade. I need to go somewhere and learn how it's done.'

After lunch the next day he unwrapped it again, balancing it in his hands, holding it up to the light as though it were a holy relic.

'It's beautiful ... makes me want to be an officer if you can use one of these!'

He attached the scabbard to his belt and stood to attention

beside the kitchen sink, then drew the sword and started to make theatrical lunges, bending his knee, one hand on his hip. It was so incongruous that even Lily was laughing. That doesn't happen very often! She looked over at Jim, leaning back watching his brother's antics, smiling.

'Do you know how to use that thing?'

'Haven't even tried it yet. But no doubt I'll learn if I need to.'

He didn't sound sure. Maybe he was anxious to play down the likelihood of meeting the enemy at such close quarters.

'I hope you don't. I hope you never have to take the horrible thing out. Not ever.'

Even so, she watched, mesmerised, as Ivan swished the weapon over Lily's head, making her flinch.

'D'ye think I'd make a good knight, Elsie? In shining armour? I could be Lancelot and you can be Guinevere, what d'ye think?'

He grinned at her, then abruptly replaced the sword and unbuckled the scabbard from his belt. He handed it over to Jim, then he was off, back to work.

The last few days were spent in the shop and doing the rounds of friends and a few cousins. It was only going to be four and half months this time, then he'd be home on leave before embarkation to France and his battalion. In spite of all the banter and the raising of glasses, it all felt very final. She knew he was putting on a brave face for her – she could read as well as he could the daily list under 'Officers Killed' in the newspaper. Ivan could lark on with the sword, but there was nothing in the least bit romantic in what Jim was going to do.

They were at the station very early on the Friday morning; he needed to spend Saturday in London before reporting to Cambridge on Sunday evening. He'd sent his gear down ahead on the trap, but they wanted the last ten minutes alone so he waved Will off and they followed on foot. It was bitterly cold as they walked down, hand in hand, their breath clouding the air. On the platform he hugged her to his chest, kissing her forehead, stroking her back in its heavy wool coat. There must have been a few people there, waiting, but she didn't notice until the others began to move forward as the train approached, trundling down from Riccarton to Hexham on the single line. A skirt of steam billowed onto the platform as the engine snorted and squealed to a halt, briefly clouding Jim's trunk and valises, piled together. Two porters, both of whom they knew, manhandled Jim's gear up into the guard's van at the back, then jumped back down to shake his hand. Once they'd gone he gave her one last hurried kiss and climbed up into the second of the two carriages, his haversack catching on the narrow door. As the whistle sounded and the engine began to edge slowly away, Elsie stood with her arms wrapped round herself as if to replace his. Tears dribbled down her cheeks. Jim had warned her that he wasn't going to stand and wave and that nor should she. She understood. He was afraid of her seeing him cry, of seeing her cry, so there was nothing to watch but the back of the train disappearing from sight.

Back at Erringtons she went about her work in a daze, feeling disconnected from the buying and selling. Lily wasn't openly sympathetic, she hadn't expected her to be, but she wasn't unkind either; in fact she even admitted that she'd felt a little bit sad as she opened up the shop without Jim that morning. Between them they managed all the tasks: Elsie at the counter, Lily in the office behind unless there were customers waiting. Not that waiting was a problem, generally; when locals came into their shop it was as much an opportunity to catch up with the news as it was to buy groceries, so being delayed by a queue was helpful. Conversations continued at the back of the shop, then out in the street. Nearly every customer who came through the door that Friday knew that Jim had just left for officer training; each of them said a few words of support. God bless you lass, we're all pulling together.

By evening she was tired beyond reckoning. A damp weight seemed to have landed on her; the weeks of preparation were over; now there was the long haul of waiting. But for what, and for how long? One of her customers – an older woman – had been talking about the war as if it were just a temporary inconvenience, a thunderstorm on a sunny day: 'We all have to take the rough with the smooth in this life'. She was so calm about it. Elsie smiled and nodded, but she was livid; she wanted to argue with her, to shout into her stupid cow face for saying something so foolish. How could warfare, men being slaughtered and left to rot in a French field, be described as 'the rough', as if it was just a spell of bad weather, or a bit of arthritis! The rough with the smooth? What is this smooth, anyway? She was aware, every minute of every hour, of Jim on his journey south. And Ivan … she couldn't stop it, it was like picking at a scab. Her life had no smooth at all.

She packed up some ham and a few bits and pieces for supper, hoping he'd be there when she got home. No, hoping he wouldn't be. Lily took her coat and hat from the hooks as well as her own, and turned out the lamps. United for once, they began the short walk back to the house, if not together, not as apart as they might have been.

Ivan had just set out to meet them when they reached the square. Elsie started as he emerged from the semi darkness, as if she'd conjured him up with her thoughts. He took their bags, asked about their day. Had Jim's train left on time? Here, give me those parcels. When they arrived they found the parlour fire already alight and the kitchen warm from the banked up stove. It was utterly strange, knowing that Jim wasn't going to walk in and join them. For want of anything else to do, Elsie tied her pinny and began to peel some potatoes; they had to eat. Her reserves of good will running out, Lily went through for her glass of sherry, feet up. Elsie concentrated, turning the potatoes as she pared off the dirty skins in thick, flat curls. Ivan leaned with his back to the draining board, watching her work.

'So.'

'So?' Her heart was thudding. What did he want her to say?

'So, how do you feel?' His voice was gentle, soothing.

'I don't know. Sad. Worried.' She washed the peeled potatoes, chopped them into a pan. She was good at such things. Efficient.

'You know I want you, don't you?'

'Ivan, Jim's only just gone. How can you?'

'How can I? Because now, or later … some time … what difference does it make? It has nothing to do with Jim; it's you and me this is about.'

She turned on him, her voice an angry whisper.

'How can it have nothing to do with Jim when he's my husband and your brother? It's … it's shameful.'

She wiped her hands then began to lay the table, banging the cutlery in place. Her eyes were brimming.

'Shameful? Elsie, what I feel for you isn't shameful. It's the reason I get up in the morning and it's the reason I can't sleep at night. If you don't feel the same, I don't know what I'll do.'

'It's not that I don't feel the same! It's just too …'

'Too soon? Is that how you feel?'

She nodded miserably.

'So it's a matter of timing then. Not shame. You think I'm trying to take Jim's place … when he's only just gone.'

She nodded again, tears slipping down her cheeks.

'I'm not, you know. I don't want to come between you and Jim. If I did ... if I thought I might ... I'd go away, start again somewhere else.'

He was trying to be honest, she was certain of that, but surely he didn't believe it? It was a childish idea ... ridiculous. She felt anger rising again, frustration.

'You could start again, but where would that leave me?' Oh God, what was she saying? 'I can't love you and Jim; not in the way you want me to. It's not right.'

'But you do. I know it. And this isn't a matter of right and wrong, like some law, carved in stone. It's about being honest with your own heart ... with your soul. You'll see. But I'll wait. If that's what you want. Come on, let's get this supper finished; it's a long time since lunch.'

So that was it. Ivan was willing to wait until ... she was what? Ready to admit to him what she couldn't even admit to herself?

'You need to keep away from me, Ivan. Be strong for us both. Find someone else.'

Without a word, Ivan drew himself away from her. After supper he did the rounds of closing up the house. He badgered Lily into helping to clear up after the meal, but they all agreed that they should begin to look for extra help in the house. Sitting around the parlour fire they decided that they should find a cook who would prepare lunch and supper now that Elsie was out of the house all day. Agnes could wash the pots in the morning and then sort out the fire and the beds. This conversation, practical issues, did more than anything else to keep her mind away from Jim and the war. Only when she was at last in bed, alone for the first time in over four years, did the other battle flame into life again.

NINE

Frank

He was chuffed to hear about Lily's brother: gone to war at last, snooty bastard. He was beginning to think it would never happen. When he parked up outside Erringtons on the Monday afternoon Lily met him at the door, nodding towards the lass at the counter, mouthing 'I'll tell you later'. He was bent over with the weight of his case; he hadn't been north of the Tyne on business for over a month and he had some new lines. He wasn't slow; he could see what was going on; didn't need to be told. The skinny lass wrapping butter – bonny face mind – must be the sister in law. What's her name again? Ellie? Cheap as chips, according to Lily, but looking quite smart from where he was standing. So she was working in the shop now the husband had gone to face the Hun. He let the case drop onto the wooden boards, flexing his creased hand to bring the feeling back. Bloody thing got heavier and heavier. He took off his hat and gave Lily one of the *phaw* looks she liked: ample chest and rounded arse: get in there, Frank lad. He winked at her, mimed a discreet kiss behind his hand. Carefully does it. He raised his eyebrows and nodded his head towards Elsie as she took payment for the butter and pushed the heavy cash drawer closed. Lily walked him over to the counter.

'This is my friend, Mr Liddle. Frank, this is my brother Jim's wife, Mrs Errington. She's just helping me out until Jim gets back. We've been walking out for a while now, haven't we Frank?'

'We certainly have! Delighted to make your acquaintance … Ellie is it?'

He put his hat on the counter and offered his hand. She took it, but he knew straight away that he ought to have used 'Mrs Errington'. Nothing specific. Lovely little hand she had, but he could just tell that she wasn't best pleased to meet him. Now, would that be as a salesman? Or as her sister in law's 'friend'?

'It's Elsie. Good afternoon, Mr Liddle.'

He was right – no flies on Frank Liddle. Got the name wrong as well, dammit. Frank lad, you're slipping.

'Lily, are you going to look at what Mr Liddle has in his case, or should I? I know it was Jim's job, but you know more about what he has to offer than I do.'

So: deliberately formal, a bit trying-to-be-posh. She ruddy knows Lily's itching to get me on my own.

'That's true, I'll do it. We'll go through to the office, where it's quiet.'

'You do that. I'll not disturb you.'

Lily was already making her way there, lifting the hinged section of the counter and holding it up so that he could follow. He grabbed his hat and gave Elsie his best smile as he brought up the rear, his bulging case extended in front of him through the gap. As he closed the office door firmly behind them he had to force himself not to laugh. No wonder Lily was cool about that one!

He crouched down to unlock and open out his display, but then rose quickly to his feet and pulled Lily towards him, as if his passion had got the better of him. Well, it had really, so not much of a show; it was a while since he'd had it and she was a tasty bit of woman. He kept her eyes on his as he

69

fondled her breasts through the fabric of her dress, feeling her nipples harden between his expert fingers. That's my girl.

'This is what you want, isn't it?'

He moved from side to side, pressing rigid against her. She was mesmerised, as well she might be; he had a fine John Thomas when he was in top gear and he knew he was doing exactly what she wanted him to do. Except she didn't want him to do it now. She pulled away, flushed.

'Did you bring the ring? You said you'd bring it.'

As a matter of fact he had brought a ring for her; it'd cost him a penny or two, but then, it was going to be a good investment. He pulled her back and wrapped his arms around her, his hands on her bottom. She wriggled, but he spoke softly into her ear.

'It's in my pocket, don't you worry, Pussycat. Come and have dinner with me, tonight, in The Railway. Then I'll give it you ... if you're a good girl.'

She pulled back to see his face; saw that he meant it. Just look at those eyes sparkle ... this'll make a difference; should get a bit of slap and tickle and not before time ... once that ring's on her finger she can stop this prissy missy stuff. The wedding could be soon: there's lots of people getting married without long engagements because of the war. They can get a move on. All they need is the house rented and furnished to move in. She'll mention it any second now ...

'Have you signed for the house, yet?'

"We'll talk about that later. All in good time, as my old mother used to say. I'll book a table for seven o' clock; come and collect you a half past six. Now, let's look at me stuff before I tup you on that desk!'

They put together an order which he made sure was far larger than Jim's would have been. He wrote it himself really ... her mind was already fixed on the wedding ... spring

70

would be nice ... and the dress: she'll have the dress made in Newcastle. Ann can be her Maid of Honour. If big brother's here he can give her away, if not Ivan can do it blahdy blahdy blah ... he was sick to death of the whole thing by the time they emerged from the office but he kept the grin going as she rattled on about it.

He made a point of saying goodbye to little sister ... called her 'Mrs Errington' this time round though; let no-one suggest that Frank Liddle didn't learn from his mistakes. Lily came out onto the street to wave him on his way to his next call, watching with puppy eyes as he pulled his driving gloves on. He took his time ... good to wait until there was a bit of a crowd in the street before he started his motor; still didn't understand why Jim hadn't bought them one. Never mind, she'd be driving around in his before long.

He arrived back in Bellingham in time to have a good wash and brush up, then walked through the quiet streets to collect her. As she opened the door he stepped back and whistled: she'd pulled the stops out all right, wearing a dress that made the most of her curves – none of that straight up and down modern stuff. She invited him in, and why not? Big brother wouldn't like it, but what the eye don't see ... The house looked big enough for two families – she'd have to get used to something a canny bit smaller before long. Ivan and Elsie were in the parlour waiting for them; a tray with cut glasses and a decanter sat on the occasional table. Lily was all gracious lady when they went in, wanting to show him off a bit. Though he said it himself, he was looking very dapper: smart overcoat and silk scarf against the November cold. He laid on the charm after the introductions, asked all the right questions about Ivan's work at the smithy. Hard going, though; he didn't say much. Probably retarded. Another ten minutes of formal conversation and they were ready to leave. He held Lily's coat for her and stepped back to allow her through the door first; he knew the ropes.

As they strolled round to The Railway he only half listened to her chatter: his mind was on the evening ahead. Would she expect him to get down on one knee? He had a bit of a gammy left knee, actually; a childhood injury. That's why he hadn't volunteered. It didn't hurt; he didn't limp or anything, but he'd seen the doctor about it, and he'd said not to enlist. Well, not in so many words he hadn't, but that's what he'd been implying, thank God. He had enough cash in his pocket to do them proud tonight; he'd called in and ordered champagne earlier on – it should be waiting for them at the table. Pity it wasn't in his room, but there you go; time ahead for getting into her drawers. Tonight was all about getting into other things, especially her good books. Not that it was hard.

He helped her off with her coat and pulled her chair out. The champagne was a good idea by the look on her face, all lit up at the sight of the green bottle in its bucket of ice, and the fancy glasses. He'd thought hard about when to do it: before or after they ate? Hard to be sure, but the main thing was an audience. He'd play it by ear. It didn't take long: after a couple of glasses of champagne he knew the time was right; there were quite a few locals in by now, sitting down for dinner. He cleared his throat and put his glass on the table. Before he could change his mind he was down on his sound right knee, her hand in his.

'Miss Errington. Lily. Will you marry me?'

There, he'd done it. He saw the look on her face, saw her glance round to check if people were watching – he knew it – before she accepted.

'Oh Frank, of course I will'.

Time to stand up again, carefully does it. He drew a small

box from his pocket and opened it with a flourish. He lifted the ring from its velvet nest, then leaned over and slipped the ring onto her finger; he needed a bit of help to get it over the knuckle, but even so it was a slick operation. Then he pulled her to her feet beside him. Holding up her left hand he planted a kiss on her cheek, then made an announcement.

'Ladies and Gentlemen, my beautiful fiancée.'

He turned her round to face the room. She was blushing like fury, bless her! The other diners clapped politely, one or two came over to offer their congratulations. It was perfect. He decided not to bring up the subject of the house until tomorrow; he had her good and hooked now, so there was no point in spoiling the dinner by talking about money. When the waiter came he ordered for both of them, taking charge. She loved it ... they all do. And they ate well; the food was always better out of the city, especially the beef. Every now and then he leaned across the table and patted her hand. The ring looked good for what he'd paid for it. He concentrated on his next move as she chattered away about churches and wedding breakfasts and God knows what else. Actually, he did get drawn in at one point, when she started on about getting her portion; her old father had left her some cash for after she was married. Now, there's a thing, and never a mention before now.

'Happy?'

It was like fishing in a barrel. Give a girl a grope and a ring, not necessarily in that order, and she's putty in your hands. Lily's face was flushed with the champagne followed by the wine he'd ordered with the dinner, a classy red. He preferred a sweet white, but he'd read the book: red wine with red meat. She'd certainly drunk her fair share; if he could get her upstairs now he'd be rogering her in no time. Good looking woman, mind. He could feel his dick twitching ...

down, boy, not tonight.

'Oh Frank, of course I am. I can't wait for us to be walking back down the aisle together, as man and wife.'

He patted her hand, nodding as if he was lost for words at the idea. Which he was, come to think of it.

TEN

Ivan

He was laughing out loud as he returned from closing the door behind Frank and Lily.

'What an oaf! He's exactly what she deserves. Can't she see what he's like?'

Elsie was gathering up the dirty glasses as he spoke, but she set the tray down. Why was she looking at him like that?

'Well, he's not to everyone's taste, but aren't you being a bit harsh? He's nicely dressed, and chatty at least. It's not like you to be so unpleasant about someone. I don't like it. You should be glad for her.'

'Nicely dressed and chatty?' He picked up the tray and carried it along to the kitchen, talking back over his shoulder. 'That's damning with faint praise, and you know it. And I am! I *am* glad for her. They make a good pair – completely artificial, both of them. I'll be delighted if he whisks her off her feet and drives her off into the distant sunset in his fancy car. I bet *he* has a different voice for everyone he speaks to, as well.'

Ha, she smiled at that. He was right: Lily did have a little repertoire of voices: posh for the phone and for their higher class customers; normal not-so-posh voice for ordinary use and a slight Northumbrian accent when the old wifeys were in for a gossip. It drove him mad to hear her at it, especially on the phone.

75

'Frank may be an open book compared with us. Have you thought of that? Maybe it's us that's false, not them.'

Elsie was standing clutching the decanter of sherry, looking down at the floor. He didn't want to have this sort of conversation ... not when she'd had three glasses of sherry. He could hear it in her voice: it was a bit blurry and she wouldn't be fit to talk about it properly if he started on at her. He came over and took the decanter from her hands, making sure the stopper was secure before putting it on the kitchen table.

Elsie, we're not false.' He drew a long breath. 'We're in trouble; our feelings are in the wrong place, but false? Not me.'

She leaned against him, allowing herself to relax into his arms as they folded around her. She was sleepy, seemed content just to be warm and secure with him. He rocked her gently, smoothing her back with his hands and kissing the top of her head. God, that smell ... her hair.

'You're tipsy.'

He led her back to the parlour and sat her in the big armchair next to the fire, carefully lifting her feet up onto Lily's footstool. He put some more coals on the fire, replacing the guard in case of sparks. As she dozed he went back in the kitchen, clattering around, sorting out their supper. I can do this.

He woke her gently and walked her through to the kitchen where two places were laid at one corner of the scrubbed oak table. The lamp was low; its familiar hiss took the place of any conversation. He looked up from his own plate once in a while to satisfy himself that she was eating as well: no wonder she was so thin, the way she picked at her meals. If Jim was there he'd be saying something about it. He began to clear, carrying their plates to the sink in the scullery. When she followed him through to help he stopped her, indicating the door with a spare little finger.

'I think you should get away up to bed; you've got an early start.'

He began to fill the sink, avoiding her gaze, concentrating on the task. He could pile them up for Agnes in the morning, but he needed something to do. She came over and took up a cloth, then began to dry as he washed the pots.

'Go to bed, Elsie'.

He still wasn't looking at her, but he felt her close beside him.

'If you don't go, I'll make you go.'

'Can't we sit for a while, talk a bit?'

'No, I don't think so.' Why was she trying to persuade him to spend time with her, after what she'd said?

He placed the last pan upside down on the wooden drainer, then took the cloth from her hands.

'I'll finish this. Off you go.'

'Is this about not being false?' She looked lost.

'It's about you having had too much sherry, too much strain and not enough sleep. Now, do I have to tell you again?'

He wasn't joking and at last she understood. She said goodnight and left the room. He waited a few seconds then followed her into the passage and watched as she climbed the stairs, unsteady but careful. Only when she'd closed her bedroom door did he return to the kitchen, turn out the lamp and leave by the back door.

He made his way through the town, a scarf wrapped round his mouth and nose for warmth. Every door he passed was closed. Tar smoke from the coal fires was thick in the night air. He glanced up at the town hall clock as he passed; he was a bit late. He turned off the main road and strode, hands in pockets, up the hill towards his smithy. He slackened his pace to kick a loose stone neatly off the pavement onto the cobbles: goal! There'd been no serious football for a while and he missed it, but most of the team had gone by now ... some permanently.

He paused and looked around in the semi darkness; there weren't many people about at this time, but he was hoping Isabel had managed to get out of the house to meet him; it wasn't easy for her to slip out of their only door without being seen. He waited, leaning against one of the trees that lined the road, hidden in its shadow. Just as he was about to give up and set off back home he heard clogs clattering on the road as she dashed up the steep bank. She was out of breath, but even in the poor light he could make out her beaming smile as she threw herself against him.

'Thought you weren't going to make it.'

He wrapped his arms tightly around her, feeling the warmth of her body against his; she was glowing from her race through the town.

'It was me mam: finishing off some sewing instead of getting hersel off to her bed. I kept saying that I'd do it and the light wasn't good enough, but you know what she's like. Dead stubborn.'

'So that's where you get it from. Come on ...'

He pulled Isabel's thick woolen shawl up around her neck and smoothed her hat down to cover her auburn hair; it wouldn't do for her to be recognised out alone at night. She took his hand and he led her the remaining few hundred yards up the hill, keeping a close watch as they walked for any curious eyes. He unlocked the heavy door and pushed her through quickly, taking one last look around to be sure they hadn't been seen. It was unlikely, given that there were no houses immediately around the building, but even so ...

He fastened the door behind them and lit the oil lamp,

turning the wick down low, although the soot-blackened walls absorbed most of the glow; only the tools gleamed back at them, hanging on their racks.

'It's cold. I thought it would be cosy… because of the forge and that.'

'The heat doesn't stay long once the fire's damped down. Come here; I'll warm you up in no time.'

Isabel stayed where she was, looking round, her shoulders hunched against the chill air. He leaned against the door, arms folded, and looked her up and down, wondering whether she was going to put him off or run away like she did the other day. Embarrassed, she opened her shawl to release her arms, and then held her hands out towards the cool embers of the fire.

He was fond of her, with her kind heart and her silly sense of humour. She was a bonny lass, too, no doubt about that: pretty teeth and soft skin; if Elsie really meant that he should find someone else, well, Isabel would do nicely. He really hoped she wasn't going to grow all coy on him again. In his experience, once a girl let you touch her as he'd touched Isabel, it was only a matter of time. But she made no attempt to come over for a cuddle, and he was beginning to wonder what she was after.

'What's up? Wish you hadn't come?'

'No, it's not that. I like being here with you, Ivan.'

She took her hat off and looked round for somewhere clean to put it, but there wasn't anywhere, so she hung it on the same hook as his blacksmith's tongs. She came over at last, slipping her arms inside his coat and round his back, kissing him full on the lips. He straightened up and returned her kiss.

'Howay, we'll go in the back room. There's some blankets and stuff to make you comfy, keep you warm.' He picked up the lamp, but as they reached the door she resisted and pulled away from him.

'No, I'll not. I love you Ivan, but a lass wants a ring on her finger before she lies down with a man.'

'You mean, you do.'

'All right. Aye ... I do. I know I'm not your first lass, but you're my first real man. I know I joke around a bit, but ...'

'It's not a joke to let a man see you half naked. He could get the wrong impression.'

At least she blushed: she knew he was right; she'd led him on the other evening, but only because she needed him so badly, he was sure of it. What she wanted was a promise that he wasn't just going to have his way with her then move on. Or be forced to marry her if she got in the family way, like her friend Daisy; Daisy who'd gone too far with John Hall at haytime last summer and had a baby this April gone. They'd been married in the October, but only because her father had threatened to take Albert's head off if he didn't do the right thing by her. Not a happy story for anyone, really: he could see why it made Isabel cautious. What she wanted was an engagement ring, and then a proper wedding with flower girls, not like John and Daisy's muted affair ... her parents had been too ashamed to have much of a do.

'Sorry. I really do want ... but it's wrong and it's dangerous. Me dad'll kill us and me mam'll die of shame if she finds out.'

Ivan laughed out loud. The idea of a tumble with Isabel being 'dangerous' seemed absurd. But he knew what she meant; it was different for a girl. Her dad was a right bruiser; a pitman with muscles the size of coal buckets. And there were two younger brothers, both of them hard buggers. He put his arms around her and held her until she relaxed, then he kissed her again. Standing back, he took her left hand and put it to his lips, then singled out her fourth finger and eased it between his lips, sucking it, looking straight into her eyes. He could see her melting again. He took her finger from his mouth and held it in front of her face.

'So, if I promise to put a ring on this pretty finger, you'll feel that it isn't wrong and isn't dangerous for us to be together. Is that it?'

It hadn't been quite what she meant and he knew it. What she was really hoping for was for him to respect her enough to want to wait, and she wanted him to have enough willpower for the both of them. God, these women! He was as hard as one of his own pokers down there … it was painful. If she only knew how much he was longing to have her in that back room. But maybe not as much as she needed to be as pure as wind-blown snow when she walked down the aisle.

'Yes, that's it.'

She pulled away from him and he let her go.

This wasn't what he'd expected when he'd brought her up here, but he ought to have seen it coming. She'd dropped quite a few hints in the last few weeks and her mother had even invited him for tea when the father was on the four 'til midnight. He'd spent an entertaining couple of hours with the two women and he liked her mother, no bother. And it wasn't that she wouldn't make a good wife for him, either; he was sure she would, although she'd be a right handful. So why wasn't he taking the next train to Hexham to choose a ring, then? He knew that her father and brothers would be glad to have him in the family, so why the delay? He could rent – no buy – a cottage for them; he still had money from his father. Maybe she was right. Maybe he had no business expecting to get inside her drawers without making her a promise at least.

'A penny for them?'

She was standing in front of him, gazing at his face, trying to read what was going through his mind. He gave a long sigh, then pulled her back to him, holding her hard against him. Was this what he really wanted? And how would he know if it wasn't?

'All right then ... we'll get engaged.'

There, he'd said it, and he might as well keep going so there'd be no going back:

'I love you, Isabel, and I want to marry you.'

Isabel was tense in his arms, but he felt her relax as his words found their way home. There were tears wet on her cheeks and he smiled down at her, smearing them away with his thumbs. He kissed her deeply, his hands cupping her face as her hands crept round under his coat again, this time pulling up his shirt, her icy fingers spread on his warm back. His patience failed him as she played her nails up and down his spine and before she knew it he'd slipped his arms around her waist and lifted her through to where he'd left the pile of blankets. As he set her down, she started again.

'You do mean it, don't you? You are going to buy us a ring and everything? I mean, you really do love us?'

He knew she just wanted him to say the words again, but he wished she didn't. He lay down beside her on the makeshift bed, the faint glow from the lamp just enough to see by. He began to undo her dress and kept on whispering, reassuring her, saying whatever she wanted to hear. Cold as it was, he wanted her naked. Thank God she was only wearing drawers and a shift under her dress; nothing with fancy hooks and ribbons to untie, not even stockings; her feet must be freezing. He sat back and looked at her, then quickly pulled his shirt over his head and unfastened his breeches, yanking them down so that he could press his flesh against hers. He explored her body, cupping her firm round breasts and gradually easing his hand down over her smooth

82

belly to where her triangle of dark hair was just visible in the near darkness. Her eyes widened and her body arched as his fingers crept firmly but gently between her legs and began to ease inside her. He kissed her again and again as his fingers stroked gently, until he could feel her growing restless.

'Do you want me to stop?

'No, I want ... don't stop ...'

She whimpered softly and reached out for him. She was ready, and as eager for him as he was for her. He eased his lean body up over hers and guided himself inside her and began to move, in control, looking into her face to sense if he was hurting her. She took his rhythm straight away and they were bound together, her arms wrapped around his neck, until he came to a shuddering climax, unable to hold back any longer. He lay down beside her, pulling the blankets up for warmth and stroking her hair. He could do a lot worse than marry her, if only he could do the right thing and forget Elsie.

'I love you, Ivan.'

She cuddled in to him, needing a response. He turned towards her and kissed her, his hand resting on her belly under the blanket. She wasn't plump, but her flesh was soft: there was so much more of her than there was of ...

He sighed, eyes closed. 'Elsie, I love you too ...'

They both tensed as what he'd said sank in. Without saying anything, Isabel sat up and fumbled around on the cold stone floor for her drawers and yanked them on, then her thick woolen dress, standing up to fasten the buttons with shaking fingers, ignoring him as he stammered an apology, trying hopelessly to unspeak his words. That word.

'Where's me clogs?'

She pushed her feet roughly inside them without doing up the leather laces.

'Isabel, don't go. I don't know why I called you that. But

it doesn't mean anything. Come here ... look at me, will you!'

He grabbed her arms above the elbows and tried to make her look at him, but she strained away, wriggling to free herself, her head twisted to one side. He let her go, worried that he might hurt her if he didn't, which was when she turned towards him, as furious as she was hurt.

'Doesn't mean anything? You call me by another lass's name just after we've ...we've ... been together, and you don't think it matters? And Elsie! Elsie? Why her name, eh?'

Sobbing now, she dragged her shawl on and ripped her hat from the hook, bringing the tongs crashing onto the flagstones. She stumbled to the door and felt for the lock in the gloom, shaking as she turned the heavy key. Ivan followed her, dragging his trousers up, tucking his shirt in; he could just make out the knocking of her clogs as she bolted down the road towards the town. What a fucking mess. He went back and folded the blankets away, then extinguished the lamp, burning one of his fingers as he fumbled with the glass chimney. He sucked on it as he locked the door and set out down the hill, glad of the darkness. So ... that was clever! Isabel knew it wasn't a slip of the tongue; she wasn't dim. A confession, more like ... and she'd understood.

He walked down to Percy Row and stood in the shadows, watching to see if there was any movement in Isabel's cottage. There wasn't, and anyway he doubted whether there was much to be said. Not yet, at least.

ELEVEN

Elsie

Postie brought the letter into Erringtons with the business post, instead of taking it to Hareshaw House.

'Here we are, Mrs Errington, he hasn't forgot you yet!'

He popped the envelope in front of her on the counter, hoping for a cheerful response; it wasn't often these days that he could be sure of one.

'Well, thank you, Mr Nunn. I wasn't expecting a letter!' She gave him a big smile. She was lucky, knowing her husband was safe for the time being, unlike a lot of them.

'No-one likes a man who brings bad news. The sooner this war ends the better, pet.'

It was kind of him to bring the letter directly, but she put it in her coat pocket to read at night, after work. Jim had said he'd write straight away but she hadn't expected to hear from him quite so soon ... it was typical of him. She needed to reply, tell him about Lily and Frank. Instead of working out in the back as she usually did, Lily was staying near the counter that morning, even standing beside her.

'People will want to see my ring, so I might as well just be out here today. We can work together.'

Lily was right: the engagement was common knowledge before midday, and people were calling in to congratulate her. She was chatty with everyone, even the sort of customers she normally avoided. It didn't seem to be an act, either; it was as if the engagement had peeled away the old Lily leaving a fresh one in her place. There was no guarantee that it would last, but in the meantime it made working alongside her a different experience altogether. Maybe it was a good thing, in spite of Ivan's reservations, and no doubt Jim's when he heard. Every customer gave Lily an opportunity to talk about 'her Frank', his plans for a lavish honeymoon, the new house ... she never stopped. And when the shop was empty she would stand there, just fiddling with the ring on her finger. *Good grief, she's gone all soft.*

Frank left Bellingham in the morning, after calling in at the shop to say goodbye. He whipped his hat off and came straight over to kiss Lily's cheek.

'Good morning ladies! I'd love to stay, but duty calls. I'll do my rounds as fast as possible and be back by Friday afternoon, my angel.'

Lily was radiant; he would be there for the weekend, staying at The Railway. They would have time to plan the wedding. By then she would have seen the vicar and asked Ann to be her bridesmaid. He leaned over the counter and kissed her cheek again; he chucked her chin playfully, then took her left hand with its ring and put it to his lips. Just as he was leaving, he turned back and casually asked Elsie if she could pass him a couple of packs of Players from the shelf behind her. He tapped his pocket.

'No cash on me, just make a note of it ... I'll settle up on Friday.'

She glanced at Lily: do I do this?

'Don't be silly, my love.' Lily rushed to the shelf and took three packs. He pocketed them with a wink of thanks and then left. His cologne loitered in the air behind him.

'Will I write that down?' Start an account?'

'Good heavens, no – Frank's my fiancé. He's family.' Lily's

face flushed with the pleasure of using the word. 'I'm the luckiest woman alive, Elsie.'

'I'm glad for you ... glad you're happy.'

She was glad, but the little she'd seen of Frank was helping her understand why the men didn't trust him. She wasn't going to tell Jim about the cigarettes, not even Ivan. As she picked up an order and began to gather up the items on the list, Lily came over and put her hand on her arm. It shocked her; Lily never touched her other than accidently.

'Elsie, I'm sorry I've not been a better sister to you. I'll try harder.'

That was all she said. It wasn't much, but for Lily to make any kind of apology was so rare that it left her speechless, and by the time it had sunk in, Lily was already busy with a new customer. For the life of her she couldn't work it out. Was it one of her games? Or a new leaf? Assuming it all went well ... fingers and toes crossed ... Lily would be leaving home soon; maybe she wanted to clear her conscience or something, like people did on their deathbeds? Whatever the reason, it was going to make her life easier by the looks of it. Thank God for small mercies. Ivan had been up and out before them that morning, so Elsie had suffered Lily alone over breakfast. She'd heard more than once about the champagne, about how romantic the proposal had been, how the other diners had been entranced by Frank's glamour and style. She'd admired the ring, then admired it again. Five years ago, when Jim brought her home the day after they were engaged, Lily had all but ignored her. She'd been nasty then and worse ever since, but here she was, saying sorry. Who would have thought it? She wondered what Ivan would say when she told him. She'd tell Jim when she wrote, too; he'd need to be sitting down when he read it!

She opened his letter after supper, leaning against the

range. Lily was through in the parlour: her pleasant mood had continued all day, and they could hear her humming cheerfully to herself as she pottered about. It was curiously disturbing; Ivan said it was like the purring of an ill-tempered cat. He was reading the newspaper, which he'd taken to doing since Jim left, now that the news wasn't filtering down to him any more. He was restless and looked grey and tired, which wasn't surprising given the time he'd come in the night before. She'd been asleep when he left the house, but her sherry-induced drowsing hadn't lasted long and she'd lain awake for hours. His tread on the stairs in the early hours of the morning had set her heart hammering: what was going on? And although he'd arrived home for supper at the usual time, he was tense. She wanted to ask him where he'd been the night before, but she couldn't. The strain was exhausting. Was it her? Was it the war? He'd mentioned that during the day there'd been one lad after another hanging around the forge to talk about the Government bringing in forced enlistment if the Derby Scheme didn't attract more recruits. He could see it coming ... maybe next year, just after Christmas.

'Jim said it wouldn't be long. He warned me.'

'Can't you appeal? I thought being a blacksmith was important?'

'It is, but they need us over there, too. Where the horses went. At the front.'

'What about the tractors? Who'll look after them if you go?'

'They'll find an older man. It's easy work, once you understand the mechanics. Didn't take me long. If I go they'll find an engineer from Hexham soon enough.'

She watched his face as he talked. He was young, fit and unmarried; his time had probably come, and fair enough. Was this why he was so on edge, then? She didn't think so:

he seemed resigned to being called up, in spite of hating everything about war. He hated violence, hated taking orders, hated being part of a team unless it was to kick a ball about … but he was ready to go if he had to. She wanted him not to be, she wanted him to want to stay, but she couldn't say it.

Jim's letter was interesting. He'd always written well. When they were courting he used to send notes to her, nearly every day. At first she'd been surprised by them; he could write better than he could talk. When she'd mentioned how impressed she was he'd admitted that he'd won the English Composition prize at St Bees more than once. She'd been self-conscious about her own lack of schooling – still was – but he'd encouraged her to read over the years. Now she read his first letter to her since their wedding.

He wrote that it'd taken him a while to get going with the letter because he couldn't even decide how to start because nothing he said seemed exactly right, or enough. In the end he began, 'My Darling Elsie', because that's what she was, he said. He told her about the train journey.

> … long and cold, but interesting to see different landscapes. We can travel down together after the war. At home every view is framed by layers, everywhere we look there are rolling fields and hills overlapping each other into the distance. We see only fragments of sky. As the train steamed south through county after county that's what I noticed most, the open skies filling the window. We steamed through acre after acre of level landscape, with villages scattered low on the horizon against a vast grey sky. And another thing, the churches have spires instead of towers. They point up like swords on the skyline …

He said that he was glad that next time she would be

in Harrods with him. It was awful, he'd thought, far too lavish, but she would enjoy the choice, the colours. There'd been Christmas decorations, fancy lights; he'd felt impossibly lonely without her beside him to filter the substance from the glitter. She would be entranced by the range of goods displayed, but there was too much choice for his liking. It had taken him an hour to choose a scarf for her, each one had seemed more beautiful than the last until he'd opted for soft wool in a rich blue to match her eyes; he'd send it as soon as he could. He'd found the trench coat he needed and it was there, hanging on a hook beside him. She would hate it, but Harrods boasted that it was the only one certain to keep the French rain out.

... I'll need it tomorrow because it's even colder here than in the North, which I wasn't expecting. All these miles south and it's still freezing! My room is small but comfortable, with a tiny grate for a fire, unlit as yet. I hope the students know how lucky they are to study here. My window looks out over a courtyard where, as I write, there are groups of men hovering about, smoking by lamplight. I passed through earlier, led by the college porter. He's a decent chap, invalided from France. Some of the men are in groups; they obviously know each other already – from school by the look of them: Elsie, they are so <u>young</u>! Surely they ought to be shaving before they're allowed into battle? There are a few older men, my age or even a bit older, which is a relief. I'll tell you more after tomorrow, when I've had a day to learn the ropes. We have a 5.30 start according to my orders, which I'll finish reading later.

You'll still be in bed when I'm out there lining up, no doubt with snowflakes as big as farthings melting between my collar and my neck. I'll be thinking about you, all warm and comfortable under our eiderdown as I stand out there in the icy darkness for roll call.

God bless you, I enclose kisses for your pretty lips. I love you, Jim. P.S. I'll post this now; go for a walk to find a post box. It will be good exercise and will warm me up – and I'll see a bit of Cambridge by night!

She nudged Ivan until he put his paper down and looked at her, eyebrows raised.

'He says it's really cold down there, and they start at 5.30. He won't like that.'

She folded the page, then unfolded it again.

'Do you want me to read it to you?'

'No, you just tell me the important bits. Has he used his sword yet? He's a great shot ... have they started target practice?'

'Not yet; give him a chance! This was written on his first evening in Cambridge. Sunday. It's mainly about the journey and Harrods.'

Ivan picked up the newspaper and began to read again. He answered from behind its pages.

'Just tell me when he starts doing some proper man's stuff will you? Something interesting.'

He grinned as she kicked him under the table. Friends again, thank God.

TWELVE

Frank

On Friday evening, after a long, hot bath, he walked round to Lily's for six thirty, as arranged.

'Sweets for my sweet!' He presented her with a box of chocolates as he stepped into the hall.

'Bring Frank through, Lily!'

He was whacked after his weeks' tour of north Northumberland towns but he wasn't going to refuse the offer of a drink. It would've been pleasant to have a little kip, feet up in front of that roaring fire, but he knew what was expected and he came up with a smooth flow of chat: stored up tales about his travels, little bits of gossip, especially now there was a war on. He kept them all entertained while he downed a couple of malts, then looked at his pocket watch and announced it was time for their supper at The Railway. He helped her on with her coat and she stood there with her arm through his, gazing up at him. He was used to women fancying the pants off him, but this adoration thing was a new one; he could get used to it, mind.

'You must eat here with us one evening, if you haven't already booked elsewhere.'

'Well, thank you, I'll be pleased to.'

Now, that sister in law knew how to make a man happy: full board didn't come cheap. And he could see why she wanted him around for a meal; old Ivan wasn't exactly a bundle of fun and what with the husband away soldiering she must be desperate for a bit of decent company.

Over at The Railway he wasn't quite as relaxed. Of course, it was good to see Lily; she was looking gorgeous as they took their seats at the table. But after a grinding week he just wanted a slap up dinner, not a sheaf of lists and dates to think about. Bless her, she'd obviously been working hard to get everything sorted out. The vicar's agreed to a date, March the eleventh, and her friend Ann's said she'll be the bridesmaid. There's a list of people they must invite, then a second list of those they might invite if there's enough …. *Christ!*

'Lily, pet, let's just have a nice dinner, eh?'

He touched her hand in a jokey way, ordered some more wine. *Here goes:*

'Perhaps we should talk about the house.'

He had to be very careful here: relax; no sign of any worry … keep her comfortable. As far as she was concerned he'd found an ideal house in Newcastle; they'd talked about it. It was small but it was in a fashionable area, quite close to the town centre near the theatre and restaurants, which made up for its size.

'When are you going to take me to see it?'

He knew she'd ask. He'd mentioned the idea of a trip down to town in his motor several times in the past, and now that they were engaged and Jim wasn't here to disapprove there was no excuse for putting it off.

'Well, there's a bit of a problem. The house I was after …' he leaned over, took her hand, '*we* were after? It's gone.'

'Gone? What do you mean, *gone?*'

Of course she had no idea what he was talking about.

'How can a house *go* anywhere?'

He saw a flicker of something – was that irritation in her eyes? She'd have to watch her step, getting shirty with him.

'I mean, my own darling, that someone else has taken it. Or will do if I don't come up with enough money to secure it. Damn shame: I thought we had an agreement, but this war's changed everything. I was hoping to surprise you, have the keys this weekend, but the bounder of a landlord wants a huge deposit. Shortage of houses, apparently.'

'Can he do that? Legally I mean, can he?'

'Of course he can. It's his property. Nothing's signed, so he can let it to whomsoever he wants.'

Time to look downcast. She was looking puzzled, reasonably enough: he'd more or less told her weeks ago that he'd signed some kind of agreement for the house. But he'd made it vague, so she couldn't be sure. He kept up the miserable face and waited; if his hunch was right, she'd come up with an offer any minute now.

'What if *I* have the extra we need?'

There we go! She looked embarrassed. Her sainted mother will have told her that ladies don't talk about money, which was odd when you thought about it, when she'd been in business all those years. She was probably hoping he wouldn't be offended. Fat chance of that, but he needed to show some reluctance.

'No. No, my sweet, definitely not. A chap can't accept money from a lady. It's not the way things work. I wouldn't hear of it.'

He withdrew his hand and turned away.

'But … I'm your fiancée. The money is for our home. Surely that makes a difference?'

'No, I'm sorry, but my mind is made up. We'll just have to delay things … the wedding.' *Trump card.*

'Frank, listen, I can have the money I mentioned – from my father – once we're married. It's in trust. All I need to do is to get hold of it early, somehow.'

This was better than he'd hoped for: getting hold of the inheritance, not just the savings. He looked at her face. Poor lamb, she was finding this hard. How long before he should allow her to convince him? Just a bit more.

'When he was dying, my father wanted to leave something to me as well as the boys. Jim got the shop and the house, of course. Ivan got his share when he set up on his own as a smith; I think Father bought the building for him, and his tools. Anyway, he got more than enough. So Father put some money into a trust for me, but I can't have it until after I'm married. I think it's meant for when we have a family … children. School fees, that sort of thing.'

She was blushing, as well she might! What would her mother say if she could hear her talking to a man about having babies?

'So, how much is it?' He couldn't help himself.

'Quite a lot, I think. About four hundred pounds. It's been gaining interest. I'd have to ask Mr Gibson.'

Frank squeezed her hand and looked down, because God alone knew what expression there'd be on his face. Had he heard that right? Four hundred pounds? And what was hers was his now, or would be soon; he wasn't going to be all proud and defensive about it.

'I can't deny that having the house sorted will take a weight of my shoulders.' *Big sigh.*

'Then it's settled? You'll let me do it?'

'All right then. Just the once.'

He beamed at her and took a large swig of his red wine – it was growing on him, this claret. Lily was so delighted to see him smiling again that she looked as if she could weep with relief. Just how he felt, mind you. He needed to say something but couldn't think what for once, so he just smiled and shook his head to suggest that he was reluctant but prepared to compromise, for her sake.

'Let's not mention it again, then. I'll sort it out as soon as I can, so you can tell the landlord not to let those other people step in.'

That's my girl; he'd sort it out first thing Monday.

Their meal ended well. He threw off his tiredness – what a difference four hundred quid made to the spirits – and was back on top form. They started a conversation with Mr and Mrs Iveson at the next table and he bought drinks for everyone and told some more of his amusing stories, as well as a few of other people's. Afterwards they walked back home arm in arm, close together. Despite the bitter evening gloom he felt warm and relaxed, what with a lovely woman on his arm and the prospect of a healthy bank account. He went in for a 'nightcap' as she called it. The fire was nearly out in the parlour so he rekindled as she busied herself with the drinks. She liked a man who was practical, so why not? She poured a large glass of whisky for him and a sherry for her. Once the fire was going well, he stood up from the hearth and came over to her and took the glass from her hand. He put it back on the table and pulled her towards him.

'You're a beautiful woman, Lily, do you know that?'

He put his hands on her hips, then on her bottom; kissed her hard on the lips, then the neck where the lace of her collar brushed her skin. She obviously didn't know what to do with her hands, so he took one of them and pressed it to where he was rapidly growing as solid as the proverbial rock. She took her hand away as soon as he let go of it, but he laughed and pulled it back.

'Come on, Lil, we're getting married, remember.'

He cupped her breast. He'd like to get inside the blouse but there were loads of tiny buttons, so he stayed safe, fingering her nipple as it hardened under the soft fabric.

'There you are now, that's nice, isn't it?'

Her face said she was enjoying herself. He undid a few buttons, slipping his hand in to cup her full breast.

'Frank, isn't this what you're supposed to do on our wedding night?'

He heard the whisper and drew back to see her face, keeping his hand where it was. Dear God, she didn't know what was what! Didn't her mother explain these things to her?

'No, this is what you do *before* the wedding. Afterwards it's even more fun.'

'Frank, I'm not sure if …'

Before she could finish the sentence they both heard the front door open and close. He quickly withdrew his hand and she fastened her buttons. *Bugger, it must be Ivan. I bet he knows a bit more than his sister does about the old in and out.* They heard his footsteps along the hall, through to the kitchen. He picked up his glass and by the time Ivan came back along they were sitting on opposite sides of the hearth in the armchairs, both with glasses in hand. He gave her a wink and took a slug as Ivan put his head round the door.

'I'm off upstairs. Make sure the fire's low and the lamp's out before you come up, Lily. And I think it's about time Frank went back to The Railway; they'll be locking the doors.'

Cocky little bastard. Who did he think he was? Lily was his sister, fair enough, but she was older than him, and she could be alone with a man if she wanted, especially her fiancé. Even so he decided to call it a night; there was plenty of time to get his hands on those beauties when they were married. He pulled her to her feet and kissed her goodnight, lingering with his lips on hers. Aways leave them wanting more, as his old dad used to say.

THIRTEEN

Ivan

'You must eat here with us? Good God, Elsie, where did that bright idea spring from?'

'I'm sorry; do you mind a lot? I just thought it's the right thing to do. You know.'

She looked at him, obviously hoping he'd agree; it would be ten times harder for her if he didn't play along, or worse still if he went out on the night, he supposed. He winced at the thought of an entire evening with Frank and Lily, but Elsie was willing him to go along with it.

'You will be here, won't you, when he comes? Mrs Binns can make us something, so it won't be much extra work.'

Elsie and Lily had lost no time in finding a cook – they'd asked around and within a few days of making the decision they'd found Grace Binns to prepare some of their meals; even their small town already had a raft of war widows looking for work.

'With Prince Charming? Where else would I be? You couldn't drag me away; I'll be spellbound by Liddle the Loverboy recounting More Tales of a Travelling Salesman'. He shook his head. 'What the hell does she want to marry him for?'

'She wants a wedding and a house of her own. She wants babies.'

Elsie flushed at the word. She knew that Jim had talked

about their problem with him, that he knew, but she'd never mentioned it. He watched her face; the pain of it roiled in the air between them.

'Come here, lass.'

She stepped over, her eyes brimming with tears. As he hugged her, the hidden grief of the last few months – *years of it* – overwhelmed her. Now she sobbed; she gave her whole body over to it. He said nothing; just stroked her hair, shushing now and then, but only to comfort her; he didn't want her to stop until she was spent. When she finally did grow calm he found a hankie and wiped her eyes and face.

'My poor girl.'

They found the supper Mrs Binns had left for them and ate in the warmth of the kitchen. Every now and then he would make her laugh by inventing a Frank-style anecdote, delivering it in a fair likeness of his nasal tone. He *loved* it, being there with her like this, just her and him. He sat back in his chair, fingers laced behind his head. Without Jim and Lily to notice he could gaze at Elsie, her eyes now damp with tears of laughter. She'd surrendered; she was enjoying the comfort, the freedom to giggle, her hand clasped over her mouth. But she was on her guard. When at last he leaned over and touched her she flinched away, then stood up and began to clear. He tried to make her relax again but she couldn't, or wouldn't, and finally he left the house and spent an hour or so in The Crown just to settle himself down. It didn't help that Lily and Frank were there when he arrived home. He did what Jim would have done, said the right things, but he was still feeling roused and restless when he went upstairs, passing Elsie's room – hers and Jim's – on the way to his own.

The following evening was the same, at first.

Lily and Frank had been invited to the Armstrongs, so they were alone together again. After supper Elsie sat down to write to Jim. She'd sent a short note earlier in the week, to tell him about Lily's engagement, but now she was going to fill in all the details. He lit a cigarette, picked up the newspaper, then he watched her; the end of her tongue was sticking out in concentration, following the pen across the paper as she wrote. It made him smile. She looked up.

'What?'

'Nothing.'

He went back to the news, but couldn't take anything in. He'd have to go out, have a pint with the lads. He couldn't sit here and watch Elsie like this; he was in torment being in the same room, just watching her write a letter.

'Right, I'm off out to the pub.'

'Again? Really?'

'Yes, really. I'll be late back probably so I'll see you tomorrow. Send big brother my regards or whatever, will you?'

He knew he sounded offhand, but it was the best he could do. To lessen the injury he brushed her hair with his fingers as he passed her on the way to the back door and she turned to smile up at him. It was all he could do to muster the will to grab his scarf from the hook and leave the house. He was doing the right thing for sure, but was he doing it in the right way? God only knows. He went over the options in his mind, trying to avoid admitting that the best thing all round would be for him to sign up and go. He might even end up doing artillery training at the camp up on the moor; that way he would be near enough to walk down when he had time off. Maybe work with the horses up there, too.

* * * *

The route to The Crown was so familiar that he didn't need to think about it. He was nearly there when he sensed

100

movement on the gloomy path ahead: black forms loomed out of the shadows, breaking his thoughts.

'Well, will yer look at wor blacksmith!'

'Are ye gannen to meet a bonny lass, Ivan?'

Even in the darkness he knew straight away it was Isabel's brothers that were blocking his way. His instinct was to turn and run, but he remained where he stood, waiting to see what would happen. He'd been expecting something to come of that night. Isabel hadn't been near him, and she hadn't replied to the messages he'd sent with Alfie, but he'd known it would catch up with him.

'Wor Isabel's not happy, Ivan. She says yer let 'er down. She says yer promised to marry 'er, then yer let 'er down.'

This was Joe, at seventeen already half a head taller than Ivan and far heavier; his brother George was a year older and a year bigger: God help the Boche if these two ever joined the ranks. He didn't respond. There was no sign yet that Isabel had told them the whole story, but then, why else were they there? Or had they just run into him by chance?

'Got nowt ter say?'

'Isn't that between Isabel and me?'

'Not when wor bairn's cryin all the time it isn't, yer pansy toff!'

He was fast, but not fast enough. He saw it coming and ducked, but George's fist caught his temple and he staggered off the pavement onto the rough cobbles, buckling as Joe rounded behind him aiming a brutal kick to the back of his knees. There was a brief pause while they checked no-one was in sight then they started again, using their hefty boots to do as much damage as possible without killing him. They weren't that stupid. At least he hoped they weren't. He took the pounding, wrapping his arms round his head to block the worst of it, twisting round on the freezing cobbles trying

101

to avoid one agonizing kick after another. The lads were growing winded before there was a shout from the square – someone leaving The Crown had seen what was going on. They stopped abruptly. He could hear their chests heaving as they bent low over him.

'Mess with wor sister would yer?'

'A man's got to keep his promises, isn't that right George?'

'It is, Joe.'

Through the jagging pain Ivan heard the brothers' message, followed by the heavy thud of their boots as they bolted down the street into the night. He tried and failed to straighten up as a small crowd of locals ran over to him. A shaft of light from the open door of the pub reached out towards where he lay. One or two of the younger men continued down the street hoping to catch his attackers, but they soon reappeared through the gloom.

'Lost the bastards.'

'Christ, lads, it's Ivan! Howay lads, let's get 'im up.

They eased him from the ground, but he couldn't stand on his own: blood was spewing from his nose and a split lip, and his right leg gave way beneath him. Every movement was razor edged.

'I think yer ankle's broke, Ivan lad; we'll get yer back home, but one of the lads'll hev to gan to fetch the doctor. Brace yersel: it's gannen ter hurt like hell, bonny lad.'

It took four men to carry him back to the house, all of them friends since childhood. They tried not to jerk him as they inched along the path, but even so he passed in and out of consciousness. As they drew near, one of them ran on ahead to bang on the door, warn whoever was there. He groaned, don't let Elsie see me in such a mess … it was worse than the kicking, the thought of her being upset by it. And the lads kept asking who'd done it; they knew he'd be bound

102

to have recognized the attackers. Just give us the nod and we ll get the bastards ... They were up for retribution, already planning who would do it and what they would do.

Later, she told him she'd just finished her letter when the knocking on the front door started up. It was locked but not bolted, and as she'd turned the key it had flown open. She'd stood back, not following the garbled explanation, but then the group of friends had swayed awkwardly into view, and somehow she'd known. They'd manoeuvred sideways to carry Ivan up the steps and into the hallway. Some of his blood had splashed onto the door and she'd tried to wipe it off with her hand, but that had made it worse. Still she hadn't properly understood what was going on, but when he turned his face towards her she'd felt sick. He'd tried to speak but his breathing was too shallow, and anyway the men were shouting instructions to each other, working out where best to put him: it was bedlam.

Three days on a mattress on the parlour floor. They kept the fire going day and night; his mother would have thought it a shameless waste of coal, but Elsie and even Lily wanted him to be warm at least, even if most of his body was rigid, purple and beyond painful. His left ankle was vastly swollen but not broken, thank God. But at least one rib was cracked: breathing was an atrocious effort. He turned his face away when they came in to fetch the scuttle or empty the chamber pot; he'd let them down, causing all this extra work when they had a business to run. There was no excuse for it. On the fourth day some of the lads came over and helped him upstairs to his own room, into a proper bed. They got in touch with John Graham from down the valley to come and do a day or two at the forge, to keep Ivan's farmers going; they carried buckets of coal up, lining them up beside the iron grate so that the women didn't need to; they promised to come every day, and they did, pestering him for a name … names. There were rumours, but they needed to be sure.

On the fifth day Isabel came to see him. He heard her voice in the hall, then Elsie's light tread on the stairs.

'It's Isabel Moffat wanting to see you. Can she come up?'

No wonder she looked a bit puzzled; he hadn't mentioned Isabel since who knows when, certainly not after that night. He nodded, feeling a flush of shame as Elsie turned away to call Isabel up. He knew she'd been waiting for him to explain the beating, but he hadn't, and now she would know. Well, not know … but guess, surely. Christ, what a mess.

'I'll make you a cup of tea.'

Elsie disappeared down to the kitchen as Isabel walked into the room, shucking her coat off and placing it on a chair near the door. He beckoned to her and she came over to the bed, sat on the edge. He took her hand but she pulled away, avoiding his eyes. Was she angry or upset? He looked foul; maybe she couldn't bear the sight of him.

'I didn't tell them, Ivan. Honest I didn't.'

Distressed then, not annoyed.

'I know.'

'How d'ye know?'

'Because I'd be dead, not just messed up.' He smiled feebly, wincing as his healing lips cracked and oozed.

'They're bastards, the pair of them. Daft bastards. They've gone now, mind.'

'Gone where?'

'To the war. Me dad's livid, me mam's yammering on about Joe bein a bairn still, but it was the only way. They thought you'd tell the polis.'

'No. It was between me and you. Why did you tell them? What did you tell them?'

'I was cryin all the time and they wouldn't let up askin

why. They knew it was summat to do with you, so in the end I said ye'd asked us to marry yez, and then called it off. I think they might've sort've guessed the rest, but they didn't ask us and I kept me gob shut so they couldn't be sure. I'm really sorry, Ivan.'

'It's me that's sorry.'

He was, too. Not just because he'd taken a beating. Because he'd hurt her just as badly, and she deserved better.

'I'll still marry you, if you want me after all this. You'll have to wait awhile though; your daft brothers've put me out of action good and proper. Does your mam and dad know what's gone on?'

'Not really. Me brothers didn't say owt to them and I didn't either. They like you. Mind you, so did Joe and George before ... But me Dad would've done worse, like.'

'I know.'

He took her hand again and this time she let him keep it.

'So, are you going to climb down off your high horse and marry me?'

Her expression changed, but there was no smile.

'I know ... I look terrible, but Doctor Armstrong reckons a month will see me more or less back to normal. Well, maybe apart from the nose.'

'It's not what yer look like, yer daft bugger.'

She touched his unshaven chin, briefly.

'So?'

'It's her.'

Isabel gestured to where Elsie had left them to go back downstairs.

'She's my brother's wife, Isabel.'

'But it wor her name yer said. That's who yer was thinkin about isn't it?'

'No. Perhaps. I don't know ... but it didn't mean anything.

If you'd waited a minute before running off I could've made it right. I can make it right now. As soon as I'm back on my feet I'll find a house and we'll get wed. Will we?'

'What about me brothers? And yours, for that matter?'

'There's a war on. I might have to go in the new year; Jim reckons it's just a matter of time. It'd be good to be married before it happens.'

He didn't need to say any more; there'd been plenty of early weddings in Bellingham since the war started ... men and women desperate to experience life, just in case.

'Don't you hate us, for what they've done to yer? Just look at yer!'

She was smiling now, despite the words. She pushed her nose to one side and blew her cheeks out in an attempt to mimic Ivan's swollen face. She was beautiful when she smiled.

'Not as much as I hate myself for what I might've done to you.'

He was getting through to her. This was the way out of all this: he'd get married, leave Elsie in peace, as she wanted and needed. He was fond enough of Isabel to make her a good husband, surely.

'Come closer.'

He tugged at her hand and she shifted along the bed so that she could lean towards him.

'I can't kiss you; I'd mess you up if I did.'

He put his fingers to his mouth, touching tentatively and wincing: his lips were a puffy mess of half healed cuts, more as a result of the repeated grinding on the rough ground than with any direct blows, or he would've lost some teeth. *Small mercies.* Nonetheless, she leaned over and with infinite care touched her lips on his.

'There.'

'There?'

'There's more where that came from, once yer can take it. I hope other parts of yer aren't as battered as yer face, like.'

As Isabel leaned back from the kiss Elsie walked into the room, tray in hands. She'd seen nothing, but he knew she'd take in the scene as if she'd been there all the time. She balanced the tray at the foot of the bed and turned to go, her face fixed in a tight smile.

'Tell 'er then, Ivan.'

He wasn't sure whether Isabel intended it to be a challenge, but that's how it felt. He glanced at her, then looked at Elsie, who'd stopped dead at the door then turned to face them when Isabel spoke.

'Tell me what?'

Isabel was waiting for him to speak. Before many seconds had passed it was already too late: she'd registered his silence, the faint hesitation. He watched helplessly as she pivoted up from the bed and strode to the door, pushing past Elsie to grab her coat before clattering down the stairs. He lay back, eyes closed, as the front door crashed behind her.

'Tell me what?'

Ivan turned his face away, didn't respond.

'What, Ivan?'

107

FOURTEEN

Jim

It was the evenings he found the hardest. The winter days were short and the effort needed for long, heavily equipped runs along the Cam, the drilling and the endless marching meant that he was – certainly at first – exhausted by nightfall, physically but not mentally. Evening mess he found tedious: it was as much about training in etiquette as enjoying a good dinner although, thank God, Archie had been right about the food: it was excellent and there was lots of it.

It fast became clear that the younger men, those straight from public schools or university, were already gentlemen; they were there purely to be instructed in the duties of being an officer. The rest, including Jim, were expected to watch and learn how to conform; the other ranks would expect it. As he got to know some of the other older recruits he realised that they were a mixed bunch with one thing in common: they were respectable, but not gentlemen. Some, like Jim, had been running their own businesses for years, but there was also John Douglas, a solicitor from Durham, a bit of an intellectual, who'd left a large practice to volunteer. Then there was Fred Hale, a dour bank manager from York. They were both over thirty. The best of the older crew was Edward Lovage, a newly qualified doctor who'd homed in on Jim as a likely pal on the first evening.

'If we stick together we might come through this intact.'

'What, the war?'

'No, this!' Edward gestured with his eyes at the young bucks at the end of the table, with their crisp accents and beautifully tailored uniforms.

'The Eton crew?

'Along with Wellington, Marlborough, Rugby …'

'They're good lads.'

'I'm sure they are.'

'But they're very young.'

'I've been reading about chromosomes … genetics. D'ye know anything about it?'

'Only what I've read in the newspaper.' He knew there'd been a lot of research going on, but he hadn't taken much interest.

'Well, these lot all have the "posh toff" gene.' Jim smiled at the idea. Edward seemed fairly posh toff to him.

'And the "natural leader" gene; we mustn't forget that one.'

Neither of them cared particularly, but they both knew that officer training was designed to make them into honorary toffs. If they learned it all now it would save a lot of red faces when they joined their battalions. You have to know how things ought to be done. It would be a temporary elevation, for the duration of the war.

What interested Jim most was the tactical instruction. Some of what they were taught he'd already been through in the OCT, but there were a lot of new ideas to take in. They spent whole mornings in class, then afternoons in fields outside the city, learning about trench warfare, grenades, types of bombs, explosives. The younger trainees were full of enthusiasm: Labrador puppies Edward called them, stumbling over themselves, volunteering to demonstrate new skills: construction and repair of trenches, loopholes, entanglements. Jim and the other older men took it slowly, perhaps more aware of the need to understand every detail.

'My old father always used to say, "It's the last screw that holds it all together, Edward my boy." I could never decide whether he was being practical or just philosophical.'

'Either way, if my life depends on it I want to get it right.'

'You're not wrong there.'

Unexpected to Jim was the rapid establishment of his natural authority in the training unit. Before many days had passed he sensed that the others, including many of Edward's posh toffs, deferred to him when decisions had to be made. If they were put into groups he was assumed to be the leader; if he wasn't appointed, the man in charge tended to give ground to him anyway. He was used to giving orders back in Erringtons, but it was something beyond that. Another thing: he became known as "Grocer". It started life as a nickname in the first few days, when they learned that he was in trade, but it quickly became his only name, and he liked it. All this he tried to explain in his letters. He was missing her in a way that he couldn't properly express. Yes, he'd grown used to his narrow student bed ... but not to the absence of Elsie beside him. It must be easier for Edward, without a wife at home.

> ... Darling, I do so wish you could be here with me, <u>now</u>, this second. It's snowing and the younger men (they're boys really) are throwing snowballs in the quad. They're a noisy lot! We could wrap up warm and take a walk down through the town before bed. As I told you in my last letter, there isn't really room in it for two of us, but I'm sure we'd manage somehow. I'm looking forward to watching your face when you first see the beauty of the buildings here, especially the chapel at King's College. I can quite understand why men want to come and study here. You'll

like Edward, I'm sure. He's a farmer's son who went up to Oxford and studied medicine; he's in his late twenties, so an old man like me. He's very funny and clever, but not married yet.

He'd asked Edward early on whether he had a wife, or a fiancée perhaps.

'Never had any time. When I go home for the weekend my mother's always lined up some poor local girl, but then I'm back to town and into the surgery.'

'What about in town? After work?' He reminded Jim of Ivan: no doubt there was a queue of young women, just waiting to be asked.

'I've had a girl or two, and I'll probably find a wife eventually, but she'll need to be a saint; I'm called out at all hours of the night and day and there's always someone banging at the door. It drives my housekeeper distracted.'

Some of the men, even the married ones, were taking the chance to enjoy a bit of flirtation with local women. Sometimes more than that. Their training discouraged using any pubs where other ranks could be drinking, and getting drunk in public was out, too: a gentleman doesn't allow it to show that he's been drinking. But they did leave the college grounds, and when they did they experienced the age-old allure of a uniform: there was no shortage of female company in the town. One of older men, Mason, was already taking full advantage and wanted everyone else to know. As the port made its way around the table, he couldn't resist bragging about it.

'By God, she's a sport! We were going at it like rabbits; she's got the finest …'

But he quickly got the message that it wasn't done to talk about such things. It occurred to Jim, looking down the table, that most of the men at the other end were probably still innocents as far as women were concerned. Perhaps that's why they never talked about it: the only ones they knew were sisters and mothers. Whatever the reason, their conversation rarely turned to the sort of stuff you'd hear in any bar in Bellingham ... and when it did there was no admiration for it, and certainly no respect. As soon as Mason began to describe the pleasures of his night out he was shouted down:

'Damn you for being a dirty dog, Mason!'

'Keep it to yourself, old boy. Let's honour the ladies, hey?'

'Mason, it's not something you brag about.'

Jim found it all quite entertaining, but it was hard to become excited about freedom he hadn't wanted in the first place. Without being unsociable, because that was frowned upon too – loners don't make good officers – he spent most of his spare time reading official pamphlets and textbooks to supplement the work, or talking about the day's instruction with Edward and the others over a whisky in the mess. That, and writing to Elsie. The longer his training went on, the more it seemed to him that he needed to get over to France and fight. Then he could get back home, to normal life.

> ... This halfway house between me and the real war is starting to grate. I doubt whether much of what we're being taught will ever be of any use; military law and all this marching and saluting for example. What I really need to know I'll probably learn on the job far quicker. One exception is that we have been doing night operations this week. It's been bitterly cold and wet, but we've spent hours out in the icy countryside being instructed in how to find the enemy and do tasks in total darkness. It's been challenging to say the least, but it's at least more like the real thing. Mind you, I rather wish I'd

volunteered in summer instead of mid-winter, especially without you to keep me warm.

Two further issues disturbed him. The first was the rumour that the whole system for officer training was about to change, in February '16. There would be new Officer Training Battalions with all sorts of would-be officers, including men brought back from France who'd missed out on commissions in 1914. Presumably the army was realising that it couldn't be as selective now that so many of its first intake of officers were slowly mouldering in French and Belgian mud. What worried Jim was that they were saying the new course would take four months. If he hadn't been gazetted by then, would he have to start again? The other concern was that it seemed certain that compulsory conscription would begin in January. If this was true, it was only a matter of time before Ivan would either be called up or would feel honour bound to volunteer.

... I'm hoping that they won't call Ivan up for duty; he's needed in Bellingham, unless they plan to take all the horses, but even then, how many mechanics are there around? None as good as him. As you thought, I'm anything but happy about Lily's engagement to Liddle. I don't get the feeling he's a <u>totally</u> bad sort, but nor do I entirely trust him. What does Ivan think, I mean about his character? I know things are not easy between you and Lily, but if you feel you <u>can</u> talk to her, please ask her to wait longer before committing herself. I would love to see her married, but not to him, I'm afraid. I have written to her, you may have seen the envelope. I don't know whether she has told you what I said, but it wasn't perhaps the letter of congratulations that she'd anticipated. I'm afraid I was a bit heavy handed, which I felt I ought to be in the absence of our father.

Elsie later confirmed that he'd been right: Lily read his letter in the shop and her face had been thunder as she took in what her brother had written. She'd folded it, put it back in the envelope, then she'd gone through into the office and slammed the door behind her. Lily's letter to him, written later than Elsie's note, had been a rhapsody about Frank's many virtues; she was obviously desperate for his approval. *Why?* On the other hand, although Elsie hadn't exactly damned Frank, her lack of enthusiasm had been plain. Ivan had even scrawled a note at the bottom telling Jim he was "very lucky to be somewhere he didn't have to see them together". Underneath, in Elsie's girlish hand was a further note: "He should not have written that! It is so rude!" But he got the picture. It merely confirmed his own impression of the man.

The tone of his response had obviously been a serious blow to Lily, and he soon understood why. Within ten days of posting his letter to her he received a letter from Gibson, the family solicitor, about a meeting he'd had with Miss Errington:

> ... Your sister made it clear that she wanted access to the trust fund set up by your father in her name. As you know, Mr Errington, the trust was established with a considerable sum, made greater by the accrued interest of some nine years. At first I was concerned that the family business must be suffering from some financial difficulty as a result of your absence; the war and so on. However, Miss Errington reassured me that this was not the case, going on to explain that she had recently become engaged and that she was anxious to use the funds for various aspects of proposed expenditure, referring in particular to

114

their wedding, which I gather is to take place in a mere four months, in March 1916.

I explained to Miss Errington that her father's trust specifically stated that the monies should be made available only <u>after</u> her marriage. I suggested, further, that she and her fiancé might choose to wait until your return for their wedding; this war cannot continue for long and their engagement, as it stands, will be very short. To be blunt, I was a little alarmed by the haste that she was expressing, a state of mind made more acute when I enquired as to whether she had already mentioned the trust and its extent to Mr Liddle, her intended. She denied having done this, but I'm afraid that I remain unconvinced, and feel that her visit to me might well have been proposed by the gentleman, her lack of candour no doubt being the result of her loyalty to him.

I'm afraid that Miss Errington was less than happy with my answer, although as your family's legal representative I could give her no other; your father was most particular about the release of the trust, possibly envisaging just such an event as this. As you know, the trust also dictates that you should be a signatory to the closure of the trust and subsequent release of Miss Errington's inheritance. Your sister was quite unaware of this, and she was, if I may say so, most vexed when she heard of it. She asked about the legal position if you should be absent or killed after the wedding, when she might fairly expect to receive the funds. I explained that one could set up a proxy signature, if you were to agree to it in writing, and that in the case of your death the decision would lie with your executor, that is to say, with me. I went on to suggest that in the light of the proximity of her forthcoming nuptials and the likelihood of your being gazetted and posted overseas, it might be a good idea to set about arranging the proxy signature immediately. Unless of course you are returning to Northumberland before then, in which case you should come in to see me. I could have the documents ready for signature.

I have no doubt that Miss Errington will be writing to you about our discussion, and trust that you will be in touch with me in due course with instructions in this matter.

Yours etc

Jim could just picture Lily's face. He, who'd married a miner's daughter, could withhold her inheritance if he disapproved of Liddle, who in Lily's view was a perfectly respectable businessman. As Ivan suggested, he was lucky not to be there!

FIFTEEN

Elsie

She had the house to herself for the first time in weeks. Lily was spending the afternoon with Ann, to talk about the wedding – again – and Ivan was out for the first time since the attack. He'd appeared fully dressed at the kitchen door as she sat doing the polishing ready for Christmas: a simple job, transforming candlesticks, cruet set and napkin rings from matt grey to gleaming silver by the light of the kitchen lamp. It was dull outside, the sky heavy with rain, the colour of used bath water.

'I'm going up to the forge.' He was defensive; he knew she wouldn't like it.

'You shouldn't be going out yet.'

'I've worked with worse after a match.'

'Football never caused injuries like that.'

'It was weeks ago.'

'Just go then, if that's what you want.'

She watched as he reached his jacket and scarf from the hook. He twisted his shoulders slowly to shove his arms through the sleeves; his chest was still tender, even if his face was back to normal apart from a sunset of bruising. He was still limping a bit, too, but he wouldn't use his father's stick. It was there, dull with disuse behind the umbrellas in the hall stand, but he wouldn't take it.

'You're daft. What if you slip? It's icy out there.'

117

'I won't slip.'

It'd been like this ever since. She hadn't asked a fourth time what it was Isabel wanted him to tell her, and he hadn't offered any explanation: not for her coming to see him and not for her leaving so abruptly. She'd been running up and downstairs, changing his dressings, fetching his meals and stoking the fire until this last week, but he'd never asked her to stop and chat; not once. And she hadn't really wanted to; she was outfaced by it ... there was too much that needed saying. She didn't even know who'd hurt him like that, or why they'd done it. The worst thing was being polite as strangers.

When he'd gone she finished the silver and began to gather up the ingredients for the Christmas cake. It ought to have been done weeks ago – there was no time for it to mature now – but she couldn't help that. For two pins she'd not bother, but she'd promised Jim that she'd save some for him to take back with him, whenever that might be.

It was evening and the kitchen was heady with mixed peel and brandy by the time she put the blended ingredients aside to rest. Later, after supper, she would finish the job. It occurred to her that Lily might like Frank to come for Christmas. Jim wouldn't be there: with only two days' leave it wasn't possible. He'd written to say that he was going to his friend's; Edward, the doctor, had invited him to the family home. He'd sent a parcel with gifts, she'd sent hers. He would ring her when he could.

That evening was the most relaxed they'd all spent together in weeks. Ivan looked better; he'd managed the journey up to his forge and enjoyed the exercise. He hadn't fallen. He'd returned in the late afternoon, numb from walking slowly into a biting wind but wearing a triumphant grin as he collapsed onto a chair as she worked at the kitchen table. She'd stirred in the last of the walnuts and fruit as he told her who he'd seen on the street, what he'd need to do to start up again after weeks off. Alfie and John Graham had done a good job, but he needed to get back to work.

'So, when are you going to start?'

'Next week. I've been three weeks without lifting a hammer. My arms are like a lass's.'

'It takes longer than that to heal properly; you'll need to go slow at first.'

'I'll need to do some lifting you mean, or I'll end up knitting for a living, like the wifeys. I'll have a fat belly and no muscles.'

They both laughed at the vision of Ivan joining the old women with their baskets of yarn and wooden pins. It changed things between them, this lightness, putting the last few gloomy weeks aside.

Even Lily was mellow, after an afternoon with Ann and her wedding plans. She joined them, bringing the sherry decanter through from the parlour. She commented on the silver, lifted the muslin cloth to admire the result of Elsie's weighing and stirring. She even helped with the supper, and instead of eating in silent concentration she chattered about her dress, the house in town that now seemed certain. Elsie had never seen her be so open; perhaps now was the time for some gentle pressure?

'Lily, wouldn't it be nice to wait a bit, until Jim can be here?'

No answer. Ivan stopped eating, eyebrows raised.

'He's very disappointed to be missing his only sister's wedding.'

That was the least of it, but what else could they say?

'Frank and I have discussed it, and we've decided that we don't want to wait any longer than necessary.'

Elsie didn't even try to argue with her. It was as if Lily

had prepared her statement. She probably had, come to that. She'd held out long enough for a husband, and what if Frank had to go to war after all? If she wanted a wedding ring on her finger before that could happen, well good for her, really.

'You do know, you two, that you'll have to find a housekeeper.'

It was a casual comment, or at least her tone was, but it splintered the air. Ivan looked at her, frowning, waiting for Lily to go on.

'You two can't live here together on your own, if you see what I mean.'

She did, but she hadn't given it a thought. Had Ivan? He certainly hadn't mentioned it.

'People will talk if you don't have someone living in when I go. Ask Jim, I'm sure he'll agree.'

Ivan put down his knife and fork.

'You're right, our Lily. I should have thought about it as soon as you told me you were leaving home. Can you and Elsie find someone? Elsie, would Mrs Binns be interested, d'you think? It would save her rent.'

Lily had succeeded; the rest of the meal was spent talking about the practicalities of taking on a full time housekeeper. It shouldn't be difficult to find one: even if Mrs Binns didn't want the job, there were several war widows who would be only too happy to find a place as good as this one. Even so, she couldn't decide what to think about it. It would be a relief to have the house in good hands when she was working all day, but she wasn't sure about the idea of a stranger living with them.

Ivan cleared away as Elsie greased and lined and greased again a large square cake tin that was older than all of them. They called Lily through to make a wish as the final stirring took place, then Elsie dolloped the mix into the tin, scraping the bowl clean. She covered the top with greaseproof and newspaper and Ivan tied the string holding everything in place. The bottom oven was warm but not too warm: if she woke in the night, as she did more often than not with Jim away, she would come down and turn it so that it cooked evenly. Hot with all the effort, she brushed the damp hair from her forehead and grinned at the other two. They felt like a family.

She did wake up in the night. The room was pitch black and she lay for a minute, hugging the blankets around her before she remembered. The cake … She pulled on a pair of Jim's heavy wool socks for warmth and crept quietly down to the kitchen, the stairs lit by a rectangle of winter moonlight slanting through the long landing window. As she opened the kitchen door the smell of baking met her like an old friend. She lit a candle – no point in fiddling with the lamp for only a few minutes – and placed it on the floor beside the range. She knelt down, feeling the chill of the tiles through her nightdress. The metal door of the bottom oven stuck, as it often did, and she had to yank on the handle to open it. Using a thick tea cloth for protection she began carefully to lift out the heavy cake.

'Do you need any help?'

It was Ivan, standing at the kitchen door. She froze, her outstretched arms weighed down in front of her.

'No, I'm managing … thank you. You go back to bed.'

She was actually struggling to hold the awkward tin, but she badly wanted him to leave her to it. She knew he hadn't gone; he was leaning against the door jamb as she completed the cake-turning and clunked home the iron door. As she clambered back to her feet he straightened up and came into the kitchen, closing the door behind him. Now that she was upright she noticed that he looked respectable compared to

121

her, wearing yesterday's shirt and thick pyjama bottoms. But his feet were bare; it made her cold just to see them on the unforgiving quarry tiles. She leaned against the kitchen table for support, holding the warm cloth across her chest.

'You didn't need to come down; I've done it loads of times before.'

'I didn't come to help really; I just heard you creep past my room.'

'I didn't creep, I tiptoed.'

'What's the difference?'

'I tiptoed to be as quiet as I could. Creeping's what you do when you're up to something you shouldn't be.'

'Well … I crept down here.'

He came over to her and took the cloth from her hands.

'I love the socks.'

As he spoke he lifted hanks of her hair and arranged them over her shoulders, as if he was preparing her for a photograph, or a painting.

'They're Jim's.'

He paused.

'I know.'

She stood utterly still, unable to breathe as she felt the warmth of his body so close to hers. Without losing her gaze he slowly reached down and lifted the folds of her nightgown so that her legs could be seen, slim and pale in the candlelight. With a quick movement he nudged her up onto the table and ruched the material up over her thighs. She whimpered but made no effort to stop him. It was too late. His fingers explored gently until he heard the sharp intake of her breath, then he smiled and kissed her. She closed her eyes so that she would only sense him releasing the cord of his pyjamas, then easing himself inside her. For several seconds he didn't move: he just held still, his arms holding her to him. It was

Elsie who began to push her hips against his, inviting him to finish what he'd started. As he moved she arched her back and propped her hands behind her on the table top, her legs wrapped around him. Her socks, Jim's socks, fell to the floor at Ivan's feet. At last he grasped her up urgently, almost lifting her from the table.

'Like coming home after a long journey.' She whispered in his ear, as he held her there.

She shuffled forward and dropped onto the floor so that her nightgown unravelled back down to her ankles. Modest again. She wondered whether he would remember, but then he responded.

'Not the boat without a paddle, then?'

He took her face between both his hands and kissed her, long and tenderly.

'Are you all right?' She touched him low on his chest where a metal boot cap had done the most damage. The skin was just losing its disturbing ochre.

'Elsie, do you really think I noticed how much it hurt me, to make love to you? Did I hurt you?'

She shook her head. *Not yet*

SIXTEEN

Frank

He wouldn't be in Bellingham for Christmas Day. He'd told Lily his brother and sister in law were expecting him in Wallsend; the kids love their uncle Frank. It was true, but if he was honest he didn't really fancy the idea of spending the day up there anyway; he'd want to collapse in an armchair after dinner, take his shoes off and have a snooze. And he'd want a beer or six; he couldn't really do that with Ivan the Good watching. Mebbe taking notes. It was a shame not to be with Lily, but there you are. Next year they'd have their own home and invite everyone down on Boxing Day. Odds on they wouldn't come. Who was it that said, "The best of all possible worlds"?

He drew up outside the shop on the twenty third; Lily wasn't expecting him, but he was going to whisk her out for tea. He was hoping that what she had to tell him was worth the effort of the extra miles.

'Can you spare her, Elsie? Let's get your coat, Lil … we can't have you going out there without wrapping you up, can we? Bitter out there, isn't it Mrs …er…?'

He was irresistible; even that tight-mouthed old biddy was simpering and agreeing that it was indeed very chilly. He popped Lily's hat on her head and gave her a peck on the cheek, commenting with a wink that some mistletoe wouldn't come amiss. Having made his presence felt he bundled her out of the door, giving Elsie a perky little nod as he clipped it closed behind them. He'd given the women waiting at the counter something to gossip about as they crossed the street: Miss Errington's fiancé ... what a charming young man.

Over at The Railway it was busier than usual and they had to wait for a table. He ordered tea with cakes once they were seated, then leaned back in his chair, waiting. She should have news about the trust; it'd better be good. Mind you, she didn't look like someone about to produce a large cheque. In fact, she looked a bit nervous. Bad sign.

'So, you went to see the solicitor?'

She nodded, then told him. She related what had happened during her meeting with Gibson, quoting him on the 'unalterable legality' of the trust. So: no chance of getting it before the wedding and her fucking brother held the purse strings. Christ, is nothing simple? But he had to hand it to her, she had a back-up plan.

'I've been thinking.' *She'd* been thinking? Not as much as he had. He'd been thinking about nothing else. A few hundred quid in his bank account? He'd been bloody dreaming about it.

'It was on the train back from Hexham, after the meeting.'

'Yes?' Get on with it. Never mind where you were, what's the idea?

'I'm going to borrow from Erringtons ... a sum of money each week. It'll be easy because I do all the book keeping and banking.'

Genius. His woman's a genius.

'When I see you I'll give you the money ... and you can secure the house and put some by for furnishings and so on.'

House, yes; furnishings can wait. 'And what about the rest? The trust money?' He didn't want to appear greedy, but this said, he wasn't going to wave goodbye to it on the say-so

125

of Soldier Jim.

'Once we're married, Jim will see how happy and settled we are and he'll release my inheritance. Then I'll pay back what I've borrowed somehow and the rest will be ours.'

She seemed very sure.

'You're sure?'

'Of course!'

'That's my girl. I love a woman who's resourceful! How much do you think you can borrow a week without anyone noticing?'

She handed him an envelope, smiling.

'Here's two pound notes and four half crowns.'

Good grief, she'd started already. He would never have guessed she could be so shifty.

'Enough for the time being, Frank, I'm sure of that; I was thinking of two pounds each week after the three today. If our rent's going to be fifteen shillings a week, the landlord can't want much more than fifteen pounds in advance, and you've already saved most of that.'

He took a sip of his tea; gave her the 'little boy lost' look.

'Well, my own love, I had saved most of it but what with one thing and another I've had to dip into the old pot a bit.'

He tried to sound casual, but he could see she was taken aback. Time for a touch of flattery.

'And you know why, my angel? Because I'm so much in love with you that you're a distraction. Haven't been putting all the usual energy into the job; been daydreaming a bit too much.'

She was melting, so he decided to finish the job while he was on top.

'Truth to tell, the pot's bally near empty, what with staying here at weekends ...'

He allowed his explanation to trail off. Lily stared at him.

126

She looked puzzled, which he could understand really, but fuck it. A couple came in and took the table next to theirs and she turned away from them, whispering to him anxiously.

'Well, how much do we need, then? I can't take too much or it will be obvious, and anyway, you really oughtn't to have spent all that money, Frank. You need to make a budget and stick to it.'

He tapped the table with his spoon. Now she was being irritating. Bossy. He gave her a long, hard stare and watched her reaction. It was enough; she looked flushed.

'Please don't get cross. Look, I have my own savings in the bank, here in Bellingham. I was going to use them for … well, all sorts of things, but I can give you twenty pounds today. Now, if you like. You'll have twenty three pounds then, so please go tomorrow and pay the wretched man what he needs, then we can relax and start to plan properly.'

That's better. Relax, Frank my son. He stopped tapping.

'I was going to buy fabric for curtains, some honeymoon clothes … but they can wait.'

She looked embarrassed; was it the honeymoon talk, or the money, or what?

'My own darling, you are the best girl in the world. Look, let's finish our tea … we don't need to talk about this for a minute longer. Then we can go to the bank.'

He spooned some jam onto a scone and held it to her mouth, licking his lips. She flushed and took a little bite, smiling again. God, if there was a university for charm he'd be a professor.

He made sure that they left in time for Lily to go to Lloyds to draw the twenty pounds. It wasn't what he'd been hoping for when he left home that morning, but it was a relief nonetheless. He waited outside, but as she emerged, four crisp five pound notes in her hand, he went straight over and took her arm protectively, steering her along the street to where he'd parked his motor, in front of Erringtons. He opened the passenger door and took a parcel from the front seat.

'For Christmas, my sweet. It's just a little something to make you even more beautiful.'

Actually it was a bloody good bit of stuff: a gold bracelet that had belonged to his dear old mother. He'd damn nearly pawned it several times, but here it was, safely where it belonged. As she took her present, Lily passed the banknotes discreetly into his open hand.

'You'll go and see the man tomorrow? About the house?'

'Tomorrow, my angel.' He kissed her hand, then her cheek. 'Don't you worry about a thing. I'll be carrying you over that threshold and up the stairs before you know it.'

SEVENTEEN

Jim

It all added to the sense of disconnection he'd felt in the last several weeks. They'd driven up in Edward's Rover, arriving as the sun started to dip behind the high walls of the kitchen garden. Back in comfortable civvies, he savoured his drink as he looked around the room. It wasn't at all grand, but it had effortless style: the product, he guessed, of confidence and old money. It was the sort of parlour, or 'sitting room' as Edward called it, that he would like for himself and Elsie.

He would have enjoyed just sitting there peacefully all evening, but there were other plans. Within the hour there were the sounds of people arriving at the front door, the rapid clip of the maid's shoes as she rushed to take coats and hats. Edward and his father rose immediately and went out into the hall to greet Marion Enderby, Edward's older sister, with her four children. He half rose, unsure whether to go with them. Instead he remained where he was, beside the great stone fireplace, admiring the way the bed of ash spilled unchecked onto the deep hearth. Within a minute the room was filled with the excited clamour of a family being reunited after eight months.

'Uncle Edward why aren't you in uniform? Mama promised us you'd be wearing your uniform, didn't you Mama?'

Edward stood to attention.

'Sorry, Sir, will be wearing it for church in the morning,

Sir!' He caught the boy up in a hug.

Edward's mother appeared from the hall with a very young child in her arms and a little girl holding onto her skirt.

'Mr Errington, you must be wondering what on earth you've come too! Marion, William is going to be climbing the Christmas tree if you don't come through immediately.'

Marion flashed a greeting at Jim and disappeared through to the dining room, calling back over her shoulder, 'A very large sherry, Pa, if you're asking!'

Before long, Jim found himself on all fours on the rug behind the sofa, helping George and William, the two older children, set up their toy soldiers in formation.

'I've got Papa's battalion, this time. You can be the Boche. Mr Errington, can you help him set his up? Mind you, they shall all be down again once my lot advance!'

The boys' father, George Enderby, was a captain with the Scots Guards; apparently a nod to his Scottish ancestry. It was clear that someone, perhaps Marion, perhaps their other grandfather, was keeping them up to date with battles on the Western Front.

'Have you ever been to France, Sir? My father says it's a beautiful country, but not where he is at the moment. He says the villagers are having to move away in case they're hurt by the shelling. At Ypres, that's in Begium, they used a church as their headquarters. Mama says so much for the Christian message of peace on earth, but we want to be soldiers when we grow up, don't we Will? Did you know our Great Great Grandfather fought at Waterloo?"

He was charmed by their chatter. As he listened, helping to arrange the lead battalions, he thought about Elsie and her aching need for a baby; *their* aching need. God only knows how long it'll be before there's any chance of that happening.

At dinner, Jim was seated next to Marion. She made no

attempt to hide her curiosity, asking a string of questions about him, about his family. Where did they live? What was Northumberland like? Was his business being harmed or helped by the war? At one point he looked over at Edward, who raised his glass.

'Don't tell her everything, Jim; she won't give up 'til she knows your shoe size!'

'You be quiet, little brother. It's so interesting to talk to a friend of yours that I haven't known most of my life!'

It was Elsie that really seemed to interest Marion. He found himself describing the deep blue of her wide-set eyes, the way she always liked everyone unless there was a good reason not to.

'Is she very pretty?'

He nodded.

'She's younger than you are?'

He nodded again. 'She was only eighteen when we married, four years ago.'

'You obviously miss her a great deal.'

He nodded. Was it that obvious?

'I certainly do miss her. To be honest, I don't feel whole unless she's beside me. I'd rather lose a limb than lose her.'

'Then she's a lucky woman.'

He suddenly felt self-conscious; it wasn't like him to talk about feelings, least of all to someone he hardly knew.

And what about you? Edward tells me George is serving with the Scots Guards. You must have your hands full with four children and no husband at home.

Marion put her hands on her head in a gesture of mock dismay. She told him about George. He was the son of a major and had been to Oxford, then Sandhurst, before joining the Regulars. When he came out after his seven years he was listed as a Reservist.

'So when the war started it was inevitable that he'd have to go?'

'Commissioned almost as soon as the war began and already wounded once, although not severely, thank God.' She described how he'd returned to his battalion after two weeks in a Base Hospital, and now she counted every day that passed as a gift.

'It's like being in Limbo. I feel ... queasy nearly all the time, you know? Mary doesn't remember her father and Lucy hasn't even met him yet! But the boys are absolutely in love with the whole thing, as you might have noticed, even though they've seen one of our chaps come home with a leg missing.'

Her husband's family had a small estate in Wiltshire which in peace time George ran with his father. She'd found her own war time niche taking over her husband's duties, helped by a team of girls from the Women's Land Army to replace their workers.

'Jim, they are such wonderful women. They'll try anything, you know. We're producing better crops now than we ever did before. George can't believe it.'

She smiled, modestly delighted at her own success.

'Well I can. I won't be at all surprised if Lily and Elsie haven't doubled our turnover by the time I get back. I fully expect to be a kept man.'

'Good for them. Mind you, I'll have to clear the girls out before George comes home; he'll be in his element with all those rosy cheeks and firm limbs!'

He didn't believe this for a minute. Marion shared the same good looks and gentle temperament as her brother; he had no doubt that her George worshipped the very ground she walked on, as well he might. With part of his mind constantly returning to Elsie in Bellingham, Jim listened to Marion describing her work on the estate and the sorrow of losing so many friends and workers. It was good to be sitting beside a lovely woman after weeks with only male company.

'You know, when George left the army to work on the estate I thought we'd seen the last of uniforms and service overseas. He's not really a fighter, George; he's much happier shooting pheasants than the enemy. Did you hear about what happened this time last year? At La Boutillerie?' She raised her eyebrows.

'The truce, you mean?'

He'd read accounts in the newspapers, even seen photographs of Allied and German troops shaking hands in no-mans-land. He knew people who'd been disgusted, alarmed even, but he'd found it astounding. According to the Mirror, the Germans lit candles and placed them along the parapet of their trenches; they'd sung carols. Maybe it was that, the voices carrying over no-man's land in the sepulchral ceasefire silence, which stopped the war for an hour or two. They'd ended up exchanging cigarettes and chocolate, even alcohol. The top brass had been livid; bad for the fighting spirit and all that, never to happen again.

'Yes, I heard about it. I don't suppose it'll be happening tonight: not after the trouble it caused last year.'

'Sadly, no. But George was there. He wrote to me afterwards about it; said it nearly broke his heart to go back to the fighting after sharing a drink. In fact ...' Her voice petered out. She put her hand over her mouth and looked away from him for a few seconds, then turned back, her eyes pooled with tears. 'Sorry: I keep doing this at the moment.'

'Don't be. Would you rather talk about something else?'

'No, it's all right. What he said ... George I mean ... was that it had been like a sacrament. Like taking Holy Communion. They shared a bit of food and drank together. Not exactly bread and wine, but ... So afterwards, when they had to go back and try and kill each other, it somehow felt like sacrilege.' She glanced at him. Had he understood?

'That makes sense to me. I'm not particularly religious, but Christmas …'

'It's a tragedy. You know, he showed the German a photograph of me. Me and the children. Apparently there was a lot of that – sharing pictures of girlfriends and wives and families. You'd think it would be the last thing you'd want to do, but perhaps it was … I don't know … '

As she sat there beside him, her face pale in the candlelight, Jim understood perfectly why George would want to show her photograph to his enemy that night in no-man's-land. He'd already chosen the picture of Elsie he was taking out with him.

'Marion, I hope you aren't giving away any of my boyhood secrets!' Edward changed the tone of their conversation. She gave him an arch look and then leaned towards Jim, pretending to whisper something outrageous in his ear. He took her cue, grinned and wrung his hands.

'Really? How many times? Just wait 'til I tell the mess about this!' He raised his glass to Edward, who roared with laughter. In other circumstances he might have been totally happy.

The few days' leave passed too quickly. Christmas day followed a familiar pattern: church, a good walk along frost-rimed lanes under a cold sun, the boys running ahead, dodging behind trees, finding sticks to use as rifles. Then a huge lunch, with most of the food from their own farm, followed by a gathering in front of the warm fire in the sitting room. They exchanged gifts in the late afternoon, the boys fetching the parcels one at a time from beneath the tree in the dining room. Jim had brought whisky for the Lovages, and chocolates; they had bought him a cashmere scarf, much to his embarrassment.

'We couldn't have everyone else with gifts and you empty handed, now could we?' Mrs Lovage gave him a motherly peck on the cheek as she handed it to him. 'We're so very pleased that you joined us. After this beastly war you must come again, and bring Elsie with you.'

He thanked her. Elsie would love this home, this family.

They left early on Boxing Day. The sky was heavy and grey; there were flakes of snow hovering in the air as they said goodbye on the gravelled driveway. The boys, by now his firm friends, begged to be given one last cantering piggyback to the stables and back. Marion stood and watched their antics; she hoped they weren't being too much of a nuisance. How could these fine sons be a nuisance to anyone?

'Stay safe.' She shook his hand, looked him in the eye. 'And please watch out for my little brother. He's rather a pest but I'm fond of him.'

Her eyes were brimming as she looked over at Edward, standing beside the car pulling on his driving gloves. Edward saw her look and came over for a final hug.

'Don't worry, Sis, I'm too fond of myself to get hurt. That right, Jim?'

'Right. You'll be back wearing a stethoscope before anyone can miss you.'

'Quickly now, let's go before Mother goes all weepy on us.'

* * * *

In the post, early in the new year, was a letter from Gibson. He'd made a few telephone calls on Jim's behalf; written a letter or two. He had the picture. No criminal activities exactly, but Liddle had a sheaf of debts, some going back a long time. There were rumours of an illegitimate child, its mother abandoned, their whereabouts unknown.

135

He read and re-read it, too tired after a day's march really to know what to do about it. Lily was an adult. He'd written and warned her that Frank didn't appear to be a man of integrity; he'd advised her to wait before committing herself to him, but she hadn't listened. If, as it appeared, he was greatly in debt and – possibly – a totally bad lot, would that make any difference? She was in love. She didn't want to hear any criticism of the man.

He lay back on his bed and considered the Trust money that was hers, if he agreed, after the marriage. Did Liddle know about it? If he did, Lily was a gullible fool. And if he was minded to refuse to sign it over, what then? Would Liddle just abandon her? Damn, blast and bugger it! He decided to write to Elsie, telling her about his and Gibson's fears and asking her to keep a close eye on Frank when he was around, and on Lily.

> ... I'm sorry to have to say this, sweetheart,
> but I think you shouldn't leave him alone where
> there is any cash to be found. By now he must
> be aware of the various places used in the shop,
> and if Gibson's to be believed, and I'm sure he is,
> I doubt whether a chap of his sort would be able
> to resist the temptation. All in all it would be
> better not even to put it in his way. Gibson also
> mentioned a girl left by him 'in the family way'.
> This must not reach Lily's ears, not least because
> there is a chance that this is rumour, not fact. But
> it does make me worry a great deal as to what
> Lily is thinking of, wanting to marry him. She
> must have some idea of his past, don't you think?
>
> You should show this letter to Ivan, so that
> he can be aware, if he isn't already, of what we're
> dealing with.

I hope to hear very soon from Archie about my commission, and will let you know as soon as I hear anything definite. I love and miss you more than I can say, my darling. I should be with you by the end of the month, all being well.

He'd contacted Archie about an early commission. It was time to go home.

EIGHTEEN

Elsie

Her body was doing what was expected of it: it worked in the shop, it did more than its fair share of chores in the house, it even wrote to Jim. Meanwhile, another Elsie was in a trance. Minutes mattered only if Ivan was in the house or the garden or anywhere else she could see him. There was this weight in her chest, a coiled snake too heavy to carry. She'd forgotten how to feel even remotely normal. The day after their lovemaking she panicked while they were having lunch and had to leave the table, keeping out of the way until he went back to work. The shop kept her occupied all afternoon, but by the evening she'd eaten virtually nothing and felt weak and sick. After supper, when Lily went through to the parlour – she was sewing these evenings – Ivan closed the kitchen door and stood, arms folded, as she replaced the pots, wiped the table. She blushed as her cloth passed over the place where she'd perched, half naked, the night before.

'Are you going to come over here?'

He spoke quietly, but the question made her shiver. What would it mean? If she went across? She put down the cloth and took a step towards him.

'Over here, Elsie.'

'Why?' But she went.

'Turn around.'

She looked at him. What now? He took her by the

138

shoulders and swivelled her so that she was facing away from him.

'Don't look so worried, I'm just going to undo your pinny.'

She laughed out loud. Seconds later he turned her back to face him and held her head in his cupped hands, kissing her with such passion that she stopped breathing. He folded her to his chest; she could feel both their hearts beating, but not together. There was a battle going on.

'I'm sorry, Elsie, but I'm not going to keep away from you. Not for you, not for Jim. I can't do it. I've tried for years, but not any longer.'

There were tears in his eyes as he kissed her again: her forehead, her lips, her cheeks, tens of tiny kisses as if to make up for lost time.

'You won't try to stop me, will you? Tell me you won't. I won't let you.'

She said nothing, just listened as he whispered that he wanted her, only her, always her. She knew she ought at least to attempt to pull away from him, to remind him – as if he should need reminding – that of all the women there were, she was the last one he should love in this way. But she didn't.

So now: a double life.

Shortly after supper on Christmas Eve, Luke Routledge from Boat Farm arrived with their goose. They sat round the table, whisky bottle out, and toasted their men. Even Lily came through, leaving her pins and measuring tape.

'Jim and George!'

'May they stay safe!'

Luke's brother, George, was serving on Gallipoli with the Northumberland Fusiliers; his mam wasn't taking it very well, what with it being Christmas and George not there to help with the plucking and the Turkish campaign failing, or so they said.

'Bloody Turks, sorry Mrs Errington, sorry Miss Errington for the swearing, but they're a bad lot. We've lost loads of our lads out there. As soon as I've had me eighteenth in May I'm going to be out there and kill a few; even things up a bit.'

Elsie shook her head as she listened to the threats of the pink-cheeked boy. She was fairly sure that his experience of violence so far would be limited to the occasional clip around the ear from his father.

'It'll all be over by then, Luke. You won't need to go, and George can come home.'

'It bloody better not be, sorry Mrs Errington, sorry Miss Errington for the swearing.'

His face was flushed by now; the two whiskies were beginning to show. 'Me and Dan Lazenby's got it all planned. His birthday's two days after mine, then we're down to the recruiting office and away. Me bag's packed already, like.'

He looked around with the cheerful grin of someone about to spend a week in Scarborough.

'Does your mam know?'

'Nah! I dursn't tell 'er; she'd lock us up!'

It was after eight o'clock when Luke went out into the freezing night air for the return journey to the farm. He'd left his horse and cart in Erringtons' paddock while he made the dozen or so deliveries at that end of town, so Ivan pulled on his coat and went with him to open and close the gate. As Elsie washed and dried the glasses she thought about how it must feel to be Luke and George's mother, with a son hundreds of miles away, facing who knows what horror, perhaps injured or dying. The very idea of young men killing other young men was disgusting. Jim should never have volunteered. If he'd waited, none of this would have happened. What if the war doesn't end soon? What if Jim has to go and kill other people's sons and husbands? It made her ill to consider it.

She'd stuffed and trussed the goose by the time Ivan came back; he was carrying a hessian sack full of holly, a gift from one of his farmers. Lily bundled up all her sewing so the tables were clear in the parlour, and together they decorated the mantelshelf and sideboard, lighting far too many candles so that they didn't need to bother with the lamps.

'Jim should be here.'

She'd said it before she knew she'd even thought it, but it was true. Jim had always been the one to do this; he would have insisted that the holly was up before now. She closed her eyes and pictured his bulky frame bending down to pick the best branches carefully, as if something rested on the result. More than anything she wanted to conjure him there, there in the parlour, just by willing it to be so. If she could wish the last month undone, then she would. They could have joined in the carol singing around the town as usual, and she wouldn't be feeling like this.

'He should.'

Ivan took out another sprig of holly and handed it to her.

Lily brought out the sherry and a decanter of brandy for Ivan. She refused her glass at first, but Ivan insisted she should drink it: it would relax her and help her to sleep. In the end the cards came out and they enjoyed a few games, but by ten she was drifting off; her eyelids were drooping even as she tried to sort out her trumps. Lily nudged Ivan as she placed a card.

'Do you think we should wake her? She should be in bed. And there's no rush in the morning; we can all sleep as long as we like.'

'She wants to go to church, I think.'

He knelt in front of her, gathering up the cards that were beginning to spill from her hand. She turned sideways into her armchair, as if she were already in bed. She didn't want to move: if she did, she would wake up and she'd never get back to sleep again.

'Come on, Elsie.'

'Leave me alone.'

'No, let's get you upstairs.'

She tried to push him away, but he drew her into his arms so that her head rested on his shoulder. He climbed carefully up the stairs, bracing himself before each step and resting with both feet on each tread before he moved on. It must be hurting his ribs ... she should rouse herself, walk on her own, but she was too weary even to try. He struggled to turn the handle of the bedroom door with her in his arms, and when it clicked free the door swung open suddenly, so that he nearly fell into the room. She heard him gasp with pain as he struggled to stay balanced, then he carried her over to the bed and set her down. The room and the bed were stone cold and she turned onto her side, drawing up her knees for warmth as he pulled the eiderdown up and tucked it round her shoulders.

* * * *

She woke again later, suddenly, as if someone had tapped her on the shoulder in the dark, but the room was empty. It was uncomfortable, sleeping ... trying to sleep ... in her clothes. When she couldn't bear it any longer she twisted out of bed to undress: by the time she'd struggled out of her skirt and blouse in the dark room, pulled off her stockings and pulled on her nightdress, her teeth were chattering. Then she lay awake until Christmas morning dawned.

When it did, there was an adamantine frost in the valley. They opened the front door to a town that was utterly still, hushed apart from the irregular clang of the bells of St Cuthbert's. As they stepped gingerly onto the street they found that it had been newly paved overnight with thick ice. Within seconds, Lily grabbed Ivan's hand to prevent herself from sliding, so she took his other arm. And so they walked, carefully, to the morning service. As they took their places in the pew, the choir was singing softly *O Jesu so sweet, O Jesu so mild*, the harmonies as subtle as the winter light that leached through the tall arched windows. The Charltons were there, fuddled Mrs Jobson … their icy breath was visible, clouding the air inside the nave as they sang jaunty carols to the wheezing pipe organ. Prayers were said for sons and husbands. Elsie felt her chin begin to tremble as they recited together the Collect for Peace …

O God, who art the author of peace … in knowledge of whom standeth our eternal life, whose service is perfect freedom … defend us thy humble servants in all assaults of our enemies; that we, surely trusting in thy defence, may not fear the power of any adversaries; through the might of Jesus Christ our Lord. Amen.

As the prayer ended her body began to heave with sobs as she thought of Jim, of Fred Charlton. How could the new year make things better, really? Even peace wouldn't bring peace … not for her, not now.

NINETEEN

Frank

It was the beginning of the third week in January before he next pulled up outside Erringtons. He'd sent a note to Lily explaining that he was working flat out, trying to boost his business before the big day. She'd written back: she'd been missing him, finding it hard that she hadn't seen him for nearly a month, but even so the time was flying, especially with dress fittings, and her bottom drawer was nearly complete. She loved the bracelet. He was wearing the driving gloves she'd given him.

Goody Two Shoes was there at the counter again and the shop was quiet. He took his hat off and offered her his hand. He quite fancied giving her a peck on the cheek, but maybe that should wait. Mind, she looked a bit pale and cold, but then it was winter and Big Jim wasn't there to warm her up.

'Happy New Year, Elsie.'

Buggered if he was going to call her anything else; he was as near as damn-it a member of the family now. She didn't seem too happy to see him. Surely she could do with some snappy conversation after Christmas with Ivan the Invalid. He'd have to find out from Lily what he'd done to deserve a kicking. Apart from having such a pretty face that is.

She reached behind and opened the door to the office; he could see Lily's face as she looked up and saw him. He'd never seen her move so fast; she was out of her seat and round the front of the counter like a chased rabbit. He kissed both of her hands and her cheeks.

'Let's have a look at you. I'm a lucky man!'

That did the trick: she didn't know where to put herself.

'Come into the office and we'll do your order, then perhaps we can go somewhere for tea.'

He went back to the motor to fetch his case of products and soon they were alone in the back room. She left the door ajar. Look but don't touch, eh? Never mind; won't be long now. The order complete, he packed up and they walked together to The Railway for tea. God, what was it like, walking round this place? Everybody they passed wanted to stop and talk, even the old wifeys. Especially the old wifeys. Give him the big city and anonymity any day.

Once the girl had brought their tea, he asked casually if she'd brought the money with her. Maybe he should have waited a little longer before mentioning it; he hadn't thanked for her Christmas present yet, but first things first. She handed over an envelope with four pound notes. He checked the contents. Just a minute ...

'Didn't you say two pounds a week, my lovely? I was rather expecting six, not four.'

He tried to keep the tone light, for now.

She was hoping to borrow a bit more at the end of that week when she did the banking ... perhaps she'd manage five pounds by next week. He tried to look satisfied, but hell, two quid's two quid. She was keeping an account book of the money she was borrowing, but it didn't stop her feeling a bit ashamed, as if it was stealing. Didn't he realise this ... yackety yickey? Of course he bloody did, but it wasn't as if the business couldn't afford it. Christ, now she was trying to tell him what to spend it on.

'At least we'll have a little nest egg to spend on the house.

I think Chapmans for the furniture, don't you? I was talking to one of our better customers and she said ... what? Frank, what's wrong?'

She'd seen the look on his face. He'd always been an open book, even when it led to a good hiding at school.

'There are more important things to think about than fancy furniture, Lil, my darling. Now that we have the house I have ... one or two outstanding accounts to settle.'

It was a relief to be able to say it. He'd paid over the very modest sum actually required by the landlord before Christmas; the rest of Lily's money – nearly twenty pounds – he'd spread over a number of people waiting for cash from him: he who shouts loudest, so to speak. He wasn't out of deep water, but at least he could breathe a bit. He'd been getting out of the car the other night after a bloody long day on the road, when a couple of no-necks had come from nowhere.

'Evening Liddle. Wor boss wants a word wi ye.'

'Wey, he wants what's owing to him forst, like. Then he'll have a word. Aboot rats that borrow of 'im and then keep 'im waitin fer 'is intrest.'

There was one on either side of him, as big as fucking trams they were.

'He knows he'll get his money.'

'And the interest, Mr Liddle.'

'And the interest.' Now fuck off.

'Because if yez keep 'im waitin much longer, we're gannen ter hev ter tek yon car instead.'

'And teach yez a lesson.'

He had money in his wallet, but he didn't want them to see how much.

'I'll bring it round tomorrow morning. Nine o'clock sharp.'

'Wey Liddle, yer a reasonable man. Howay, hev a fag.'

One of them offered him a packet of Players while the

other lit a match. All pals until he took his first drag, then the no-neck on the right reached out and calmly took it from his hand as the one on the left grabbed his arms behind his back. Right Man gripped him by the back of the neck and yanked his head down. Smiling, he took a long pull on the fag, then pointed the glowing end so close to his eye he could feel the heat beginning to singe his lashes.

'Nine o'clock, Liddle, or yez'll be needen a white stick, see?'

'That's a joke, Liddle ... "see"... because yer won't be able to.'

Very funny. Where did the snake Jew find comedians like him?

'All right lads, I get the message. I'll be there, with the money, on time.'

They'd let him go, but he'd been shaking so badly he could hardly lock the car. He managed to get himself inside all right, but then he'd drunk the best part of a bottle of brandy before collapsing onto his unmade bed. It was only the knowledge of what would happen if he didn't that made him struggle back up a few hours later. Westgate Road at eight fifty five prompt and the motor was safe for a while: ten quid gone in a flash to keep the greedy little Jew bastard happy. Then he'd paid a few quid each to his tailor and current landlord; the rest had already gone on Christmas presents for the nephews. He was hoping to settle a few more debts before March – at Erringtons' expense.

'But Frank, what's more important than a bed for us to sleep in and a table to eat at, and some chairs?'

Bless her, she looked mystified as to what his 'outstanding accounts' could be; she'd lived a sheltered life, she'd been spoiled. Time to put her right.

He sat up straight and withdrew his hand from Lily's to

147

get out his cigarettes and matches. He lit up and looked at her across the cups and saucers. He took a long drag, then sat back, arms over the back of his chair, his eyes focused on a painting to the right of her head.

'Lily, I think I'd better make myself clear. You may be the boss in Erringtons, but you're not going to be wearing any trousers in our house. I will be saying where the money gets spent and you'll be doing as you're told.'

He smiled to soften his words.

'You're my precious girl; I don't want you to worry yourself about these things. Do you understand?'

He sat up and patted her hand. If she cut up rough, well too bad: he'd done very well out of her. If she didn't, well better still; she'd be docile as a lamb before he'd finished. She was staring at him, as if understanding him and not understanding him were equally not what she wanted. He repeated the question, this time with a definite edge to his voice. She was nodding, and he could see the tears begin to well.

'Out loud please, Lily.' She had to force herself to speak. Made a change.

'I understand.'

He made a show of looking behind him and to either side.

'Are you talking to me? Because if you are, you'd better use my name.' He was leaning over the table, speaking slowly, every word enunciated for effect.

'I understand, Frank.'

'That's better. Now, let's order some more tea.'

He beckoned to the waitress, holding up the pot to indicate that he wanted a fresh brew. It was all over: he could go back to being Frank the Friendly.

He stayed in Bellingham that night, and they had a good dinner together back at The Railway. It was grand, drawing other diners into their conversation and buying drinks all round. He could see Lily wondering what it was all costing, and whether it was her four pounds that he was using to pay, but she didn't question him ... *she's learning*. Anyway, in six weeks she was going to promise to love, honour and obey him, so she might as well get in some practice with the obedience now. To make his point he strolled over to the bar and bought a cigar.

TWENTY

Ivan

Lily'd gone back to the shop early, so they were alone; he loved it when they had a bit of time together after lunch. He'd been hoping for something else when she asked him if he had a few minutes to spare, but as soon as Lily closed the front door she handed him the letter Jim had written about Frank. She watched his face as he read it.

'Ivan, he's even worse than we thought, isn't he?'

'Not really; none of this surprises me. Certainly not the debts and so on.'

'I saw Lily give him something the other day. I couldn't see it clearly, but it looked like an envelope. I'm worried about it now, reading that.'

'Where was this?'

'Outside the shop. I was standing at the window and they crossed the street together. He got into the car and then I saw her.'

'Saw her what? She just handed him an envelope? Probably a love letter. She'll have sprayed scent on the paper and enclosed a lock of hair.'

'Well, yes, I suppose so. But she looked round first, as if it was some sort of secret.'

'Elsie, there's nothing wrong with passing someone an envelope. Postie does it all the time.'

He tried to make nothing of it, but he had to admit it

sounded a bit ... what? Elsie was frowning; he ought to be taking it more seriously.

'Shouldn't we say something? To Lily, I mean. Warn her about him?'

'Tell you what, let's wait for Jim to do it.' If Jim had the power to cut her funds, it was his job to tell her why he was doing it.

'It's such a shame.'

She was right. Anyone could see Lily was looking wonderful; much happier than she used to be before Frank. It was all going so well. Mrs Binns had agreed to move in as housekeeper for the duration of the war – as they'd expected, she was glad of a position where she could live in. Given that Lily was right, she was a good choice. They'd also advertised for a general book-keeper to take over Lily's responsibilities; Elsie was hoping to find someone who'd be willing to take a turn at the counter when the shop was busy. And Will, the deliveries boy, was keen to do extra hours, so Erringtons wasn't going to suffer too much when Lily left in March. The ordering was the only thing.

'I've never done it before. I suppose there'll be lists to work from.'

'You'll be the boss, Elsie. You can bring in all sorts of new stuff, with no-one to argue with you!'

'What about Frank?'

'How d'you mean?'

'When he comes as a salesman, after the wedding? If he thinks I'm going to go into that back room alone with him!' She shuddered. He hadn't thought of that.

'Why, he hasn't tried to meddle with you, has he?'

'No, but it makes me feel *slimy* ... just to be near him.' The look of dread on her face was so comical, he laughed out loud.

'Just as well, or I'd have to challenge him to a duel.'

'Jim would, you mean.'

He handed the letter back to her, then pulled her to him and kissed her. She relaxed into his arms, returning his kiss.

'You know, I don't think I have the courage to tell her.'

'Really?'

He looked at her face; was she joking? She wasn't.

'It's not just that she'll get all angry and defend him, it's that she'll be really upset. Whatever we think about him, she really does love him. What'll she do? Break off her engagement? Then what? She'll become even more bitter and horrible than she was before. It's only money, Ivan. Maybe his debts can be sorted out so they can start without any.'

'And the other woman? The one with the bairn? If it's true, I mean?'

'I'm not going to be casting the first stone. Are you?'

He didn't spend much time in church these days, but even he was familiar with the old bible story.

'Perhaps not.'

'No perhaps about it.'

'Right, before I get a sermon I'm off up the hill.'

It was good to be back at work, feeling strong again. It still gave him gyp to use the hammer for any length of time, but he could manage everything else. His nose had a bit of a lump that might be there for good, but it could've been much worse. He'd seen Isabel the other day, with her mother, but she hadn't let on to him. How would he be feeling now, this minute, if they were engaged? He didn't even want to think about it.

He was late home. After leaving the smithy he walked down the hill, snow whipping into his face from a sullen sky. He called in at The Crown – he needed to buy a round – several rounds – for the lads. The place was empty at first and he downed his first pint in under a minute and ordered another, leaning on the bar, alone. But after five minutes the saloon door crashed open and a group of young men spilled in, some of them the friends he was hoping to see: the lads who'd been so good after the beating. None of them was much over twenty.

'Fill wor glasses, wor papers've come!'

Ivan stood up and joined the crowd. *What's going on?* Two of the five had received their call up papers that morning. One of them, Johnny Dixon, reached into his inside pocket and passed him the official letter.

The two of them stood together, holding invisible weapons, mock attention. The barman was an ex-soldier, returned from Belgium with part of his left leg missing early in 1915. He pulled their pints, but Ivan could see his face with its half smile: rather you than me. The lads remained at the bar, talking loudly, swaggering about the contribution they were going to make to the progress of the war in France.

'The buggers won't know what's hit them! Me fether says to aim fer their dicks, that way even if they survive they won't produce any baby Boches ...' There was loud laughter.

'That's nee good; Boche dicks are ower small to hit. I'm gannen fer the chest. Blow the bastards away!'

There was more laughter. By now the ale was swilling freely and cigarette smoke was hazing the air. Ivan wasn't fooled by the bluster; there was tension there: sweating upper lips, shifting eyes. He remembered 1914; the lads had been fearless then ... couldn't sleep for worrying that the war might end before they got there. But now? It hadn't taken too long for the flow of volunteers to slow down once the newspapers were publishing long lists of dead, wounded and missing in action. These boys wouldn't sleep tonight either, but not because they were excited. After buying a round or two, Ivan lit a cigarette, shook hands with the others and wished the two a good war and a safe return. He couldn't take any more of it.

He came in through the back, pushed the kitchen door gently. *What?* Elsie was kneeling on the floor in front of the dresser, the contents of one of the bottom cupboards stacked haphazardly out on the floor. There was a bucket on the tiles beside her, steam rising from the soapy water. Her hair was loose, damp around her face as she washed the shelves, scrubbing at a stain so hard that the veins stood out on her forearm. It was nearly nine o'clock.

'What on earth are you doing?'

He saw her shoulders begin to shake and he went over to her, taking the wet cloth from her hands and pulling her to her feet.

'What is it, sweetheart?'

'You know.'

'But why now ... and why the spring cleaning when you should be sitting with your feet up?'

'I'm not tired, and Mrs Binns'll have a heart attack if she has to take on messy cupboards, and I don't have much time during the day, and now Jim's coming home ...' So that was it.

'But you want to see him, don't you? We all do.'

What was he hoping she'd reply? He knew Elsie loved him and wanted him, but Jim she adored. He'd watched her when she read his letters, her face all lit up. And he loved his brother – he *did* – but fuck the thought of being around when they were together again.

He felt her nod, and just held her, rocking her tenderly and kissing her hair as he'd done months before. After a few minutes he nudged her into a chair. He knelt down and swabbed the shelves dry, then he began to replace the contents of the cupboard, asking her as he worked how she'd heard that Jim would be back so soon. Still sniffing she explained that he'd telephoned the shop, that afternoon, just before they closed. He had his commission, thanks to Archie, and was coming home before leaving for France. He'd be with them for a week, maybe.

After a few more minutes Elsie tutted and took over the tidying, grumbling she'd never find anything again if he put it away. That's better. He took the chair now, and gazed at her as she worked. She stopped suddenly, turning towards him on her hands and knees.

'What if the snow comes in worse? He won't even get here.'

'He'll walk here if he has to, snow or no snow. You know that.'

She nodded; went back to her tidying. Nearly done.

'Where's Lily?'

'At Ann's.'

'Come upstairs with me.' It was a whisper.

'Ivan, I can't. We can't. Apart from anything else, Lily might come back in.'

'Not yet she won't; you said she's with Ann, remember. It'll be all bride this and bridesmaid that.'

'But she might. Anyway, I feel guilty enough without carrying on when Jim's coming home, and so should you.'

She was serious now, but she knew she was in a weak position. He knew her so well; they were immoderate in their passion for one another. It wasn't reasonable at all.

'I do, but it won't stop me.'

He leaned down, took her by her upper arms, then picked her up and threw her over his shoulder, ignoring her whispered fury. She thumped his back, tried to reach up and pull his hair.

'Now, don't struggle or I might drop you.'

For the second time in weeks he carried her up the stairs, this time nearly tripping because he was laughing so much at her efforts to escape. He took her past Lily's, along to his own room at the end of the passage. He swung the door closed and dumped her on the bed, holding her there with one hand as she tried to escape.

'It's no use, you'll just have to give in.'

He unbuckled his belt and lay down beside her; she was panting, still agitated, so he took her hand and placed it where she would feel how much he needed her. With a moan she began to undo his buttons, tearing at his trousers as he hitched up her skirt. She helped him pull her drawers down, right down, over her feet and off. She was whimpering, but very quietly, as he shifted onto his back and pulled her up on top of him so that she was straddling his chest. She shuffled down, then raised her hips and lowered herself onto him. He waited a second, smiling, and then made long, gentle love to her.

'There, that wasn't so bad, was it?'

She leaned over and picked her underclothes from the floor. He lay back and watched as she straightened her stockings and pulled on her drawers with their lace and ribbons.

'I don't know how Jim functions during the day when he's got you beside him all night. He must feel worn out!' He was joking of course, but it would be true, for him it would.

'How am I going to get out of here if Lily's back?'

She had her hands on her hips; she'd gone all school-mistress on him. He gestured her to be silent as he stood up and walked past her, then opened the bedroom door briskly, as if he'd been in there to fetch something. He strode to the top of the stairs and looked down to where the hall lamp gave a faint light. As far as he could see Lily wasn't home yet.

There were no wet footprints by the front door that he could see; no brolly or melting snow. He beckoned and she slipped out and back down to the kitchen to finish what she'd started.

TWENTY ONE

Jim

As he'd hoped, Archie Pumphrey didn't have much difficulty in finding him a commission. The Northumberland Fusiliers badly needed a draft of good officers, and the CO of the local territorial battalion was one of his shooting friends. The old Major's recommendation would have come as good news at a bad time. It only took a couple of weeks for the envelope to arrive at Trinity OTC. The porter was used to the ropes by now and handed it to him personally, with a friendly handshake.

'Congratulations, Sir.'

He'd been increasingly anxious to be away from Cambridge after Gibson's letter, and the feel of the textured paper and the opening words, 'George, by the Grace of God … King', made his heart race. He read on. The King sent him greetings and was expecting him to do his duty in the Rank of 2nd Lieutenant. He read the entire flowery commission, strangely overcome by the idea of his King trusting him to lead men in his name. He folded it and pushed it respectfully back into its envelope. It was nearly time to eat, so he dressed for his first mess as an officer, although it wouldn't be public knowledge until it was posted in the London Gazette. Before long he'd have a batman to take care of his gear. Strange thought. He could hardly restrain a silly grin when he greeted Edward and the other cadets over their first drinks.

'Just call me Sir, you lot!'

It took a few seconds to sink in, but then there were warm congratulations, handshakes and a fair amount of banter about his new rank. He wasn't really a drinker, but by the end of the dinner they'd all got through far more than usual, particularly Edward. He watched his friend as the night wore on; it must be tough for him to be left behind. He raised his glass, and Edward responded.

'To Jim. A good man, and as fine an officer as the King could wish for.'

The others, all the oldies, joined the toast, and before long the news reached the far end of the table, where the real gentlemen were enjoying a fairly boisterous last bottle or two. He saw the reaction, a few raised eyebrows. Even so, several of the youngsters left their seats and came over to shake his hand, offer cigars. It was a grand final evening.

By mid-morning on Thursday 10th February he was on his way north, this time in full uniform; he'd bought his regimental badges and Lieutenant's star in London. It was a good feeling, acknowledging the respectful nods of the other passengers as he entered the compartment. He touched his cap, smiled, but he didn't want any conversation; his chest was tight with anticipation; he was just marking time until he'd be with Elsie. He'd rung the day before, telling her that he'd be arriving in Hexham in the mid-afternoon, but that she shouldn't come to meet him in case he was delayed. In the event he wasn't much held up, although it began snowing heavily in Yorkshire, blurring his view for the rest of the journey. He tapped his fingers in frustration as the train slowed down occasionally to push through fresh white drifts, leaving the tracks behind them smutted and soiled. It was already three o'clock when the engine hissed to a standstill in Central Station, only just in time for the connections west and north to Bellingham, even without the snow. Cursing under his breath he shouted for a porter to fetch his trunk and charged over to where his next train was gathering up steam.

As the local train bowled along beside the Tyne he closed his eyes to picture her. She would have been watching the clock, stepping out into the street and looking towards the station. She'd be wearing her warm boots, but wouldn't bother with a coat. He could hardly bear the idea of losing one of his six nights with her; the train from Hexham to Bellingham had better be running. If not, he'd leave his trunk and walk home.

As it was, the iron rails that snaked up the valley from the Hexham junction were fairly clear. He knew the old couple waiting for the Bellingham train with him: the Fenwicks, retired farmers, customers. They chatted politely about the war, his commission. He noticed their deference and felt humbled by it; how many men from this valley had already died in uniform?

'You know that I'd be joining this war officer or not? They've brought in conscription.'

'Not sure how good a soldier'll be that's forced into the job, like.'

'We'll see.'

'Will yer brother be gannen, Mr Errington?'

'Depends if they can spare him. Probably. If not this week, then next, or later this year.'

'Well, God bless yer, hinny. Bless yer both.'

Mary Fenwick patted his arm as the five sixteen to Rickerton Junction clanked to a halt alongside them.

It was market day, when the shop was always very busy, even in the early evening; they stayed open later than other days. From the dark street he could see her through the misted window; his heart lurched as he watched her chatting to old Mrs Morris, helping her to pack the parcels of food into her basket. Lily was there too, but they were both too occupied to see him with his face against the glass pane. He saw her glance up as he opened the door, then stop what she was doing. He stepped in, took off his cap. Mrs Morris and the other customers gathered what was going on and the bustle in the shop petered out, the chatter hushed as everyone took in that he was there, in his shop, in his officer's uniform.

There was a pause, then he was vaguely aware of a round of applause as Elsie slipped under the barrier of the counter and flung herself into his arms. He caught her in a bear hug, at the same time acknowledging with a smile, over her head, the cheerful support of their customers. Holding Elsie with one arm he reached round her to shake hands with those closest to him. Home.

'Well, if my wife here isn't going to serve you good people then I will.'

He took off his greatcoat and lifted the wooden barrier, taking his place behind the counter with Lily. He looked up expectantly, ready for the next customer, but she seemed a little hesitant. He smiled and reached out to take the packets from her hand:

'It's still where I belong, you know. Don't take any notice of this get-up.'

Once they'd closed up he walked them home, one on each arm. The women chattered on, even Lily; he couldn't think when he'd last heard her talk so much and so freely. Perhaps tonight wasn't the night to start up about Frank; it could wait a while. His trunk was where he'd left it in the hall on the way from the station.

'Not that again! Are we going to be packing the wretched thing all week?'

She was laughing, but he could see that the damned trunk was a dirty great reminder of why he was home.

'Just leave it, I'll see to it.'

He wanted these few days to be as normal as he could make them. Only better.

'Jim?'

It was Ivan, calling from the kitchen; he strode along to meet him. That was another conversation that could wait: Ivan wasn't going to open up about the attack in front of the women. They shook hands, hugged briefly. He looked Ivan up and down.

'I like the new nose.'

'Thanks. I didn't exactly choose it myself.'

Supper was simple but tasty; Mrs Binns had left them shepherd's pie and apple sponge. He wanted to hear about Bellingham, the business ... who'd gone to the war? They wanted to hear about his training.

'Show us your stick stuff, Jim!'

He'd written to her about the hours spent drilling: tucking the stick under the arm, taking it in the hand again, cocking it up in the air, smartly down by the side ...

'Right, watch carefully.'

He took a wooden spoon from the drawer and executed the whole drill, there in the kitchen, head up, back straight, transformed into a soldier by the precise movements, mimicking the strident yelling of the company sergeant major.

'How does that help when you meet a German? Do you tap him on the head with it?'

'Little brother, you may well ask.'

He slumped down at the table, suddenly embarrassed by it all.

'It's all about discipline, isn't it? They want you to be like

162

machines.'

She could see it; he knew she would. He took her hand and stood up again.

'Would you mind if Elsie and I leave you two to do the clearing up tonight?'

He wasn't bothered whether Lily and Ivan would mind or not; it was time for bed. He kissed Lily on the cheek, patted Ivan's shoulder as they left the table. Ivan would understand him wanting an early night with Elsie, that was for sure. Did he have a girl at the moment? They'd talk tomorrow.

The following morning they had breakfast alone, later than usual. He wasn't going to have Elsie doing nothing but work at Erringtons on his last few days at home. They'd agreed that she'd join Lily there now, while he sorted his trunk, then after lunch she'd return to work for a couple of hours, the busiest part of the day, while Jim went up to the forge with Ivan; they needed to catch up with each other. But after that he would come along to meet her and the rest of the day would be theirs; Lily could finish off and close up in the early evening. They'd received a number of applications for Lily's job: she was hoping to leave the business a week before the wedding. Not long now, so filling in for Elsie when Jim was on leave wouldn't trouble her at all, especially when Frank wasn't there.

His two hours with Ivan were spent at the forge, chatting as he worked on the hooves of a couple of mares from Hainingside. There was time to talk, but they didn't cover much ground.

'So, why the kicking?'

'It was about a lass.'

'The father?'

'The brothers.'

'Was she … is she …?'

163

'No.'

'Do I know her?'

'Possibly. Probably. Look, it happened, it was my own fault. Can we talk about something else?'

So they'd talked about the work he was doing with farm machinery, and whether it would keep him safe from conscription. By three thirty Jim had been home to wash, changed back into his uniform and was on his way to fetch Elsie. They'd been hoping to go for a walk before dark, up out of the town and along the burn to the waterfall, but the sky was slate grey and charged with rain or snow. An arctic wind skated across their faces as they left the shop.

'Let's just go home.'

Elsie tucked her arm through his. Jim put his hand on hers and squeezed it, knowing that the house would be empty for at least two hours. But as they stepped out briskly towards the square a car negotiated the corner and drove past them towards the middle of the town. Elsie looked back through the gloom of late afternoon.

'Jim, wait a minute ... I think that's Frank Liddle. What's he doing here? He's supposed to be coming next Tuesday. I'm sure Lily isn't expecting him – she would have said.'

She looked up at him, uncertain.

'Come on.'

He wasn't happy at having to turn round, but on the other hand he didn't want Liddle in the shop with only Lily around. By the time they'd retraced their steps Frank was already leaning on the counter with his back to the door, lighting up a cigar he'd clearly just taken from the humidor. Lily was still behind the counter, but as they came back in she blushed and nudged Frank. He straightened up and turned to face them.

'Well, Errington, good to see you! I was hoping we'd meet before the wedding.'

164

The same old Liddle, only cockier than ever. He passed the cigar to his left hand, offering his right. Jim shook it, briefly.

'We weren't expecting to see you today, Frank.' Elsie looked enquiringly from Frank to Lily.

'Frank's just called in to see me on his way back to Newcastle, haven't you Frank. He's been up north, Alnwick and Rothbury.' Lily looked uncomfortable.

'And villages in between. I've had a busy few days.'

'On the way back?'

He'd been driving on the wrong road from the wrong direction.

'Well actually, I made a detour because I couldn't wait 'til Tuesday to see my Lily.'

Liddle leaned over and took her hand. It was a smooth response, but only Lily believed him, and she was beaming, *God help us*. Jim took his coat off and helped Elsie out of hers.

'I tell you what, Lily, why don't you and Frank have an hour together, since he's come out of his way.'

'Well, if you're willing to take over, I'll take my girl out for tea. Come on Lily; get your coat, my sweet.'

For once Lily seemed slightly reluctant to go out, but Frank swept his hat off the counter, took her arm and bustled her out of the door. Elsie closed it behind them and turned back to him with a long sigh.

'Oh, Romeo!' She put on a Lily face.

'He's a first class idiot and a cheat. Look, while we're here on our own I think I'll take a gander at the books without Lily hovering around. I know the shop's doing well, but I ought to have a glance at the figures. Is that all right with you?'

He left the office door wide open so that he could see her.

'But before I do …'

He pulled Elsie into the back office and kissed her, his hands cupping her bottom through the fabric of her dress. Within seconds the bell above the door jangled as a customer came in. Elsie laughed as he swore under his breath and let her go. She reached for her Errington's pinafore and blew him a kiss as she went back to the counter.

He sat down at the desk and pulled open the drawer; the ledger was there, where the accounts had been kept for as many years as the shop had been open. He lifted it out and set it on the desk, turning the heavy pages until he found the current figures. The takings were reasonable, but not as good as he'd expected from what Elsie had told him; the bottom line was lower than last year's. He shuffled through the other books and papers in the drawer. The only unfamiliar thing was a little notebook, tucked under everything else. He flicked it open, not expecting to find anything of interest, but there was a short list of dates and figures in Lily's neat hand, beginning in mid-December. The dates went on until the beginning of March, but not the figures; they ended last week. He was sitting, elbows on the desk, when Elsie came through.

'What is it, love?' She was flushed. He stood up and came round the desk towards her.

'Jim, I don't … I think … I'm not sure … there's money missing from the drawer. A five pound note. Unless Lily's put it somewhere for safety.'

She glanced over at the desk, as if the five pound note might be there.

'I know it was there because Mr Benson paid his account this morning. I took it from him myself.'

Jim reached over and picked up the little notebook and looked at it again, at the entries and the dates.

'Was Liddle here just before Christmas, then not until mid-January?' He knew it seemed an odd question, but after a second or two Elsie nodded.

'In that case, I think I know exactly where your five pound note is.'

He left the ledger open with the little notebook beside it while he and Elsie served the last few customers of the day together. They were busy making up a few orders for the following morning when Frank and Lily returned, emerging arm in arm from the semi-darkness. As they came in, he glanced to check the time then circled behind them. He locked the door, turning the sign to closed. For a matter of seconds he stood in silence barring the exit. Liddle just looked at him.

'I want a word with you, Liddle. Lily, you go into the office with Elsie, please.'

Lily looked from him to Frank but didn't move.

'*Now*, Lily.'

He waited for her in silence, but as she reached the office door she stopped and turned back: she'd seen the ledger and the notebook where he'd left them.

'It was my idea, not his. He's a good man.'

She stared at her hands, still in their gloves.

'If he's a "good man", why is he taking money from you? Why would you take money from Errington's to give to him? Does he know you're stealing?' He gestured to Liddle.

'I am *not* stealing! How dare you say I'm stealing!'

Lily reached into her pocket for a handkerchief and pressed it to her eyes.

'Well, what would you call it?' Elsie was genuinely puzzled.

'I've been borrowing money that's due to me, that's all. To help my fiancé. Not that it's any of your business.' She glowered at Elsie, the old Lily back in her voice and attitude.

167

'Just look at you!' She gestured towards Elsie. 'You come into this family, no family of your own, without so much as a penny as I remember, not a farthing to your name, but you sit there all virtuous, judging me for wanting what's mine. Or will be, once I'm married.'

'Lily, I'm not judging you, I just don't understand what's going on.'

'Just ignore her, Elsie. Lily, I'm not going to drag this out, and I'm not going to try and alter your view of this man, although perhaps I should. As I understand it you've been helping him out, maybe settling his debts? I gather you've been taking money from the business, viewing it as an advance on the money that Father put in trust for you. Is that right?'

'So, what's wrong with that?'

She looked so aggrieved; could she honestly not see what was wrong with it?

'You also know, because Gibson mentioned it, that I can veto the payment of the trust if I have doubts about the integrity of the man you marry. Is that right? I mean is it right that you understand it?'

Lily's teeth clenched. She began to shout, stabbing her finger in Jim's direction.

'Why should you be able to control my money? It's outrageous!'

'Because Father and Gibson believed it to be the wise thing to do. And standing here, looking at Liddle, who's had … how much, already? It makes me relieved that they were so careful. Now, this is what I plan to do.'

Lily was about to start again, but Frank put his hand on her arm.

'First, this will be your last week in Erringtons, Lily. I'll be leaving the country next week for … I don't know how long … a while … and I want Elsie to be able to spend some time with me, so until then you can work your notice; you were going in a couple of weeks anyway, so no-one will think anything of it. I gather you've had some response to the advertisement for your position? Well, let's get it sorted out while I'm here to help.'

He paused, looking to see if there was going to be any argument, but none came.

'Secondly,' he looked Liddle directly in the face, 'I don't want you in my shop again. Not as Lily's fiancé or husband, and certainly not as a salesman. Is this clear?'

Frank looked away; his face livid. He threw the cigar down and stubbed it out with his foot, twisting hard, mashing it to pieces on the wooden boards. Lily took a step towards Jim, so angry her teeth were clenched together; she could barely articulate.

'What about my trust money?'

'I've been thinking about that ever since I heard about your engagement; nothing to do with this.' He gestured towards the accounts ledger. 'I'm not convinced that the money – it's a large sum, as you know – should come to you directly ... or straight away.'

'What do you mean, "not directly or straight away"? Whose money is it? We need it for ... all sorts of things.' She glanced at Frank, then back to him.

'Lily, I'm about to offer you a compromise. No, don't interrupt! I'm going to instruct Gibson to set up a new trust which maintains the capital invested and allows you so much a month.'

There was a long, uncomfortable silence. It was Elsie who began to move first.

'Let's go home; have something to eat. It's cold and I'm tired.'

She was right. He strode over to the door and unlocked it,

holding it wide so that Frank and Lily could pass. Lily went first, but Frank paused on the threshold and coolly took out a cigarette, cupping the match in his hands against the icy wind as Jim held the door. He slouched against the door jamb and took a long, slow drag then looked at Jim, a smirk playing at the corner of his mouth.

'How much?'

'How much what?'

'How much a month?'

Before he could think he had Frank by the throat, up against the wall outside the shop; his cigarette flew into the gutter.

'One more word, Liddle ... just one. Go on!' *You can struggle all you like, but you're too puny.*

He held Liddle with his chin tilted up so that the back of his head was grinding against the rough stone. His hat fell off and landed at their feet. 'Not smiling now, eh?' He pressed harder, forcing Liddle up onto his toes. It was only Elsie standing in the doorway, hand over her mouth, that stopped him. He released Frank and stepped away in case he changed his mind and brayed him one.

'I just hope Lily knows what she's doing.'

Jim stood by as Frank regained his balance, bent down and picked up his hat, straightened his tie. Give him his due, he wasn't running ... far from it. In fact he was taking out a fresh cigarette. He lit it, but the brief flare of the match showed trembling hands. *So, not as fearless as he made out.* Lily was looking from one to the other of them. Liddle turned his back on him and took her by the arm.

'Come on, Lil, I need a drink.'

'Have one on me, Liddle. You've got that fiver.'

TWENTY TWO

Frank

He lay on his back in his single room at The Railway, one hand behind his head, his fingers exploring the tender lump where that oaf soldier had smashed him against the wall. Bastard. Three pints with Lily snivelling at him across the table hadn't helped. A small amount a month was no fucking use; he needed a rock solid chunk of cash to get the Jew off his back again. The others could wait, but he'd had more late night visitors about the car money. He'd managed to put them off – listen lads, he can have the whole lot in March – but that was only if Lily got her Trust. Big Jim wasn't going to listen to him or her now, so who would he listen to? He got up and stood at the window, looking out over the dark street. Poky little place with poky little people. Once he had Lily he would wave it goodbye. He'd see her in the morning, take her out for lunch – see if he could find a way. But then he was heading off back to Newcastle.

At eleven thirty on Sunday morning he was sitting in his motor, waiting for Lily as arranged. He'd seen them – not the baby brother, the other three – coming back from church. Then Soldier Boy and the pretty little wife went out again. He was going to quiz Lily about something she'd let slip after the set-to on Friday. She'd had a few sherries and some interesting stuff came out. Such as the blacksmith was banging away at more than just his anvil. Seemed unlikely,

171

but you never know. And if she was sure about it he had a plan. He just needed her to give him a few juicy details.

Lily was there at the front door; he climbed out of the car to greet her. She looked a bit peaky, but then so did he. He would need to tread carefully with his little beauty of an idea; didn't want yet another sleepless night. She'd need persuading – a few glasses of wine would help.

'Good morning, my angel. I hope you're hungry.'

He gave her a kiss and took her arm.

'We're going to have a good roast dinner and a bottle of something tasty.'

It was cold as the Arctic again; pity, he would have liked a walk up the burn, a bit of a cuddle. Never mind … four weeks to go and if he played his cards right they'd be married, well off and debt free. And being a married man might help him keep army service at bay, especially if he could get her in the family way straight off. Gammy knee, father to be … So, no need to rush things. At The Railway he ordered two beef dinners and a bottle of red wine, with a pint for him and a schooner of sherry for Lily while they waited. Let's oil the wheels a bit.

'So, you don't think Elsie's as innocent as she looks, after all?' No need to be vulgar – she'd know what he meant.

'All I said was that I'd heard them one night. Upstairs. I went to Ann's, then I came back – I'd left my wedding lists behind. I didn't see anything but I heard them all right.'

She flushed from the neck up. She'd need to drop all this coy stuff when they got married – he liked gutsy women between the sheets.

'Look pet, I don't mean to be dirty, but are you sure they were … you know? It's important.'

'Why?'

Oh here we go … Why? Why ask so many damned questions?

172

He needed to spell it out.

'Why? Because I'm going to suggest to Ivan that he should persuade Soldier Jim to give you your money as soon as we get married. The lot, I mean. That's why.'

'He won't go against Jim. Not Ivan.'

What? So rogering his wife isn't going against him then?

'He might, if he knows what'll happen if he doesn't.'

He watched Lily's face to see if he'd got through. No. *God in heaven, she's slow.*

'What I mean is, he might if I threaten to tell big brother about him and his pretty little missis.'

This time the lights went on: she understood. He could see her trying to get to grips with the thought.

'But isn't that blackmail? Sort of?'

'Yes, I'm afraid it is. But if you want something badly enough ...'

He left it there. Lunch had arrived and he wanted her to have a few glasses of wine before he found out where Ivan was likely to be today.

It was easy. She wanted her money every bit as much as he did, so it didn't take long to get her to agree to help him put some pressure on her precious little brother. He settled the bill and they walked back up through the town towards the house; apparently Sunday afternoon was usually football – if it was on, because numbers were low – then a snooze in front of the fire. He should be in.

* * * *

And there he was, the weary footballer, dozing in front of the parlour fire, just as Lily had said he would be. He sat down in the armchair facing Ivan across the hearth, then coughed. Bless him, he was all surprised when he sat up and found him sitting there in his parlour, and without any invitation.

173

'Can I have a word? And Lily … a brandy would be very welcome, thank you.'

Lily went to fetch some glasses. Little brother here was going to need one. No point in wasting time; who knew when the other two would be back? He smiled, leaned forward in his chair, all matey. He offered Ivan a cigarette, took one, lit up for both of them. Very cosy.

'If I found out that my little woman was "enjoying herself" with my brother, d'you know what I'd do?

No response; not even 'bugger off', which is what he'd expected. He'd have to keep going.

'I'd black both her eyes for her, then I'd show her who's boss in bed.'

That's better. The face said it all – Lily wasn't wrong then: the look of a guilty man.

'Why would I want to know that?' He was stubbing out his cigarette.

'Because it's interesting, how different people react. I mean, who knows what your big brother might do to Elsie if he found out about you and her?'

'That's a disgusting thought.'

'Not really. I might have had a go myself if it hadn't been for Lily. She must be quite … easy.' He sniggered; couldn't help it.

Ivan was up and coming for him but he stayed where he was, leaning back in the chair, with his hands up to protect his head.

'Get up! Come on you slimy bastard, we'll talk about it outside.'

'Now, now, let's not be rash. You need to think about this. We need to work together, you and me. If we can persuade Jim to free up Lily's Trust next month, I'm not going to tell him.'

'Tell him what?'

'Oh, come on, Ivan, don't be shy. And sit down. Lily lives here, remember? She's not deaf.'

He watched Ivan's expression as Lily came in with the tray of glasses and the brandy. Not a brotherly look, that one.

'You two won't be spoiling two houses when you get married. You know that?'

Frank smiled at the expression. So, Ivan thought they were made for each other, did he? Well, so they were. Lily'd flushed, though. She actually liked her little brother; didn't want him to not like her. Bit late for that, pet; you've already meddled too far. Anyway, the little bugger shouldn't be making the beast with two backs with his sister in law when Lily's in the house. She's a delicate flower, his Lil.

Ivan pushed away the glass she offered him with the back of his hand.

'Lily, you really are a total bitch. Was this your idea, or his?'

He could see Lily didn't know how to respond to that one. Either way, Ivan was going to hate her: for knowing about the little liaison, for not letting on she knew … and for telling him.

'Hey, careful with the language; that's my fiancée you're talking to.'

He took a long pull at his brandy and lit another cigarette. This was going well.

'Well, are we on, then? You tell Jim that I'm a fine fellow, and that I can handle Lily's inheritance with my eyes shut. I keep my mouth shut about what you do in your spare time. Agreed?'

'You can fuck off. Both of you. I'm not being blackmailed.'

He knew when it was time to go. He finished his drink and stood up, smoothed his hair and put his hat back on. He

175

made for the door, turning to face Ivan.

'I'd think very carefully about it if I was you, Lover Boy. You've got tonight to cut the mustard, before tomorrow – when Soldier Jim trots off to Hexham with his "little bit a month" plan. Lily'll let me know how it goes. If Jim gets on that train tomorrow morning, I'll be back here at night.'

'You can do what you like; I'll be gone by then.'

Frank let go of the door handle and stared at Ivan. Was the little bastard serious? Would he run?

'Not wise, my friend … I'll come back anyway. Are you going run off and leave little Tippy Toes to take what's coming? I don't think so. Better this way. Just a few chosen words of support? Not difficult, really.'

TWENTY THREE

Jim

They'd been invited to the Pumphreys for Sunday lunch. The sky was clear, with a pale cream button of sun that made little difference to the gnawing cold; their boots made no impression in the brittle snow as they took the Redesmouth road. Half way there they stopped to watch the buzzards wheeling overhead: their plaintive cries were the only noise in the frozen silence. Elsie was holding his arm as they walked, but he kept forgetting to match his stride to her smaller steps as he churned over the idea of having to leave her. She ended up almost running to keep pace with him.

'Are we going to be late or something?'

'I'm so sorry, sweetheart. Just kick me if I go too fast.'

'If I stop even for a second to take aim, you'll be out of reach.'

She was laughing, breathless from trying to keep up. He stopped and wrapped his arms tightly around her; her nose and cheeks were pink with cold but he could feel her body, warm in her wool coat.

'Come on, we're nearly there.'

He knew she was a bit worried about eating with Archie and Enid: going to their house as a visitor was a different matter from serving them in the shop and chatting after church. In the event the two daughters were there along with a riot of small grandchildren, so the atmosphere was relaxed

177

and cheerful. Archie had a twinkle in his eye as he introduced Elsie to his daughters.

'Come and meet the Belle of Bellington! She's the reason why I do the shopping these days.' *The old fox.*

At the end of the meal, when the nannies brought the children back through, Archie turned to him and offered him a cigar in his study. He could leave Elsie alone with the women by now; she looked relaxed with the Pumphrey daughters.

Archie heaved a rich sigh as they settled in the study.

'Lovely children ... entrancing ... but I must say I enjoy them best at bed time.'

'I'm sure!' Although he wasn't, not really. He would have given a great deal to have his and Elsie's children running around with Archie's grandchildren today.

'You seem a bit pensive, Jim. Not surprised, mind you: it's never easy.'

Archie poured them both a stiff brandy and set Jim's down beside him.

'I'm ready, Archie. Ready to go. Ready to serve the King. But you're right; it's not going to be easy.'

He took the cigar Archie offered and leaned forward to light it. Once it was drawing, he looked Archie in the eye and asked him if there was anything important he should know – he'd been a good officer in his day by all accounts; what did it take? Archie took a piece of paper from his pocket and handed it to Jim.

'I rather thought you might ask me that.'

He'd already given it some consideration and had jotted down four points in his elegant handwriting:

1. Know your men, their names, families, occupations et cetera

2. *Be consistent; friendly but <u>not too familiar</u>.*
3. *Look after their feet – inspect daily*
4. *Never eat until your men have been fed*

Jim read the notes then looked up. Archie nodded, as if to confirm what he'd written.

'There are other things of course – weaponry, defences and all that – but these are the most important, whatever they've told you at OTC.'

'There may be lads I know. In the Company. Perhaps even in my platoon.' He was worried about it: would they accept him as their officer if they knew him as their local grocer?

'However well you knew them here, it'll be quite different over there. Don't worry about it. But you'll need to keep your distance a bit. For example, by all means watch them have a game of football – the men like that – but don't be tempted to join in. That sort of thing.'

Jim could have listened to Archie all day; years of service had made the old man confident about his place in the world, and he was a good talker. When they left, an hour later, Archie shook his hand and patted his arm. Edith was very kind, too. She kissed Elsie's cheek.

'Who knows what lies ahead, my dear. You have other friends and family, I know that, but please feel that you can rely on us.' It was good to know.

Evening was drawing in as they reached the town; with no sun at all it was glacial, impossible to stay warm. As they reached the corner of the square they came face to face with two young women walking arm in arm, hunched together for warmth, their wool shawls wrapped over their heads. As they met, one of them looked up, and in the half-light he saw her expression alter as she recognised them. The girl – she was young – hesitated, then let go of her friend. She shrugged her shawl off her head onto her shoulders. She looked perished, her lips blue in her white face. Her dark red curls were tangled and loose on her shoulders.

'Wey, if it isn't Elsie Dunn!'

Elsie glanced up at him to see if he knew her. He did, now that her head was uncovered. It was Isabel Moffatt, a girl Ivan used to walk out. He raised his cap and greeted her politely. Something was odd about her, though. And why address Elsie as 'Dunn' when she knew perfectly well that she'd been an Errington for years? The girl stared boldly at him, then turned back to Elsie.

'Lucky, *lucky* Elsie Dunn, with one brother in the army and the other at home.'

She gave a mocking smile, then took her friend's arm again.

'Howay, Ethel.'

He watched as they stepped off the pavement and crossed the street before he or Elsie could respond. Isabel paused and looked back to them as they reached the other side. It was as if she was going to say something more, but then thought better of it. The friend yanked her off into the darkness.

'What was *that* about?'

'Do you know her?' Elsie was staring after her.

'She was one of Ivan's, a while ago. I never thought of her as rude …' He tailed off. *Why waste time on her?*

'One of Ivan's?'

'A woman scorned, I reckon; she hasn't found a man and thinks you've got yourself two.' He laughed. 'Just wait 'til I tell Ivan!'

He saw her pinched face and realized how tired she must be; they'd walked a fair distance. He caught hold of her arm and tucked her close to him.

'Come on, let's get home – you look worn out.'

When they opened the front door Lily was there, sitting at the bottom of the stairs, her face pale and drawn and her arms wrapped round her chest. She looked up as they came in, but she didn't stand, didn't greet them. It was shocking to see her there in the comfortless hallway; she looked stricken. He crouched down beside her and took her icy fingers in his own warm hands; close up he could see that her whole body was shivering.

'Lily, what's wrong?

'He's gone.'

'Who's gone? Frank?' *Too much to hope.* 'Elsie love, could you go and check the stove and put the kettle on; it's bitter in here.'

He helped Lily to her feet but she pulled away from him violently and started upstairs.

'Lily, what on earth's the matter?'

She stopped and leaned towards him over the bannister.

'It's all your fault for marrying a Dunn!' Her voice was husky. 'She's a slut, like Mother said, and now Ivan's gone …'

She collapsed, sobbing, on the stairs.

'Where's Ivan gone? Why?' *What the hell was she raving about? And why bring their mother up after all this time?* He ran his hand along the rail, trying to make sense of it. *Where was Frank in all this?*

'Lily, where's Frank?'

She looked up, dragging her hands across her cheeks to wipe away the tears.

'He's gone home to Newcastle, and I'll be going with him in a few weeks' time, thank God. Then that little trollop you married'll be all on her own.'

She turned to look through the bannisters towards the kitchen door, where Elsie was standing.

'Look at you, you skinny wax doll. Well, you'll have to find another man to keep you warm. Pity we only had one other brother, eh?'

'That's enough.' He lunged up the stairs towards her. She scrabbled round on hands and knees, trying to cover the last few steps before he reached her, but he was too fast. He grabbed her arm and dragged her back down to the hall.

'You poisonous witch! Is this because you haven't got your own way about the money? Is that it?'

He yanked the front door open: *she could bloody well walk to Newcastle to be with her money-grabbing fiancé* ... But she was struggling violently. There might be people in the street and he didn't want a scandal. He slammed the door and let her go, expecting her to dash upstairs, but she turned and shoved him hard in the chest with both hands.

'It's not *me* you should be putting out it's *her*, the guttersnipe. Ask her.'

Then he slapped her sharply across the cheek, the first time he'd ever done such a thing. Her head rocked sideways with the blow, but she was back straight away, yelling in his face.

'Go on, ask her!'

He raised his arm again, but she reared away from him a few steps then slipped past and ran up to her room. He heard the key turn in the lock.

He turned to Elsie. She'd watched the scene from the end of the passage, but she hadn't said a word. Elsie with Ivan? *His* Elsie ... with *Ivan*? Whatever else Lily was suggesting, that wasn't true. They'd sit down in the kitchen and have a cup of tea together – it was punishingly cold in the hall – and she would explain, tell him why Lily was saying these things.

He watched Elsie's every move as she prepared the tea, her fingers fumbling as she counted the spoonfuls of leaves into the pot. She placed the cups carefully onto the saucers, put

182

the sugar where he could reach it. The milk was already on the table. When, after all this, she still hadn't looked at him, had said nothing at all, he knew. Holding his hot cup for a shred of comfort, he thought back to the confrontation, out on the street.

'So, one brother in the army and the other at home. Lucky Elsie Dunn.'

He glanced at her face to see if he'd struck home. He had. How bloody stupid had he been all these weeks. Or was it months ...*years* even?

'So, Lily knows, and Isabel. Does anyone else know? Or everyone? Am I the only blind idiot who didn't know that you and Ivan were ...?'

He swallowed, shook his head ...tried to get rid of it. Was it just that he was away for a few months? *God almighty, surely not.* Then *why*?

'Why?'

Elsie glanced up at him for the first time, then looked hard into her cup. She was sitting bolt upright, like a pupil at a desk. She tried to speak but nothing came out. She cleared her throat and tried again; her eyes were still locked downwards.

'Put your cup down and answer my question please, Elsie.'

'I don't know... because he loves me. He kept on at me ...'

He grabbed her wrist. 'Did he force you? I'll kill him if he did.'

But she looked up, eyes wide, shook her head, tears beginning to dribble down her cheeks.

'He didn't force me but I didn't want him to either. At least, not at first.'

He could barely hear her, but what she said was clear enough. At *first*. He loosed her wrist and wrenched the cup

183

from her hand, then half stood to fling it into the sink. Pieces of china bounced out and onto the floor. She flinched, but stayed at the table. He could see her fiddling, trying to find something else to occupy her hands. They were shaking.

'So "at first" you didn't want him, but then ... what? You just got used to it? How often?'

She was scarlet. *Well, that was something.*

'How. Often. Elsie?'

'Not often. A few times, that's all.'

'That's all?' *Did she really say "that's all"?* 'Where? In our bed? Does he creep in at night when Lily's out of the way?'

She wouldn't look at him. Enough. He didn't want to know. He pushed his chair back and stood upright. The pains shooting through his gut made him want to double up. Without touching her he walked past and opened the kitchen door.

'I'll go tomorrow. Off south.'

As he walked past Lily's room he paused and knocked. He wanted to know what had happened to make Ivan leave. Why go now, suddenly, when *he* would be leaving for France within the week? Guilt? He doubted that: they'd talked together last night, old friends as well as brothers, without any sign of it. Lily clearly knew more than she was letting on, but she wouldn't come to the door. It didn't really matter anyway. He tried once more, rapping his knuckles hard on the panels, but there was utter silence in the house when he stopped.

He made his way to the spare bedroom and repacked his trunk, neatly and methodically, slotting small articles in where they'd fit best. He discarded his photograph of Elsie in the garden, the one he'd chosen: summer, she was smiling at the camera, the sun on her hair. He set it on the bedside table along with the silver cufflinks she'd bought him for Christmas. It was difficult to drag the trunk on his own but he managed, manoeuvring it clumsily along the corridor and taking the weight as it thumped down the stairs, snagging the runner away from its brass rods.

In their bedroom he gathered together any belongings he wanted to take with him so that his cases would be ready in the morning. He'd need to walk to the station very early and send a cart up. And Gibson; *damn! He hadn't been to see him.* He could go tomorrow morning on his way, or … *Christ* it hurt to concentrate. You know, he might as well let her – him really – have the money. What difference could it make? He'd write; sort it out. Maybe Frank would come right, be decent.

Where should he go? He needed to sleep, wanted to be unconscious to pass the hours before morning. He lay back on the bed and closed his eyes. Instantly, scenes crowded into his mind. He was appalled by them but he couldn't get rid of them even when he opened his eyes again. The walls became a dark frame for every unwanted image of Ivan and Elsie. It drained him, trying to keep it at bay, and at last he wept like a child, his body racked, until he fell asleep. Later, though, he was woken by the cold. Half asleep, he stripped off his breeches, his jacket and waistcoat; hung them up, ready for the morning. Then he climbed under the covers, too weary even to think.

It was still dark outside, pitch black in the bedroom, when he stirred. It took a few seconds before he remembered, then he felt sick. He rolled over and found his matches, lit a candle. He was aching and needed to move, so he picked up his cigarettes and candle and went to the door; he'd go downstairs and find the whisky bottle. The candle flame flickered madly in the draught as he opened the door, but it steadied and as it did he caught sight of something in the shadows. His heart jarred. Elsie was on the landing. She'd

185

been lying pressed against the door: he could have tripped over her. He knelt down, placing the candle holder on the floor beside her face. Her eyelids were swollen and her hair was loose on the wooden boards. The air held no warmth at all and her cheek was frozen, although she stirred as he touched her. He shook her awake – even through her dress and shawl he could feel that she was rigid with cold. *How long had she been there?*

'You stupid girl.'

He helped her to stand, then walked her into the room, throwing back the blankets before guiding her to sit on the bed and wrapping the eiderdown round her. She sat upright; her teeth were chattering and her limbs juddered helplessly. Without allowing himself to think, he climbed onto the bed and pulled her down to lie beside him, crooked under his arm so that she could draw as much warmth from him as possible. After a while he could feel her absorbing him, coming back to life. Her, not him.

'Love me again.'

It was a whisper. He tensed. *What did she say?*

'Love me.'

Again a whisper, but this time he heard her. Love her? How could he not love her? He stroked her hair.

'Shh, don't talk. Just get warm again. What kind of madness was that?'

'I didn't think you'd let me in.'

She was right: he would have yelled at her, told her to go and sleep in Ivan's room. He'd left her downstairs because if he hadn't he might have damaged her in some way.

'You were right. But you should have gone to another room.'

He didn't want to say Ivan's name. 'Sleeping out there was daft … dangerous.'

'Take me back. Please take me back.'

She was clinging to him, her nails were digging into his chest. Should he take her? He felt his body responding to the idea of reclaiming what was his, and within a few seconds he had yanked back the covers and was tearing at her clothing, ripping anything that got in his way until she was naked from the waist down. She made no attempt to stop him. He was rough, pushing his fingers where she was most tender ... *did Ivan touch you here? And here?* He forced her legs wide with his knee, his arms either side of her head gripping her hair, then he drove hard into her, using all his strength to slam again and again so that he knew he must be hurting her. She held his gaze, biting her lip – against the pain? What was she thinking? Not about him! He wanted to drive Ivan from her mind and her body.

When he'd finished, she turned away, crying quietly. He wasn't sorry for her; she deserved far worse. He pulled the blankets around her. Sitting up, he lit a cigarette from the candle, now guttering in its holder. He sat and smoked as Elsie drifted into restless sleep beside him. He didn't want to see her looking so vulnerable, so he got up and pulled on some old work clothes. He'd walk to the station, organise the trap for the morning.

It was still dark as he closed the front door. It was too early for the station, so he walked in the moonlight across the square and along to where they kept Daisy. She'd been fed and watered – he'd wondered, what with Ivan leaving – but he stood and stroked her soft muzzle, talking to her as an old friend, which he supposed she was. She'd be needed in the morning, for the orders. Not his concern, now, but he hoped Lily would be strong enough to manage the next few weeks. He stayed there for a while, taking what comfort he could from the familiar smells and warmth of the stable, thankful all over again that Daisy'd been too old to go to war.

* * * *

He'd walked down to the station and found the boy, paid him in advance. Now he stood for a minute and watched her sleeping: he'd always loved the soft pale mauve of her eyelids, the spread of her hair on the sheets. He'd never not woken her with a kiss before.

'Elsie? Wake up.' He tapped her arm, flushing as he noticed a dark smudge on her wrist where he'd held her down. Tarnished goods.

'Is it morning?'

'It is. Here.'

He threw her clothes onto the bed. She fumbled with the torn underclothes, putting them on because to discard them and find others would be even worse.

They dressed, avoiding any contact, too exhausted to hurry even though his train would already have begun its journey down the valley towards them. In the kitchen they sipped a final cup of tea, without a word. She sliced some bread for him, fetched the butter from the pantry; he'd need something to eat, but he didn't touch it.

Lily came warily downstairs just as the lad from the station arrived with his handcart. She let him in and stood back as he passed her to grab a handle of the trunk and heave it out through the front door, paddling mud from the street onto the tiles. Jim went through to help, but the lad had gone. He leaned down and brushed Lily's cheek with his lips where it was slightly bruised. He felt ashamed.

'I'm sorry if I hurt you and I'm sorry I won't be here for your wedding. I'll be thinking about you.'

'No, you won't.' Lily smiled, then reached up to return his kiss. She stayed at the foot of the stairs, arms folded, her

188

dressing gown wrapped tightly around her. He held Elsie's coat for her, then pulled on his own, then his cap. He took one last look up the hallway, then opened the front door.

'And Lily ...'

'Yes?'

'... you can have your money whenever you want it. I'll write to Gibson from London. I suppose Frank may be more honest than he appears.'

The route to the station was rutted with ice but Elsie walked apart from him, stumbling occasionally but never attempting to hold his arm. He felt awkward not helping her, but she needed to get used to it. On the platform they stood beside each other but avoided each other's gaze, strangers already.

'I don't want to say goodbye.' Her voice was pitiful and he didn't want to hear it.

'Well, don't.'

She took off her gloves and touched his cheek, then his mouth, with her cool fingers, then she stood on her toes to kiss him, but he turned his head away. They could hear the chugging of the engine in the distance as it pounded down the line towards the station. When it arrived, smoke billowing, there were friendly shouts as working men climbed down, bait boxes in hand, making their way across the platform. Elsie stood back as he supervised the loading of his luggage. Finally, as the guard looked up and down the platform and prepared to blow his whistle, he turned to her.

'I'm not going to look back, so don't even wait. Just go. Go now.'

He climbed onto the train and made his way to the rear carriage. There were a few passengers further up the train, but other than that it was strangely peaceful, very ordinary. The great wheels began to turn; the train started to move. He sat in the empty carriage, a fist clenched against his mouth. His whole body was painful, jarred by the rhythmic turning of the iron wheels. At the last second he jumped up and yanked open the window, leaning out to see if Elsie was there ... he might get one last look at her if she was still on the platform. But she'd gone.

TWENTY FOUR

Elsie

She stood completely still, hands in her pockets, as the train gathered momentum and shuffed away down the line towards Hexham and the south. Her eyes filled again, even when she'd believed she had no more tears left. She turned away from the track and crossed the platform. She was frozen, and he'd told her to go, so she would; he wasn't going to be watching, anyway. It was still quite early when she arrived back at the house; Lily was in the kitchen, standing against the range for warmth as the kettle came to the boil.

'He's gone then. That's both of them. Both brothers because of you.' Lily looked as weary as she did.

'I didn't start the war, Lily.'

'You started this one.'

Was that right? Maybe it was.

'Do you know where Ivan's gone?'

She realised even as the words left her mouth that Lily would take her question the wrong way; of course she would.

'You little bitch. You see Jim off, then straight away you start sniffing around after Ivan again. What sort of woman are you?'

'I didn't mean that. I meant has he gone to sign up, or has he just *gone*?'

'He said he was going to fight, if that's what you're asking.'

It was. So, what now?

'I'll go and get changed before we have to open up. There's the orders to see to.'

She couldn't bear the disgusted look on Lily's face any longer. They had to work together until they found someone else, whatever Jim had said about Lily leaving immediately. He'd probably prefer *her* to leave, now: there are worse things than taking money, especially when you intend to pay it back. How could she pay this back? She shivered as she stripped off to wash, to put fresh clothes on. Her thighs were bruised and tender where he'd made love to her ... except he hadn't been making love. And why should he? Lily was right: it was in her blood, this weakness, if that's what it was. Her mother had been the same, but her da had been a different man from Jim.

She'd been five or six. She'd heard noises, padded barefoot down the wooden stairs in her white nightgown, looking through the narrow rails. There was only the one room at the bottom where the staircase ended. Her mother was standing against a wall, palms pressed flat at the level of her head, as if she were trying to push her way through it. Alfred, her da, had the buckle end of his thick leather belt wrapped round his fist and was lashing first this way, then that, at her back, her thighs, her legs. Her mother wasn't trying to escape – there was no point, he was blocking the door – but she yelped at each stroke, eyes closed with the pain of it.

She remembered being transfixed at the sight of his arm, raised again and again, the belt whistling through the thick air of the room; it was summer, hot and sticky, even in their dark cottage. She stood and watched, flinching with her mother at every blow. Alfred, his back to her, must have sensed that she was standing there. She remembered his face when he turned and saw her: he was furious. She wanted to say something, to stop him, but she'd already begun to retreat. She cried down to him, 'Don't whip my Mammy', and he'd taken a step towards her, leaving off for a second.

'Get yersell back up to bed bairn, or I'll give ye a taste of it an all.'

She was still awake when she heard their uneven footsteps on the stairs as they came up to their one bedroom, her mother whispering and sobbing, her father responding in his low voice. They'd made love. Elsie hadn't recognised it for what it was at the time, but later she had understood. And in the morning, when her father had left for the early shift, he'd kissed her at the door.

'Why, Mammy? Why did he hurt you?'

Her mother had held her, pressed her head into her waist and ruffled her curls. Elsie had wanted to fling her arms round her but she was frightened of touching where it was sore. She let her arms hang instead, just listening.

'Because he was hurt. It's my own fault, poppet. I've been making eyes at someone. A mammy should never make eyes at another man. But it's over now.'

And it had been. Until her mother died when she was ten, her parents seemed to be as happy as any other couple. Maybe her father's pride had been satisfied. She never found out whether he'd had it out with the man, or even who the man was, but the matter had been settled, there and then. And she never heard him mention that time, never heard him say anything but good about his Jane. If Jim hadn't gone, could they have salvaged it. Not with a belt, not like that, but somehow? Perhaps ... if it had been someone other than Ivan, someone other than his brother. There was no remedy she could think of, not for this.

She went up to the box room where Jim had stowed his trunk for the week at home. On the floor was a small pile of clothes and books he must have decided he didn't need, and on the chest of drawers was her photo in its frame – the one taken in the garden last year, with the sun shining on her hair. And he'd left the cufflinks, her present to him. *He'd gone to war without her.*

They managed to work through Monday, serving customers and packing orders for Will to deliver with Daisy, but Lily spoke only when something had to be said, keeping apart from her as much as she could. It didn't bother her, but it was as if she had some disease. On the following afternoon, Frank arrived. He didn't bother with his usual show, just nodded a brief greeting instead. She nodded back then turned away from the knowing smile he was wearing. She couldn't bear even the sight of him.

'He's gone then, Big Jim? Off to war?'

Lily must have sent him a telegram, or he wouldn't know. In fact, he wouldn't have come.

'Yes.'

What did he want her to say … you're right, my husband's left early. He'd rather go off to Belgium or wherever and be shot at than stay with me a moment longer? He knew, anyway.

'Ivan too?'

'Yes.'

'All alone then.'

'No, I have Lily for company.'

'For now.'

What, had he taken her seriously … or was this his little joke? Did he honestly think she and Lily could be companions?'

'Well, you got what you wanted.' Her tone was flat. She had no feelings about it.

'In a few weeks I will.'

'I didn't mean you've got Lily.'

'So, what did you mean, then?'

His tone was casual enough, but why was he was pushing her like this? He must know what she thought of him by now, so why try to make her spell it out? The bell sounded as a couple of women came into the shop, so she was free to ignore him. He gave up, lifted the hinged counter and went through to find Lily, not waiting for her to invite him. What a difference in such a short time. When he left, an hour or so later, he didn't even catch her eye.

It was strange, how easy she found it to keep up a smiling face, and if she did appear tired or glum now and then, the customers just assumed that she was worried about Jim and gave her sympathetic looks. Each day passed in the same way, except that Lily chose her successor and introduced her to the job.

'She's starting tomorrow. You can show her the front of the shop and I'll do the books.'

Lily had interviewed the woman privately, on the Wednesday afternoon after Jim left, while Elsie was at home. She'd offered her the job on the spot; hadn't even told her about it until afterwards.

'Don't you think that perhaps I should have been there, since I'm going to be working with her? Employing her, even?'

'It's Jim's business, not yours. Do you really think he would trust you to replace me?' She was venomous.

'I wasn't the one taking cash from the drawer and fiddling the books.' It sounded childish: even to her it sounded childish.

In fact, the woman was a good choice: Mary Dinsdale, only twenty two and already a war widow; she and her husband hadn't been married long enough to have children. She knew the shop as a customer and found the move behind the counter easy enough. Only one more week and Lily

195

would back out, leaving them to it. She couldn't wait. Mary was still in black but she was cheerful company, and very quick to learn. When Lily was in the office – she always closed the door now – and the shop was empty, they could stand together at the counter and talk. Mary told her about her John, who'd been killed outright at St Julien, nearly a year ago. He'd been a joiner.

'He could make anything you wanted with wood, could John.'

'I know; Ivan used to work with him. He was very low when he heard about it.'

Even saying Ivan's name made her stomach pinch so she had to bend slightly with the pain. She wanted to know why Mary had let John go, when he didn't have to. She'd thought that those men, the ones who volunteered straight away, must have been either mad or wanting to escape, but surely John was neither.

'Did you try to stop him?'

'No. But I wish I had, now. If he'd gone later, he wouldn't have been where that shell landed. I didn't even know he'd left the country when the telegram came. I thought he was still in training, down south.'

Elsie didn't say, because there was no point, that he might easily have been hit by a different shell, in a different place. And now Jim and Ivan would both be there. Bullets and shells could hammer down on them at any second of any day from now until the damned war ended. And she didn't even know where they were, either of them. Jim would be with his company in the Fusiliers by now, probably, but she had no idea where because he hadn't written to her. Lily'd received a short letter posted in London a few days after he left, but as far as she knew it was just to confirm that Gibson would hand over her Trust money as soon as she was married. There was no message for her, or none that Lily passed on. They were going ahead with a wedding of sorts in March, as planned, but with only a small number of guests. They weren't even inviting the Erringtons' Newcastle relations, although Frank's brother and his wife were going to be there. Elsie could come if she wanted, but only for the sake of appearances.

She hadn't decided what to do about Mrs Binns. It seemed ridiculous, a live-in housekeeper just for her, but at least she wouldn't be alone, and they'd already promised Mrs Binns the position, so she'd given notice on her own cottage. She'd be moving her belongings at the end of February, a few days' time, so it was too late now; Will was going to bring her boxes round with Errington's trap. Until then, Elsie was spending her evenings in the kitchen, leaving Lily the parlour. The sewing had stopped; maybe there was no need now; she'd be able to swan around Newcastle, buying what she needed. Well, good for her.

* * * *

They'd eaten together, in silence, as usual. Lily left the kitchen abruptly, without any attempt to help clear, as usual. Elsie gathered up the pots and put them beside the sink for the morning. Another change to come: Agnes had found a new position in a house with several servants, where she'd have some young company; she was leaving when Mrs Binns came. Poor kid, no-one could blame her. She opened a drawer and found her pen and some paper; she was going to write to Jim, send him the last of the Christmas cake he'd wanted; he'd given her his address, care of his regiment. Before. That's what it was like: before ... after ... The world was all changed, because of her, like BC and AD, but bad. She sat at the table, but there was something distracting, a noise. Tapping, on the window. She looked up, but could

197

see nothing because of the lamplight inside. She grabbed her shawl and went to the door, unlatching it just enough to peer round and see what was doing the knocking.

'Elsie.'

The voice was a whisper from a distance, past the kitchen window, but she knew straight away who it was. She stepped out onto the flagstones – they were still flecked with half thawed snow – and clicked the door shut behind her.

'Ivan?'

She walked towards the voice, seeing nothing but shadows. Then he caught her arm and pulled her to him. How long had he been there? His coat was damp and beaded with ice, stone cold against her skin.

'I thought you'd gone. Why are you here?'

'Can I come inside? Get warm?'

He was juddering with cold; he must have been out there for a while. She stood back to look at him. He was stooped, his shoulders hunched over, his chin down against his chest; she hoped it was just from the cold.

'Go round and come in by the front door. Talk to Lily, then come through to me.'

'I don't want to even see the cow, that's why I've been waiting for her to go through to the parlour.'

'She'll think I knew you weren't gone, Ivan.'

'She won't know about it, if we're quiet.'

'That's what you said before. But she did.'

He looked at her in the darkness, then made off towards the back gate. She went straight back inside, locking the door behind her and sat at the table, paper and pen in front of her. What was she going to write? She couldn't, not now. In minutes there were raised voices at the front of the house; she couldn't just stay where she was or Lily would wonder why she hadn't come through to see what was going on, so she opened the kitchen door. Lily was standing in the passageway, lit by the pool of light spilling from a lamp in the parlour. Her arms folded across her chest, she was blocking Ivan's way. Beyond Lily she could just make him out, one hand resting on the bannister. He froze as he saw her come out of the kitchen. She stopped in the shadows at the end of the passage, and Lily turned, following his gaze.

'You can't stay here with her in the house. What about Jim?'

'What about him? He won't know, unless you tell him.' His eyes never left her face.

'I'm not having you two carrying on when I'm here, not any more. It's disgusting!' Lily was looking from one to the other of them, her voice squeaky with frustration.

'Lily, it's not for you to say whether Ivan stays here. It's his home.'

'It was his home, before you got your slutty little fingers on him.'

'Shut your mouth, Lily, or I'll shut it for you.'

He didn't move, but she took in what he said. She went back into the parlour and slammed the door behind her, leaving them in darkness again.

'Come through.'

He followed her into the kitchen and made straight for the range, leaning over to take its heat. He looked peaky, exhausted. And he needed a shave.

'Where've you been, all these days?' It was nearly two weeks since he'd left.

'I've been to Newcastle and signed up. I stayed at Albert's for a week, told them I had girl trouble. They didn't ask too many questions, considering.' So, he'd been with his cousin.

'When did you get back here?'

'Tuesday.' It was Friday.

'Where've you been since then? Everyone thinks you're away training, or in France even. I thought you'd gone without saying goodbye.' *Oh for God's sake, more tears.* He didn't come over and hold her this time, he just stared at the floor.

'I've been at the forge. One of the lads knew I was there, brought me food.'

'But why?'

'Why not come here, you mean? I couldn't. I knew what Lily would be like. I didn't know whether Isabel had been spreading it about either, but Josh would have said.'

'Then why come now?'

'Because I'm off tomorrow. They're sending me to the Royal Field Artillery, I'm going to be a proper farrier. I've come for some stuff. And to see you.'

'Where?'

'Where?'

'Where're you going?'

'Salisbury Plain, first, then wherever they send me, I don't know yet. But it'll be over the channel, away from you.'

'You'd have to be away from me anyway, you know that. Ivan, what were we thinking?'

'I wasn't thinking, I was loving.' He was looking at her, watching to see how she felt.

'But when Jim got back, after the war, what then? What was going to happen then?'

She was asking him as if he ought to know, but *she* hadn't looked that far ahead either. He shrugged. He hadn't given it a thought, not really. They were as feckless and reckless as each other.

'Wait here'.

She walked along to the parlour, knocked on the door and went in. Lily was sitting beside the fire, glass in hand. She didn't look up.

'Lily, Ivan's been hiding up at the forge for days. He's cold and he's hungry and he needs some proper rest before he goes to the war.' Still nothing, not even a glance.

'I'm going to make him something to eat and help him to get his things together, then he's going to sleep in his own bed.' Lily turned towards her now.

'And are you going to sleep in your own bed, yours and Jim's?'

'Of course.'

'Oh, of *course*.' She was no good at mimicry but she'd had years of practice with sarcasm.

* * * *

She was up when Ivan left the following morning, just before dawn. He was taking only what he could carry easily and was wearing Jim's overcoat, which was big on the shoulders but longer and warmer than his own.

'D'you reckon he'll mind?'

'Bring it back in one piece and he'll maybe never know about it.'

'He'd never have known about the other thing if Liddle hadn't been out for what he could get.' It was strange, his anger, when all she could feel was remorse.

'Perhaps not ... but we would.'

He kissed her then, gently, putting down his haversack so that he could wrap both of his arms round her. She didn't return the kiss, but she was glad of it.

'Keep safe, my darling.'

'It's you that needs to keep safe, not me. Will you let me know where you are ... how you are?'

'Of course.'

He kissed her once more, then picked up his pack and opened the front door; the air outside was still bitter, the

201

street dark and still. His footsteps echoed on the cobbles as he disappeared into the shadows. If he turned to wave she couldn't see it, but she stayed where she was just in case, shivering, her shawl wrapped round her shoulders, until he must have turned the corner towards the station.

TWENTY FIVE

Ivan

He travelled south by train. Once he'd signed up and passed the medical in Newcastle they'd issued him with the tickets along with his papers. That bit had been interesting, the Medical Officer's response to his body.

'Bit of a bruiser are you, Errington?'

'No, Sir.'

'So why all the scars?'

Although he'd had no pain from his ribs for a few weeks, he could see the officer's point: there was still quite a lot of evidence for the few minutes he'd spent in the company of Isabel's brothers.

'Blacksmith, Sir. Kicked by a horse.'

'Really ... just the one? They won't want any horseplay where you're going, Lad. Watch your step.'

'I will, Sir.'

It'd been rough, staying in town, not knowing what was happening back at home. He'd left it as long as he could before making his way up the valley, but even so he wasn't going to risk going to the house until he was sure he could get Elsie on her own. He'd left the forge a few times in the dark evenings, but there was always someone around when he tried to get to the back of the house, or he'd managed that bit but then Lily was in and out of the kitchen, or Elsie wasn't there. Eventually, he'd been able to collect what he needed and spend some time with Elsie, but she wouldn't tell him much about what had happened after he left: just that Jim knew everything and had gone away early, and it was Lily that had told him, not Frank.

'What the hell for? Why would she do that when there was no point? That's why I went.'

'I don't know. We got back after you'd left, and she just started … she was waiting at the bottom of the stairs.'

'And Jim believed her … just like that?'

'She was telling the truth, Ivan … I didn't even try to deny it. I couldn't.'

She'd been quiet, withdrawn, but she'd helped him pack and had fed him, so that he'd had a good night's sleep in spite of her being just a few yards away. Would she have come in with him if Lily hadn't been there? He doubted it; from what she'd said she regretted what they'd had. Or at least she wanted it to be finished. He hadn't asked and she'd kept her distance. He'd kissed her when he left, but he could tell she just wanted him to go, and he hadn't looked back in case she'd shut the door as soon as he walked away. He'd found her photograph, the one taken in the garden with the sun on her hair. He'd taken it … left the frame behind, put it in an envelope.

The journey had taken two days because he'd spent a night in London. He'd found a cheap restaurant near the station then walked the streets to see a few of the sights for the first, maybe the only, time. Then on to Salisbury, then the end of the line. There'd been wagons on the road out to Larkhill camp. He could have hopped on, but it was only a couple of miles and he'd needed to stretch his legs a bit; the trains had been cramped and he wasn't used to sitting still for so long. He'd been glad of Jim's greatcoat; *hell* it'd been cold on that last train. He'd gathered his pack and set off to walk, stopping only once, to stare over to his left. He'd been told about it: a massive circle of standing stones in the distance, jagged teeth breaking the skyline. The camp loomed straight ahead, a vast smudge – far bigger than Bellingham or even Hexham. He was missing the hills already; he didn't care for this flat plain.

They'd given him a uniform, pointed out his billet, and there he was, a soldier in the British Army. He'd known what to expect but he still found it hard, the endless route marching and other stuff that seemed to be designed to kill any spirit and initiative they might have had. Some of the lads were fine with it – they were used to taking orders – but he was sick of being bawled at by the bastard Sergeant-Major. He missed his own company, his forge. And the mud was terrible; the place was well-nigh impassable if you left the duck boards.

Mind you, he enjoyed the weapons: even the routine safety and care of a rifle was satisfying in some way, and he was good at it; he had an instinct for knowing how things worked. His hut was all right; draughty and cold, but the men were decent enough. He'd known no-one when he arrived, but he'd settled in faster than he'd thought he would, getting to recognize who to avoid, who liked a game of football. It could be worse.

The best thing was working with horses again. There were other lads from the ranks training as military farriers; some of them would be there learning the job for two years, but not him. He proved his skills early on and was already appointed Private Shoeing-Smith. And he wasn't just looking after their feet; they were giving him specialist training, instructing him as if he was going to be a vet. If he wanted to be Farrier Corporal or Sergeant, and they thought he should, he needed to know more about husbandry. They'd told him it wouldn't be long before he'd be posted to France, but before then he had to do all the basic infantry stuff as well, in case he was needed. Apparently, in October 1914 every last man, even the cooks, had been pushed onto the front line with a gun, so he needed to learn how to fight.

He told Elsie all this in long letters. She was writing back, telling him how she was, but her letters were friendly, not loving. She told him that Graham from Acomb was doing his two days at the forge, keeping what remained of the local horses in good fettle; the shop was going well ... But it was as if she was his sister, which he supposed she was; there wasn't a mention, not a single word, about what had gone on between them, even though he tried to say how he felt in his letters to her:

> ... I often imagine you, and always in the kitchen, sweetheart, alone apart from the good Mrs Binns – is she being cheerful company? I expect she's kind, if a little dull. Darling Elsie, I wish more than anything that <u>we</u> had met before Jim saw you and swept you up. I know he's been a good husband to you, but surely we would have been happy together. I dream about being with you again, even though I know that if we both come through the war I'll need to live somewhere away from you. This is because I am <u>certain</u> that, in time, Jim will forgive you, even though I rather wish he wouldn't so that <u>I</u> could have you. I'm equally certain he will <u>never</u> forgive me, even though I wish he would so that we could be brothers again ...

It was true that he dreamed about her almost every night. There was always just the two of them; sometimes he would wake, hot and feverish, feeling for her on his narrow bunk. He wasn't the only one, but he still felt a bit shamed by it. The other lads – the young ones, not the married men – talked endlessly about their girls at home, more from hope than experience, most of them. At first they tried to get him to join in.

'You got a girl, Smithy?' He'd been Smithy from day one.

'No, not me; too busy.' He was lying on his bunk writing to Elsie before lights out.

'Maybe these northern lads like horses better than girls, eh?'

This was Jenkins, a miner who'd been ragged mercilessly about Welshmen and sheep until he'd confessed to having a sweetheart back in Merthyr Tydfil. He was a good lad, the sort he'd like to have alongside him if he ended up on the front line.

'Watch it, Jenkins; I might be down in Merthyr after all this and I'll look up your little Welsh rarebit: I'm told the Welsh lasses love us Northerners. That's right, isn't it Sol?'

'It is, Smithy.'

He dodged as Jenkins aimed a boot at his head.

'If you 'aven't got a girl, who you writing to then?'

'Leave it, Jenkins, or I'll put you outside.'

Jenkins laughed but he stopped. Sol Laidlow was a miner from Dumfries; he blocked the light when he came through the door of the hut and you didn't argue with him. He never wrote to anyone as far as they knew, even though he was older than the rest of them and had a wife and bairns back at home. Maybe he didn't know how. He was itching to be at the Front where he could hew Germans as he'd hewn coal.

'So, who is it, Smithy? That you're writing to?'

'My old granny, Sol, bless her heart.'

That shut them up; he could finish his letter in peace. He'd received a description of Lily's wedding from Elsie that morning:

> ... I decided to go in the end, but only in case
> people thought it was odd if I didn't. I couldn't

pretend I was ill because I was in the shop all morning and I look very well, or so people keep telling me. Frank was as dreadful as you could imagine, with his fancy new suit and hair as shiny as his shoes. Lily looked lovely in her fine dress, really pretty, you would have been proud of her. Doctor Armstrong gave her away and Ann was a handsome bridesmaid. After the wedding we went to The Railway for the wedding tea. Frank had arranged champagne for everyone, paid for by Lily's money no doubt. Dr. Armstrong made a good speech and said nice things about your father and Jim and you and we all drank your health, so you must stay well. I left as soon as I could, because I was feeling a bit tired, and Frank's brother (the one that's married with two little lads) was being very attentive and I liked him even less than I like his brother…

He could just imagine Frank's brother being all over Elsie, the prettiest girl in the room by far. It made him smile to read about it, but if he'd been there it would have been different. She'd have looked beautiful; no wonder Frank's brother was paying her attention, cheeky bugger. He finished his letter, asking her to write as soon as she could. Was she writing to Jim as well? She never mentioned him unless she had to, so he had no idea whether Jim had written to her, or telephoned her at the shop, even. Surely he wouldn't have gone over to France without some contact with her, but wouldn't she have told him? What if he wanted nothing more to do with her? It was torture, not knowing.

One day after another, two months of drilling, what to do in a gas attack, how to build a trench wall … as well as hours with the horses. He could spot a problem and diagnose it nearly every time now; they were trusting him do the occasional round on his own, and so far he hadn't missed anything. Maybe after the war he could do this ... be a vet. It would be a step up. As usual, he found himself wanting to talk it over with Jim. He always had, and he felt the loss of it. It was the dark side of his joy with Elsie.

It was mid-April before he saw Joe Moffat. It was late afternoon and he was returning with his unit from the rifle range when he came face to face with him. He stopped dead, then moved quickly away from the line. Joe walked on a few paces, but then turned and met his gaze. He stood his ground. He was sturdier than ever - no doubt army rations were better than what he was used to at home - but he looked younger than he remembered. He would be what, eighteen by now? Too young to go overseas, if they knew his right age.

'No big brother with you this time, Joe?'

He didn't want to fight, but he couldn't let the lad go without a warning. He wasn't going to spend the rest of his time in camp watching his back.

'Na, he's with the Tyneside Scottish. Last time wu hord he was in France, some place in the north, like.'

'You off soon?'

'Bloody hope so; I'm sick of this fucken lot.'

'You gave me a right going over, you and your brother.'

'Aye, and I'll dey it again if I git the chance, like. Wor lass desorves better than the likes of yee messin 'er aboot.'

The lad took a step towards him, his fists up, ready. *Christ, when would he let it drop?*

'True enough, but that's between her and me, not you.'

'You all right, Smithy?'

He turned as Laidlow came up behind him.

'Just a bit of old business, Sol.'

Joe stood back at the sight of the older man, put his fists

down. Sol stood and weighed him up, one meaty hand on Ivan's shoulder.

'Ye wanting something with ma friend here, Pal?'

'Na, ye can keep him. Just divvent let him meet yer sister, that's all.'

'Ye wanting a scrap, pal? Because if ye are, why don't ye just gan over there and practise falling down, before a get ma hands on ye.'

'Na, am gannen.'

Joe turned and walked away, turning once to spit in their direction.

'That yer granny's little brother then? Will a teach the little sod some manners?'

'No and no, thank you Sol.'

Maybe that would be the last of it; one war at a time was enough.

By the time he was called to the despatch office in the early evening of May 15th he was ready and they knew it. He made sure he was fit to be seen, then marched briskly over the drilling square. Strange, but he really did feel like a soldier; the horseshoe badge stitched onto the right arm of his uniform felt ... what? ... honourable, somehow.

'Private Errington, Sir.'

Here was a man worth saluting; pushing fifty but strong as a barn door and ready for anything.

'You're on your way, Private Errington. You're with the RFA. You'll leave with the draft tomorrow morning, five sharp. Do a good job and you'll be a corporal by summer; we need reliable men in charge of the horses, so it shouldn't take long. Good luck.'

'Thank you, Sir.'

So this was it; he was going to France. He needed to pack, but he wanted one last hour with his horses. They'd be going, eventually, but for now it was just him. He walked through the stalls, smoothing a nose, a fetlock, testing his memory of everything the army vets had taught him over the last few months. He'd made notes, been given a manual, but most of it was instinct and observation. He'd manage. Afterwards, it felt strange to be sorting his gear ready for the morning while the other lads, most of them, played cards. There was jeering as someone played a bad hand, a pall of cigarette smoke; it was inviting, but he wanted to write a quick message to Elsie as well.

'You telling Granny you're off to the front?'

They'd long ago stopped believing him, but the joke went on.

'Aye.' He grinned, knowing what was coming.

'You going to tell her to keep her drawers on while you're away?'

'Fuck off, Lads.'

The dirty buggers were always on about what women got up to when their men weren't around. Only the single men, though. It was tough on the married ones, or some of them; you could tell the ones who weren't sure, always looking for reassurance. He knew how they felt. What was he going to say? In the end, he just told her where he was going and that he'd write when he could.

> ... I'll be working away from the front, caring
> for the horses like I do at home. I'll be thinking
> about you, hoping that you'll think about me
> sometimes, too. I love you with all my heart ...

It was a few weeks since he'd heard from her and it was painful to think that perhaps she really was putting him out of her mind. How could she? But then ... how couldn't she, if she wanted to mend her marriage to Jim?

The men of his draft gathered in the square before five

211

the following morning. It was just before dawn; the watery violet sky glowed beyond the ranks of huts and tents and washed over the empty plain beyond. The air was still cool, but there was a promise of warm sunshine later. He loved this time of day, when the first birdsong chased the shadows. Some of the lads were chatting, there was some laughter, but he stood apart and lit a cigarette, gazing towards the stables where they'd be mucking out in a short while. Five minutes and he'd be lining up for the last roll call of his training.

TWENTY SIX

Elsie

She didn't notice anything, or at least she didn't think anything of it, until after Lily's wedding. The last few weeks had been the worst in her life: worse than when her mother died, worse than when she'd had to face up to the anger of Jim's mother when he married her; the misery was beyond anything. She felt utterly defeated. Lonely and defeated.

And now this, feeling ill day after day until she realised that it was ... how long, since she'd bled? Weeks – at least a couple of weeks before Jim's leave and now it was the end of March. She lay still, hoping the nausea would pass, but she needed to get up, open the shop. She climbed out of bed slowly and crept carefully down the stairs, but even so by the time she reached the kitchen she had to dash to the back door, hand over her mouth. She bent, holding her hair back from her face as she retched again and again, her body doubled over with dry spasms. She hadn't eaten the night before but that didn't stop the urge to empty her stomach, and it was several minutes before it eased and she felt steady enough to come back inside. Mrs Binns, Grace, was already downstairs, busying about preparing some breakfast.

'It's time to see Doctor Armstrong, pet.'

Grace helped her onto a chair and took off her own shawl to wrap round Elsie's shoulders. She was shivering, her face clammy with effort.

'Here, get something in your stomach. That way you'll have something to bring up.'

Elsie sat, numb, as Grace cut a slice of bread for her, poured a cup of tea.

'How long does this go on for? I mean, if you're right?'

She couldn't believe she was even asking the question. It was nearly five years since she'd been married, and no child. If ... *if* ... she was pregnant, then why now? She knew why now. God in heaven, what'll she do?

'Mine stopped at three months, but my sister never had a sick day yet and Martha Stubbs went on 'til the bairn arrived, so you just don't know. Here, pet, drink your tea.'

It was good to have Grace with her. Even though she couldn't tell her the truth, at least she was there, to help her through it. She broke a small piece of the bread from the slice and pushed it into her mouth, then took a tiny sip of the tea. It felt good and she kept going until she'd managed most of the slice, but then her stomach began to heave again and she was back out in the garden, shaking as she brought it up. A thread of spit clung to her lips and she wiped it away with the back of her hand. *Oh God.*

She did go to see the doctor, on her half day when the shop was closed; he was all congratulations and smiles, full of cautions about lifting heavy boxes and eating well. If he noticed her anxiety he seemed to put it down to the fact that Jim was away, in the army. And the shop, of course.

'You look a bit tired, Elsie. You need to rest a little; take a nap after lunch – Mary can hold the fort well enough. I'm sure Ann would pop along to help now and then, for that matter. And get yourself to bed early.'

She couldn't tell him that however tired she felt, every night brought agitation, not rest, *never rest*; always this wretched guilt as soon as she blew the candle out. And now

214

the joy of at last expecting a baby was ruined by it. She wasn't worthy to be a mother, not any more. And she had to tell Jim before anyone noticed and ... God forbid ... *what if the news reached him somehow before she told him*? And what if he refused to accept it? Oh God, the shame of it. After ten nights of fretting she resolved to send him a letter. She hadn't been writing to him because she couldn't think what to say and he might not even write back, but surely now ...

> ... I know this will be a surprise for you, as it was for me, to find that we are going to have a baby at last. I am feeling well, and Doctor Armstrong believes that the child will be born some time in November. Grace is looking after me like a mother, and Mary's making sure that I don't work too hard, although I feel better when I'm occupied. We are all knitting, too; we will have a finely dressed baby, I can tell you...

What else could she say? She had no idea where Jim might be when he read her letter, *if* he read it, but surely this would allow him to claim the baby as his own. If he still wanted her, and her child.

Once she'd written to Jim, she found it impossible to reply to Ivan's letters. She always read them: they were entertaining, full of comical stories about camp life, but in spite of everything he still kept on about wanting her and loving her, even though she'd told him again and again that it was all ended. And now this. If she told him about the baby it would be worse; he would expect more than she could ever give him. It surprised her that she could put him out of her mind, but she did, except when she willed him to be safe now that he was going to war. Was it wrong? Perhaps it was? To hope that Jim and Ivan should be protected from harm when others were being killed? Wrong or not, when she couldn't sleep she found herself saying it, over and over … *let them be safe, let them be safe* … as if the words could work a miracle.

Gradually, in spite of everything, she began to enjoy the sense of the baby growing inside her, especially when the sickness passed and her dresses became tighter and her waist and breasts filled out. She slowly allowed herself to feel if not happy, at least contented. Whatever else happened, she was going to have her own child. The future was so uncertain she tried not to think about it, concentrating instead on running Erringtons and keeping healthy. She found pleasure in the time she spent with Mary; they were sharing the hours and the work. With the spring came warm weather, so that they could sit outside on the bench with a cup of tea when the shop was quiet; the valley's trees returned to their restful green and she felt hopeful.

It was the middle of May before she heard from Jim. Postie brought the letter into the shop with a big grin on his face; this was a good day: no deaths and quite a few envelopes from the Front to raise some smiles. She thanked him, accepted the letter and put it to one side for when there were no customers around. But even when she was left alone behind the counter she was paralysed with fear of what he might have written. She couldn't open it. In the end she decided to get away from the shop, on her own. Mary was in the back, sorting the stock shelves, so she called her through.

'I think I need some fresh air; could you take over at the counter while I go for a walk? I won't be too long.'

If Mary saw the letter in her hand she said nothing. She'd been wonderful, realising that things weren't right between her and Jim, but never asking the wrong questions.

'Of course … you take your time. I'd finished in there, anyway. Off you go.'

She grabbed her hat and pulled her coat over her shoulders.

She'd go down to the river, where she and Jim had first walked out together nearly six years ago; she'd been seventeen, and he'd insisted they wait for over a year before they married. Today was just as sunny, but a cool breeze ruched the water as she crossed the arched bridge and took the path west from the town. Ewes and lambs were grazing in the fields beyond the track; there wasn't the slightest trace of the slaughter, far to the south, that was changing nearly every life in the valley.

When she'd walked far enough to avoid company she sat down on the river bank where a thick beech hedge protected her from the breeze. She lifted her face towards the afternoon sun; there was real warmth, and it seemed like a promise, but her heart was hammering. She carefully prised open the envelope. There was just one sheet inside, folded.

TWENTY SEVEN

Jim

The train south was like a coffin. Even with his uniform and greatcoat it was impossible to feel anything but deathly cold. It had to be what dying feels like, this gradual numbing of body and soul. He ate nothing until London where he joined a group of other subalterns in a restaurant near the station. They saw him come in, alone.

'I say, why don't you join us?

'You can't eat on your own! Here, take a pew, old chap.'

They drew up a chair for him: it would have been uncivil to refuse their invitation but he had to nail a smile to his face. Despite his mood, he had to admit the company was friendly … light hearted even, although he was the only officer on the way out for the first time; the others were on their way back after leave or convalescence. He suspected that behind the cheerfulness there must have been a few mental battles going on.

And Waterloo Station was so damned dreary. When this bloody war had started there'd been pictures in The Times of bands playing on the platform, patriotic crowds with flags waving off whole battalions. He'd seen them: the would-be heroes with shiny faces, grinning and waving through open carriage windows at toffs with top hats and canes. Where were they now? The only civilians here were families, come up to town to say goodbye. He noticed a young mother in white, kneeling to shush a whining child. Proud fathers stood to attention in tweeds. He turned away as one of them, himself bleary eyed, held out a large handkerchief to his wife who was smiling and sobbing at the same time. The rail guards looked bored with the whole thing, and who could blame them; they'd been watching the same routine for too long.

Not that *he* wanted trombones and cheering, but he did feel sorry for the groups of shaven-headed privates from the shires. They were standing about, smoking furiously: the train from Southampton had shuddered to a halt, and nearly every one of them was trying not to stare at the walking wounded as they shuffled out of the stinking carriages and down the steps. There was a commotion as one of them – a boy by the look of him – stumbled and fell. His crutches clattered onto the oily platform. He ran over to help him up.

'Here, take my arm.' *Oh Christ, he's bleeding.* It was seeping through the soiled bandages that covered what remained of his left leg.

'Just leave me be, Sir. I'll manage.'

Sir? What, when he hadn't even got there yet, and seen what he'd seen? He took the crutches from someone who'd gathered them up and helped the lad to steady himself.

'Is someone coming to meet you?'

'My mother.'

He turned away, looked around. A woman was coming towards them, one hand over her mouth as she reached out for her son.

He stepped away, *please don't say anything.* He hadn't earned so much as a look of thanks. Then it was time to board: out with the old, in with the new. He found an officers' carriage and waited. Strange, how before he knew about Elsie and Ivan, his fear had been all about leaving her. He'd hardly given a thought to what lay ahead, other than

219

hoping it would be over quickly so that he could come back again. Now he felt a wave of crippling fear of what he was about to face.

Southampton was dull and cheerless, too. He liked the sea; at St Bees he'd taken up sailing with some of the other lads, but this was altogether different: war had made the port into a military anthill, an infestation of soldiers milling around laden with gear, lining up for embarkation. The sea was just a sullen background for the swarm of uniforms.

He had two hours to wait, so he left his heavy stuff in the care of an orderly and walked into town to buy some morphia pills – his dining companions had recommended them for certain types of wounds. With these stowed in his haversack he began to stroll back, and on an impulse pushed the heavy rotating doors into one of the grand hotels, hoping to have tea in a quiet corner. It was cosy and inviting, but near the polished reception desk was a public telephone. He stopped short. The urge to pick up the receiver and ask to be put through to Erringtons, just to hear her voice, was overwhelming. He was fishing for coins when a well-dressed woman came briskly towards him down the carpeted staircase beyond reception and bustled straight over to the phone. As he walked away he could hear her talking to the operator.

The ship looked like a paddle-steamer in extreme old age. It left England at eight, swaying unlit through the night to Le Havre between protective destroyers; dull grey boats on the dull grey channel. He stood out on deck until the last lights of England dimmed in their wake, then found a bench under cover as the rain came in. The sea wasn't rough exactly, but there was a choppy swell so that men were stumbling past him to be sick, hanging over the rails; the worst hit were vomiting like dogs in the corridors. It was the first time he'd travelled abroad and this wasn't anything like what he'd hoped for. He'd promised Elsie they'd go to Paris some day, see the huge iron tower built by Eiffel ... he had school friends who went every year, so why not? He closed his eyes, then shook his head to get rid of what he saw. Little chance of that, now.

After the ship were heaving trains, crammed with troops, trundling north to Belgium. Were all foreign trains as slow as this? He might not be looking forward to getting to the front, but it was so damned tedious. He clambered down and walked alongside; it was better to be active, and this way he could warm up a bit, take account of the foreign landscape. Others did the same, so that for an hour at a time he'd fall into conversation with other officers, occasionally with other ranks. He'd been told it was about two hundred miles to the front line, but it took nearly four days and nights of jerking and rattling over the flat landscape of northern France to reach their railhead just past the Belgian border, by which time he'd had just about enough of it.

They'd been hearing guns rattling in the distance since they passed Hazebrouck the day before, but the sight of Poperinge was still a shock; the town was broken and desolate, its houses blasted by shells aimed at the station. The missing roofs and shattered walls were the first real signs of the war that was going on within a few miles, and he felt his stomach clench.

He was lucky to find another officer from his battalion in the crowd; he obviously knew his way round so he must be returning from leave or injury. He'd seen him once or twice on the train, but he'd always been deep in discussion, and anyway he hadn't felt like introducing himself in case a conversation started that took him where he didn't want to go. Now he approached him and gave his name, rank and company. The other shook his hand and grinned.

'Spence, Harry, Lieutenant. With you; great stuff!'

Within the hour they were loading their gear onto a

low slung trap and on their way to the Fusiliers' camp at Ouderdom. It was dark now, apart from the German flares that seemed to arc from three directions, revealing the bleak winter landscape and the muddy road ahead of them. It was only a couple of miles but the horse was old, so it was very late when they pulled up at the cluster of wooden huts. The camp was blacked out, everyone apart from the guards asleep, but within minutes some servants had been roused and were helping with their trunks, showing them their berths.

After the jaw clenching cold of the journey the hut felt fairly warm. Best of all, and in spite of the men shifting and snoring around them, they sat down to a scratch meal and *glory be* a huge mug of hot tea at the long table that ran down the middle of the hut between the bunks. In spite of the hour, all this comfort was provided with great cheerfulness by the batmen. Spence was obviously from a background that included a manservant, but even so he was full of praise for his military retainer.

'These fellows are a wonder, Errington. Mine can muster eggs and bacon in a foul trench where there are no hens and fewer pigs for miles around. Extraordinary. Never grouses, never loses his nerve. He's like a mother to me, only hairier.'

'Where did you find him?'

'He was assigned; just appeared soon after I arrived, like a fairy godmother. He was a miner before this show, so God alone knows how he learned to cook.'

'Well, let's hope mine's as good.'

And he was. By the time he joined his first platoon in the support trenches at Hill 60 a few days later he was already glad to have Jim Hodgson by his side, especially when he learned that the company was moving to the front the following day. *Christ, they didn't give you long:* hardly time to meet the other officers, never mind his men, and they were too busy packing

222

up to take much notice.

With snow beginning to bleach the wrecked landscape they needed as much warm gear as they could carry as well as all their equipment. Hodgson sorted his, picked out what he needed and sent the rest for storage. Ten fifty five; they were off in an hour. *Well, here goes.* He walked through the ranks, asking names and checking that every soldier had spare socks, emergency rations ... it was good to have his mind fully occupied again. He repeated every name as he heard it; if he could remember every customer back home he could remember forty eight men there. He doubled back to one private who looked familiar; he was a Wark lad, son of the local butcher.

'Jobson, Sir. I've played football against yer brother, Sir. Five three to us last derby.' He grinned. 'On home ground, too.'

So that was it; he'd been there at the side of the pitch, watched Ivan's team lose that day. Jobson'd been in goal. A fine lad.

'Good match, Jobson. We'll have you next time, though.'
'We'll have to beat the Hun first, Sir.'
'True enough.'

Movement to the front line began after midnight. He'd been briefed: the Germans held the top of the ridge above them in a solid line, a hundred yards ahead. Their own front line had two gaps.

'Can't we fill them? What's the problem?' *Basic training: every line to be intact and secure, or the enemy will take advantage.*

'You'll see. The gaps are a swamp.'
'And we can't dig and drain?'
'Not with their snipers trained on us night and day.'

As if to illustrate the point, bullets flicked overhead

223

intermittently as they made their way along the narrow communication trench to the front line. Machine gun fire raked the top of the sandbags. He'd get used to it, but his height was a problem: he needed to bend at an awkward angle to avoid being vulnerable. By the time they were in place he was aching and stiff with it and longing for some sleep, but he was kept busy until dawn and stand to. He had the rum ration to dole out, the soldiers' medicine.

What had he expected? *Christ knows.* The next month was a grim initiation: front line, then in support, then rest, moving back and forth, and the enemy had all the advantage because of the higher ground. Worse, they had the constant stink of bodies rotting in the oozing sump between the trenches and in no man's land. It was vile; he couldn't get used it. It seemed to stick to his skin and in his throat.

'That's why they're staying put, Sir.'

'What?'

'The Hun. They're not moving forward because the air's fresher up there!'

'I hope to hell we're not still here when the weather turns warm.'

'Well *they* will be, that's for sure.'

His corporal nodded towards the swampy ground where half-buried corpses lay where they'd fallen; it was grotesque. He'd taken to leading patrols under cover of mist or darkness to retrieve identity discs; they'd found over seventy so far, but there must be hundreds out there. Would the families have any idea? He hoped not. He hoped they'd been told that their sons had been buried and their graves marked and mapped.

The shelling was rough for everyone. He'd lost two of his own men in one night with a direct hit by a howitzer shell. Although he'd been off duty when it happened he'd been there within minutes, fastening his tunic as he ran, bent double, the hundred yards. One had lost the top of his head, blown off below the hair line along with his helmet; there was still a look of shock on what remained of his face. The other was laid out in the bottom of the trench. His mates were frantically trying to staunch the blood gushing from a huge wound in his chest, but for all the desperate mopping and compressing he could see it was pointless. He organized stretcher bearers and the clearing up and the repairs to the trench, but as he gave the orders his mind was on what he was going to say in the letters home to the mothers of these two; they'd both been barely nineteen years old.

He was in reserve when Elsie's letter arrived at the end of April. He'd become very friendly with Harry Spence and was on good terms with the other officers of 'B' Company, but he'd kept off the subject of home, as far as it was possible. If they wondered why he received no post they never mentioned it; they knew he was married and had no children, but that was about it. Heaven knew what they thought, but he couldn't tell the truth and he wasn't going to lie.

His stomach lurched when he saw her girlish print on the envelope. Hodgson had left it on his bunk; it was the first time he'd heard from her since that morning in February when she'd turned away as soon as his train began to move. He picked it up, then sat for a while just holding it, staring at the various post marks. He hadn't written to her, for want of anything to say that he felt sure about. He'd sent a few brief notes to Lily, but she'd replied just the once, to thank him for releasing her money and to tell him that 'her husband' had been conscripted but he was appealing because of his weak knee. She hadn't mentioned Elsie. He'd thrown the letter away. Weak knee or not, Frank was snake enough to slither out of service even now, even when so many battalions were short of men.

So, a letter from his wife. He read it, then read it again.
Elsie … *pregnant?*

TWENTY EIGHT

Ivan

He gripped the halter tightly as a third shell shrilled overhead and landed beyond them; the explosion thundered shards of compacted earth and metal, showering men and horses. His mare was snorting, shifting uneasily, but was unharmed apart from the few nasty cuts along her flanks, the ones he'd been treating when the bombardment began. Another shell struck, this time in front of them. As the din subsided a high pitched squealing started up in the line of drivers waiting with their teams.

'Who's been hit Mikey; can you see?'

'Not yet.'

'Poor bugger.'

He concentrated on his injured horse as the piercing wail continued; the young private next to him strained to see what was going on. As the dust settled they could see the shell had landed close to one of the gun trailers fifty yards in front; a horse was down, his driver underneath. The other five horses were panicking, wracking back and forth in their shafts as the two remaining drivers tried to help the trapped soldier. Men were yelling but the crying had stopped.

'Well, he's either dead, of they've got him out.'

He wasn't looking – he hated the screaming, hated when it stopped. It was shockingly familiar now.

'Nah, he's still under the horse. I reckon they're both dead by now. How many's that we've lost this week, Sir?'

'Dozens. The bastards know what they're doing.'

He'd been promoted to corporal within a couple of months, as they'd said he would be. And if things went on this way he'd be sergeant in another couple: the enemy was targeting wagon teams – and everything else of use behind the front line – so he was moving up the chain. They'd lost several drivers and a couple of smiths in the last week alone, along with dozens of mules and horses. He'd been kept busy. All that training at Larkshill had been useful, but checking a horse's mouth every day in case its bit was rubbing, which he still did, seemed a luxury once you were dealing with shrapnel wounds and broken legs; they'd already had to shoot far more horses than he'd ever save.

He finished the job and handed the horse over to Mikey, to take her further back to where they were using a sunken road for protection. He stayed where he was, lit a cigarette. One place was as safe as another when these heavy buggers were landing, and anyway he would probably be needed soon. No point in moving far.

* * * *

A few days later and they were in support, well behind the lines. They'd bathed, had fresh clothes and the chance of a good night's sleep. Simple pleasures: safe for a while, and clean. He needed a drink – beer preferably, but wine would do if that's all there was. A few of the lads were up for a walk into Arras where there'd be plenty of both, or so they'd been told.

'You coming, Smithy?'

'Try and hold me back!'

They set off into the warm June evening; it felt little different from strolling down to The Crown after a match with some of team, apart from the whine and crump of shells in the distance.

'I'm after a pretty little Mamselle tonight mind, lads.'

This was Dan Weaver, who'd already sampled several local girls and took great pleasure in describing – in detail – their French customs.

'They know exactly where to …'

'Shut up, Weaver; we've children present.'

Ivan gestured at Mikey who was listening, eyes wide. Poor kid, at nineteen he was barely experienced enough even to understand the conversation so far, but enough was enough.

'Get lost, Smithy! How's the lad going to find out if we don't tell 'im?'

Mikey blushed as Weaver put his arm round his thin shoulders and gave him a friendly hug.

'Not embarrassed are you, Mikey?'

'Leave him alone, Dan; what would his mother think, for Christ's sake? Anyway, you'll end up catching something, you know that?"

'No I'll not: I always look out for the healthy ones, me.'

This brought a roar of laughter from the group.

'Doctor Weaver can always tell, lads!'

'I can, I'm telling yez.'

'Yer daft bugger.'

'They have a look in their eyes…'

'It's not their eyes you'll get it from …'

'And anyway, if I do end up with summat, mebbe they'll send us home for a bit. Can't lose, really, eh Mikey?' Bored with his joke, Weaver dropped his arm and fell into step with a different crowd. 'Howay, let's get a shift on!'

They pushed their way through the uniformed crowd that was spilling out of the open door of an estaminet onto the narrow street. Even the sight and din of men enjoying a

229

summer evening out was intoxicating. Inside, ranks of serious drinkers lined the bar, their tobacco smoke clouding the low ceiling above. Ivan looked round; many of them already had the glazed eyes and red faces of too much alcohol, too quickly. His group spread out as they fought their way to the front, and when he reached the bar he stayed there with Overdene, another corporal, downing a first glass and ordering a second within minutes. He'd already lost Mikey: maybe he'd teamed up with Weaver to go in search of healthy girls. Daft sod. He grinned at Overdene, suddenly overwhelmed with the pleasure of simply being alive.

'This beats being eye to eye with the Hun.'

'Beats most things, the way I feel at the moment.'

'You going to find a woman?'

'Not me. My Nancy'll have me balls off if she finds out! You?'

'No. I'm used to better than this. I don't like …'

He gestured across the room, where women in twos and threes were standing, each surrounded by a crowd of tipsy soldiers. As he glanced around, one face in particular caught his eye and he stopped talking. Fuck, it was George Moffat. As if sensing Ivan's look, George stopped talking and looked directly at him, nudging one of his beefy companions; he hadn't changed a bit. Ivan braced himself as George ploughed his way towards him, holding his beer aloft to avoid spillage. He turned towards the bar, and warned Overdene in an undertone.

'To your right: I've an old friend coming over to say hello.'

His tone was enough. Overdene took a look, then shifted his weight to close the gap between them.

'Fuck me, he's a big boy. Glad he's a friend!'

'Last time we met I saw too much of his boots.'

'Steel tipped were they?'

'Steel tipped.'

He gulped down the last of his beer and turned round to face George.

'How's it going, Moffat?'

'Well, well … still a smithy then?'

George was a head taller than both of them, but at least he'd come over on his own.

'I am.'

'Thowt ye'd be at haem with the missus, like.'

He wanted to punch the smirk off his face, but he just looked at him calmly. He could see Overdene's puzzled look: he knew Ivan wasn't married, didn't even have a special girl.

'And what "missus" is that?'

'Wey, how many hev ye got, like?' He sniggered and took a pull at his beer.

'What missus?'

'Elsie Errington. That missus. Did she tell yez she's hevin a bairn? She's got a little grocer comin alang in October, November. Or mebbes it's a smith.'

His face must have given him away, because George continued:

'Na? Thowt not, like.'

George smiled broadly and held up his half-empty glass.

'Wey, here's to happy families!'

'Why don't you fuck off, Moffat.'

George kept up the grin and took another healthy swig, then he nodded to both corporals and turned on his heel, heading back to his gang and the women.

'Well, that's not what I was expecting.'

Overdene was staring at him. When Ivan didn't respond, he ordered two more beers and stood beside him in silence, waiting.

'Look, I'm sorry mate, but I've got to get out of here.'

231

He put his glass down and turned towards the door, looking for a way through the swarming drinkers. The noise was terrible ... worse than shells coming over.

'Do I wait for you?'

Overdene was calling after him as he disappeared but he didn't turn round. The street outside was still teeming so he set off, weaving swiftly through the mass of bodies until he was passing only occasional couples, kissing in shadowed doorways. He came upon a small square where – *good God* – a dainty fountain was still playing surrounded by well-tended flower beds, all colour leeched by the rising moon. He sat on an iron bench and fumbled for his cigarettes and matches. His hands were jittering. He leaned forward, elbows resting on his knees, and took a long first drag. Elsie was, what ... he did a quick calculation ... four months pregnant? Maybe five? And she hadn't told him. Why? Everybody must know, surely, if George knew. Oh Christ, did Jim know?

He tried to stand up and walk, but staggered instead into a dark passageway and vomited onto the dusty cobbles. When he'd finished he lurched over to the fountain and splashed the cool water onto his burning face and neck, wishing he dared ignore the verdigri *eau non potable* sign on the stone vase. He went back to his bench and lit another cigarette. *Think*, Ivan. This baby ... it must be their baby, his and Elsie's ... but it would have to be *Jim's* baby. The Erringtons were respectable, Elsie was Jim's wife, therefore the baby was his. Elsie would choose – had already chosen probably – safety rather than disgrace, and whatever the Moffats thought or said, no-one would believe them. To acknowledge him as the father would be madness, like choosing hell over heaven.

TWENTY NINE

Elsie

Her hands were shaking as she unfolded the thin sheet of lined paper. There was only one paragraph, closely written in Jim's neat hand, dated ten days earlier, in Belgium:

My dear Elsie

I can hardly express how I felt on reading your letter. I know that you have hoped for this for years, and can imagine your joy and excitement as you prepare for the birth. I should be granted some leave before the end of the year so that, God willing, by the time I see you next the child may be safely born. Perhaps you might delay the Christening until his father can be present? Whatever may have happened, your child must be a blessing to us, a ray of sunshine in this dark time. Stay safe, Elsie. I think of you constantly and hope, with all my heart, for a happier future.

Jim

She set the brief letter down on the grass beside her hat and stayed sitting with her hands across her belly, gazing into the eddying waters of the North Tyne. Her heart felt as if it was blooming, like the white lilac on the opposite bank. He'd been thinking about her constantly and would be here with her, with them, perhaps before Christmas. He wanted a happier future. Surely that meant that he wanted to be with her, with the baby, whatever may have happened. Now she could look forward – properly look forward – to being a mother. They could start again, as a family. Ivan will understand … he must. She tipped her head back to catch the warmth of the slow moving sun.

It took a while to walk back to the shop because she felt light-headed, and kept stopping for breath. She knew she must have a stupid smile fixed on her face, but she couldn't help it: the relief of it was overwhelming. She wanted to knock on the doors she was passing to tell people her good news … she had to do something or she'd burst. On an impulse she changed her route and walked purposefully along to St Cuthbert's, where she and Jim had been married in the June of 1911. It was tempting simply to sit in the graveyard, letting the sun continue its work on her spirits, but instead she pushed open the studded door and stepped into the high vaulted nave. Awkwardly, she kneeled in one of the back pews and prayed … a jumbled, one-sided pleading with God for Jim's safe return, for him to say 'our' child instead of 'your' child, for Ivan's forgiveness, for God's forgiveness … thank you, thank you, thank you God for my baby.

By the time she reached Erringtons she was exhausted. Mary was cutting a wedge of butter from the slab as she walked in, and simply raised her eyebrows in discreet enquiry; she'd been away a long while for a breath of fresh air. She smiled and nodded her head as she slipped out of her coat. After a brief chat the customer left, and Mary turned towards her.

'Well?'

'I'm fine now.'

'Really? You look worn out, though.'

'No, it was good news. Wonderful news, actually.'

'It's about time. Now, let's get the door closed and go for some lunch.'

* * * *

It was late in the afternoon when they heard a motor pull up in the street. Elsie glanced through the window and saw Frank helping Lily out of his car; they were both dressed up to the nines for their ride out. Lily's hair was different: shorter and chic under a new hat. They were coming towards the shop, Frank walking with a pronounced limp. She swept her hands over her own disorderly curls, replacing a loose pin. She glanced down to where her apron just covered her swelling belly. She hadn't told Lily about the baby; in fact she didn't even know her address. The door was propped open in the warmth of the spring sunshine and she stepped forward into the light as they came in from the street.

'Lily, Frank, how good to see you both.'

She held out her hand. They were both smiling broadly as they walked in and she felt her old irritation at Lily, all smug and self-important as her eyes flickered quickly around the shop, weighing things up, looking for any changes. Why should she care, now? And look at those beautiful shoes! As she gazed at Lily's footwear she sensed the sudden change of mood and looked up again. Frank had strolled over to the counter to introduce himself to Mary, but Lily was eyeing her up and down, her mouth open. 'Gawping', her mother would have called it.

'Are you …?'

Lily was either too astonished or too prudish to say the word.

'Pregnant? I am, yes.'

She smiled brightly and held her hand out again, pushing her sister in law to take it, which she did, although she clearly didn't want to. *Now wipe your hand on your skirt, why don't you?*

235

'Frank, come here. Have you seen Elsie?'

Frank cut short his patter with Mary and returned to his wife, only then catching sight of her unmistakable change in shape.

'Good God. So you're going to be a real Auntie, my precious!'

'It looks like it. But which one of my brothers is the father, that's what I'd like to know. I bet she's not sure herself.'

She turned on her expensive heels and strode out of the shop. Frank followed her out, his limp less obvious. Elsie stayed where she was, cheeks burning, knowing that Mary had heard and seen everything. How long could a minute last? She couldn't think of anything to do or say that would make it any better. She sensed movement and turned to face her friend, but Mary was already heading for the door, her face white.

'Please ... don't!'

She caught Mary's arm as she hurried past, but she shrugged her off and was gone in seconds. Elsie followed and stood at the door, watching what was going on outside. The car was still there. Lily was sitting in the passenger seat, her body rigid ... *self-righteous bitch* ... as Frank leaned against the driver's door and smoked, for all the world as if nothing had been said. He caught her eye and stood back, away from the vehicle, throwing the remains of his cigarette onto the ground. He shrugged, gave her a little wave, then climbed in beside his wife. She watched as the car pulled away, then went back in, bolting the door behind her.

She ought to have known the way she'd felt earlier in the day wouldn't last. People like her couldn't expect to be happy – there was always something waiting to ruin things if it looked too easy. She set about finishing the day's tasks: closing boxes, wiping the shelves, counting the takings. Just as she was reaching for her coat there was a knock on the door. She turned the key and drew back the bolts – it wasn't uncommon for someone to arrive after they'd closed and she was always ready to help out: it was what they did, at Erringtons. But it wasn't a customer, it was Mary.

'Can I come in?'

'Of course.'

'I shouldn't have left like that. I should've waited and talked to you.'

'It doesn't matter.'

She closed the door behind them and went over to where she could lean against the counter. Even though it was still light and fairly warm outside, it was gloomy with the door closed, and she was glad of it. Her eyes locked on a knot in one of the worn oak floorboards, as if she'd never seen it before. She waited for Mary to speak.

'I've never asked … about what's wrong, I mean. All these weeks and we've never talked about it.'

'I know.'

'It's not my business.'

'No.'

'But it's different now. Lily's made it my business. She's a right bitch mind, isn't she?'

'She is.'

'But still. What she said?'

'I know. Mary, I'm really sorry.'

'Sorry? What about? That she said it? Or that I know? Or what?'

'I don't know. Both. About everything.'

'Talk to me, Elsie.'

'I can't.'

She looked up at last, and saw that Mary's expression wasn't what she'd expected; she looked troubled, but not angry. But

237

still she couldn't say what needed to be said.

'Do you know whose child it is? I mean, is Lily right ... could it be Ivan's?'

'Yes. No. It's Jim's ... it's *Jim's*.'

'You mean, Ivan might be the father, but he isn't, you think.'

'Yes.'

Her legs nearly gave way as she admitted it.

'I don't know what to say.'

'I don't blame you.' Her voice was flat; she was spent, worn out with it.

'And the letter? Was it from Jim?'

'I wrote to him, to tell him about the baby. He wants it to be ours.'

'You're very lucky then.'

'I suppose so. You don't know what it's like ... how it was.'

'You're right, I don't. My husband was killed before I could be unfaithful to him. And he didn't have a brother to give me his child, either.'

'I didn't mean that. Mary, I didn't mean ...'

'Well, what did you mean?'

She couldn't even remember what she was going to say. Why was Mary still standing there? Why hadn't she just stayed away?

'Are you going to leave us? Erringtons?' It was almost more than she could bear, the thought of it.

'Listen, I put up with not knowing what was wrong ... but I don't think I can stay now that I do know.'

'You think I've been ... sinful. Don't you?'

'I'm not a priest, Elsie, I'm a friend.'

'I don't deserve a friend.'

'Everybody deserves a friend. But I don't think I can work here with you ... not when everyone comes in believing ....

not realising …and I'll be part of it.'

'Not realising what?'

'You know.'

'So you're going to leave me on my own.'

'I'll wait until you find someone else. There's loads of people looking for work.'

People less fussy who they work with, she meant.

'Will you tell people? Why you're leaving?'

'Of course not.'

'Well, what will you tell them, then? They're bound to ask.'

'I'll think of something.'

'But then you'll still be lying. You'll be forced to lie.'

'I'd rather live with my own lie than yours.'

THIRTY

Jim

He hadn't realised how bleak he'd felt about the future, assuming he had one, until Elsie's letter. He'd been preoccupied day and night, the unrelenting danger making him numb with fatigue. But it was the terrible sense of loss that had harmed him the most: he'd been missing half his soul. News of the baby had changed this: he could muster a thrill of joy at the thought of it: even here, where the dead and the undead were side by side. It was like being drunk. And it was just as well he was feeling more cheerful because they were being shelled, methodically up and down their trench, or what was left of it. Every night they did what they could to rebuild the parapet, but it was getting harder as the ground grew less and less stable and there were fewer men left to do the work. They needed a fresh draft, they'd been told to expect one, but none had arrived yet. He'd been ordered to warn his platoon not to waste ammunition until supplies came up the line.

They were making use of one of their bombing posts – it was fifty yards forward, inside their own wire, little more than a fortified shell hole you could only reach by going over the top and crawling when night fell. They called it The Stink, for obvious reasons. A week before he'd taken his turn, leading a team out to see what damage they could do with Mills bombs in the few hours before dawn. The worst part of the night had been reaching the post and the return

240

crawl under enemy fire; the earth was a bit dryer than it had been, but in the darkness you couldn't see what putrid mess you were dragging yourself through. It made him retch as he found himself apologising to whoever it was whose remains he'd disturbed.

He finished his patrol and started back to the officers' dugout, hoping for a bit of rest. Some chance, when these bastard shells kept coming over: there was dirt and rubbish flying everywhere. Something hard rapped his steel helmet, knocking his head sideways. It was a minute of two before he could move on, crouching to keep lower than the breastwork.

'You all right, Lieutenant?'

'Yes, thank you Hodgson. Glad of the helmet, though. Head's intact even if my neck's a bit stiff.' They'd been issued back in April and God knew how many men were alive now who would have been dead. Including him.

'Can I get you anything, Sir?'

'A hot drink with something to liven it up would be welcome. But give me an hour, first.'

He lay back on his narrow bunk. Even though it was too small for him, just being horizontal was good enough and he was asleep within seconds. But before Hodgson could bring his tea he was awake again; one of his NCOs was beside him, apologising for waking him

'Thought you'd want to know, Sir: Huns've taken The Stink. Second Lieutenant Greenhaugh's killed and Wanless and Smith're injured, probably dead. Iveson's got back, hurt, but he's wanting to go back out there again.'

'Give me a second.' He grabbed his helmet.

'We going to take it back, Sir?'

'I truly hope so.'

'Good-oh.'

He glanced around the dugout for any senior officers, but

there were none. He was up and on his way, bent double, in seconds, following his sergeant to where Iveson was squatting in the trench. His whole body was shaking convulsively as one of the corporals tried to stop the bleeding from his right shoulder. He looked up as Jim emerged from the darkness.

'Them bastards've got me mates, Sor. Got te gan and fetch them, Sor.'

'How many?'

'Wanless and Smith, Sor.'

'No, sorry Iveson, I meant how many Germans?'

'Four, Five mebbe. I got two of 'em. Didn't stop the bastards bringin' a machine gun through the wire, though. Fuckers.'

'You sure about the machine gun?'

'Aye. I was on watch, out of The Stink, like, but you could tell. It'll be up an runnin by now. We'll need to gan oot fer them, Sor. They didn't see us gannen, Sor; they think they got us al.'

'Good man ... but you're not going anywhere. Look after him, Corporal.'

He waited as the injured private was carried off, grilling the sentries about what they'd seen. Whatever the man said, from what he was told it seemed unlikely that the two soldiers would still be alive. Why would they be? Thank the Lord the Hun hadn't seen Iveson crawling away.

'You coming out there with me, Sergeant Crozier?'

'I am, Sir.'

'We need four of us. Five minutes. Two cool heads ... volunteers if you can find them.'

The sergeant nodded and left him. They had just over an hour before stand-to and the first glimmer of dawn; minutes to take out a gun that could, would, be trained on their parapet come morning. He pulled out his revolver and checked his ammunition. Ready. He lit a cigarette and leaned back against the trench wall as he waited for his party to arrive. Interesting, to feel so calm. Just as well: one whiff of fear from an officer and a raid was over before it'd begun.

They crawled silently over the top. He took Lakenby to the left with him, a volunteer from the early days of the war and known for his manic courage; Crozier took Meekin to the right, skinny as an eel and vicious in battle. They all knew what they were doing. He blotted out the foul stench as they elbowed their way wide of The Stink, as flat as they could manage, shuffling and stopping, shuffling and stopping until they were a matter of ten yards beyond it, between their wire and the machine-gun, which would be pointing away from them. He couldn't see over to where the wire had been cut … there could be men there, ready to help the raiding party back through. No, they'd be gone by now, before his sniper could pick them out at first light. Or maybe they were the two Iveson was talking about? Too late now, anyway. From The Stink they could just make out muted German voices as they busied themselves, sorting out their new position. He reached over and touched Lakenby: the signal. As they rose up and loped rapidly forwards he could hear Crozier and Meekin doing the same. Good men! He shot the gunner before he had time even to look up, then another as he was taking aim. It took them seconds to deal with all five – they obviously hadn't expected retaliation, or not so quickly.

'Keep low, lads: the Hun'll be wondering what's going on over here.'

They waited, stock-still on their hunkers in the crowded hole alongside the five enemy dead. So far no response, but it seemed beyond likely that they'd been heard, although it was still too inky dark to be seen, not that the darkness would stop a sniper. He was right: Wanless and Smith had been finished off; the Germans had pushed them up and over the edge of The Stink. Their bodies were heaped with Greenhaugh's to form a makeshift barrier to hide the machine-gun until it was needed. He gave his orders in a whisper: he would disassemble the gun and drag it back, the others could start to shift their casualties, but only if they weren't under fire.

'We could stop here and turn the gun round; do some real damage!' This was Makin, keen to have a go at the German front line.

'Let's just do what we came to do, eh? One man each, but cut and run if the Boche start firing. Either way, make sure you take their dog tags. And their pay books.'

'What about this lot, Sir?'

Crozier was indicating the dead Germans, still lying where they fell. The air was metallic with spilled blood.

'Leave their tags and photos, personal stuff, but take everything else.'

'Weapons?'

'Everything you can carry. Take the bolts if you have to leave the guns.'

The last part of the raid was painfully slow – or felt it. He had to zigzag over no-man's land twice to retrieve the gun and its tripod and a good quantity of ammunition, lugging the heavy gear behind him, keeping low as best he could. The others dragged a man each over the rough terrain, also keeping down, but moving fast. As he reached home for the second time the expected enemy flare went up at last, and he scrambled over the parapet into the trench as the first machine-gun bullets zipped over his head like hornets. He grinned at his men as a thin violet glow appeared on the horizon beyond. Dawn.

The others were elated in spite of losing Wanless and Smith, but he felt ... what? Just tired? No, he was bone weary, but before he could sleep or eat he needed to report to his senior officer. He could use a wash and a shave, but it would have to wait; his captain had been told about the raid and was waiting for him in the dugout. Spence was there, too, both were sitting at the small table the officers shared, a bottle and three glasses between them. He saluted and accepted the generous measure of whisky offered to him.

'Good work, Errington. Very good work.'

'Thank you, Sir'.

'I'll be reporting this up the line, of course. Commendation all round, I feel.'

'No need, Sir.'

'Every need, man. And Errington …'

'Yes, Sir?'

'I hear congratulations are in order on the home front as well.'

'Thank you, Sir.' Spence must have told him, and why shouldn't he?

By the time he'd handed over the German pay books and – nearly as valuable as the gun – a trench map – he was swaying with fatigue. Hodgson was waiting for him with tea that actually tasted like tea and a cooked breakfast; he was clearly hoping for a second-by-second account of the raid, but it would have to wait.

'Platoon's proud, Sir.'

'We lost three good men tonight, Hodgson.'

'But you got the buggers what did it, Sir. And a gun.'

'Not on my own, I didn't.'

'I know, Sir, but you led the way. You had the nerve for it.'

Hodgson was right, he hadn't lost his nerve. Of all the things he'd dreaded, that was the worst and it hadn't happened. These last months, being made Lieutenant early on, leading his men, killing the enemy – every hour at the front had been a test, but he was still here, and he still had the spirit, more now than ever.

'I'm going to sleep now, Hodgson. For hours, I hope. And rather doubt.'

'Leave it to me, Sir.'

He rolled onto his bunk and reached under his pillow for Elsie's letter, falling asleep as his fingers closed round the envelope.

THIRTY ONE

Elsie

She heard nothing more from Jim, not after his brief letter. When she started to feel the baby moving inside her at the end of June she wrote to him again, wanting to share it with him, but if he read it he didn't respond, and she was beginning to have doubts again. Worst of all, she didn't even know where he was now, nor where Ivan might be. Were they in France, on the Somme? News was coming through about a terrible battle, with thousands of men killed or wounded on the first day. As July wore on, more and more customers were wearing black, out of keeping with the gentle summer weather.

She hadn't wanted it, but she was Ivan's official next of kin as well as Jim's. On that night, when he'd come in from the cold, he'd asked her if she would mind.

'But I'm Jim's.'

'I know you are, but you can be mine as well. They don't care who you put.'

'Shouldn't it be Lily?'

'Why?'

'Well, because she's your own blood.'

'Thicker than water, you mean? I don't think so.'

'Of course it is.'

'Look, I don't want it to be Lily … not now. You're the one I'd want to know, if anything happened. Not that it will. I'll not be at the front.'

So … every day, hoping not to have any news. She was holding on to Ivan's 'not that it will', but still she found herself wanting, and not wanting, to slip out of the shop to join the other women waiting in the square. She wanted to be there when the postman sifted through his handful of envelopes. Get it over with. But she couldn't, because she still wasn't one of them; when Jim took her away from Percy Row he took her away from more than just a miner's cottage: she was an officer's wife, she still wouldn't be welcome. She wasn't alone, exactly, but she was lonely, with no-one to lean on other than Grace, now that Mary had left. Their friends, Jim's and hers, were all his from before they were married; she didn't feel comfortable with them on her own. Especially now.

Mary had been right: there was a queue for the job, and she'd found it hard to decide which of the women to choose. In the end she decided to take on two of them, because it wouldn't be long before she'd need to step back – it would be expected, and anyway she was always tired now, and she felt awkward at the counter. She chose another two war widows: Annie, whose mother would look after her two small children while she worked, and Eleanor, an older woman and a friend of Grace's. They weren't like Mary, but they were friendly and competent, and Erringtons was thriving with the three of them working together.

It was a beautiful summer: there was enough rain to keep the hillsides green, but the days were long and sun-filled. In the evenings of late August she'd walk, often alone, trying to keep active as she strolled past the old ironworks and along Hareshaw Burn to the Linn, or more often across the bridge and beside the North Tyne. It felt strange to be solitary when this had been their favourite time of year, hers and Jim's. She imagined what it would be like if things were different and he was there, walking with her. He'd fuss a bit, hold her arm.

There always used to be other couples taking advantage of the warm evenings to be alone together. Not now. She saw only older people, and women with children enjoying watery adventures as the sun gradually dropped behind the hills. No young men. When she reached the bridge she would stand facing south, her eyes focused beyond Northumberland, beyond England even, over the channel.

* * * *

One morning towards the middle of September, Archie Pumphrey marched into the shop with his copy of the London Gazette, a massive grin on his face. Eleanor called her through from where she'd been filing the accounts, and as she popped her head round the office door he barely gave himself enough time to whip off his panama before launching into his news.

'My dear, my dear, have you heard? Did he tell you?'

'Sorry Major, I really don't know what you mean.'

'My dear, it's Jim, he's been awarded the Military Cross. Look here!'

He held the paper up; it was folded to the page announcing awards for bravery. She came out and took it from him, squinting to read the small print.

'Led a raid, took a machine gun post! By Jove, he's a credit to his regiment, a credit to us all!'

He beamed around at the women with their shopping baskets, answered a few questions, then turned back to her.

'My dear, you must be very proud.'

Did she look proud? She hoped so, but she wasn't, not really; she was disappointed. For a minute she'd thought it had just happened, this brave thing Jim had done, which meant he was definitely alive. That was all she cared about. But then she saw the date. His 'conspicuous gallantry' had taken place in May, for goodness' sake, not recently. It was months ago, and it didn't tell her a thing except that Jim was courageous, which she knew already. She wished he'd told her himself: she felt foolish, not knowing.

So, not a word about it, eh?'

'No, he didn't say.'

'Don't suppose he'd want to worry you … telling you about this sort of jaunt. And you know, he'll only just have found out himself, officially. Probably had a fair idea, but he'd want to be sure before he let you know.'

He went off in high spirits, but before he left he invited her to visit the following Sunday:

'Come for tea … we'll send a man and a trap for you; we can't having you walking in your delicate condition!'

It took her a while to decide what to wear. She'd managed so far by letting out and adding panels to her ordinary summer dresses, but none of them seemed smart enough for tea at Fairstead Hall. In the end she took her best dress and shortened it, then used the blue silk she'd cut off to enlarge it where it wouldn't fit any more. Good job hemlines had changed so much. Once she'd trimmed her best hat with some new ribbon she felt ready, presentable.

And of course, Edith was very kind, leading her through to the drawing room and feeding her up, as she put it, with scones and cake. She looked her up and down, as if she were a mare in foal.

'Elsie, I hope you don't mind my saying that you really are too thin. It's well seen that your husband isn't here to keep an eye on you!'

'Well, Grace – Mrs Binns – is always cooking for me, it's just that some of the time I don't feel hungry.'

'Good Lord, when I was expecting I ate all the time! Mind you, I've never been a slip of a thing like you. Even so, you need some flesh on you if you're going to … my dear, what's wrong?'

Too much kindness. She could feel the tears, fat and wet, begin to roll down her cheeks. She scraffled in her bag, but couldn't find her hanky.

'Here, have mine.'

'Thank you.'

'I expect you're very worried, my dear.'

'Yes.'

'It's natural that you should be, but you know, Jim's like Archie, he's made of strong stuff.'

'I know, but you hear such dreadful things … so many men are dead.' She was sobbing now. She must have wept a whole sea of tears since February. An ocean.

'You know … when my girls were very little, Archie was off fighting in Africa. It was quite dreadful, not knowing what was going on. But he came through it, and now he's a Grandpapa.'

'How could you bear it, not knowing?'

'Well … I just did. We officers' wives have to stand up straight and get on with it.'

'What if he's lying somewhere now, at this very minute, hurt or …'

'Elsie, listen to me. If anything happens to Jim, they will tell you. If he's wounded they'll send you a telegram. If he's missing they will send you a telegram. And if …well, whatever happens, they'll send you a telegram. And I'm sure it won't happen, so just concentrate on looking after yourself and that baby. Think how happy Jim must be, knowing that the next time he sees you he'll be seeing you *both*.'

It was impossible not to be reassured; Edith was so certain about everything. It was just a matter of waiting: for the baby to come, for the war to end, for Jim to come home.

251

She hadn't really wanted to go to the Pumphreys on her own, but afterwards she was glad she'd been and she felt stronger and happier than she had done in weeks. She would try to eat more and smile more; she would relax with Eleanor and Annie, sit at the counter sometimes. Share their conversation.

That night she slept well for the first time in months, waking only when the sun filtered through her curtains. She took her time; she ate breakfast with Grace and even wandered into the back garden. The bench had become grimy without the men using it: she should fetch a cloth and wipe it down. There were a few roses left among the brown and wilting stubs; late flowers, startlingly red. She dead-headed the bush, picked a few of them. It was warm enough to be without a coat, and she enjoyed the walk to Erringtons in the morning sun, so she dawdled, taking the longer route past the churchyard so that she could go in and lay the roses on her parents' grave; she didn't go there often enough.

It was Tuesday morning, and both women were at the counter as she opened the door. As soon as the bell sounded Eleanor lifted the hinged counter and came straight over to her, taking her by the arm and leading her to where they kept a chair for older customers to rest their legs.

'Why am I in the old wifey chair?' Why? Eleanor's lips were set in a thin line. She was flushed. 'What's wrong?' She could feel the panic rising as she looked at Eleanor's face.

'The lad's been. He missed you at the house and Grace sent him on here. He's on his way.'

'What lad?'

'The telegram lad.'

THIRTY TWO

Ivan

This'll do. It'll have to. He needed somewhere to rest the horses after they'd taken the guns forward in a few days' time, assuming the push went well that is. There wasn't a lot of cover: just a few tree stumps, ragged poles that had once been a fair sized wood by the looks of it … but they'd have the Hun under control by then. They hoped. He stowed his binoculars and leaned back to light another cigarette. It was going to be a big show tomorrow, no doubt about that. The front line stretched out of sight; thousands of men, just waiting. He looked over to High Wood where the Hun had machine guns in concrete bunkers. They'd held out there for two months and the bloody things were like last year's conkers: soaked in vinegar, smashing all comers, every game won. His side needed some bigger conkers; that was the problem.

He set off back to do his evening inspection; it was getting late and he wanted to use what remained of the daylight. He passed back along the cramped communication trench, nodding at men he knew, pulling up now and then for a word. Poor buggers, they knew what was coming. As he neared the relative safety of his own position, well behind the line, he saw a group of officers up ahead; they were standing together, deep in conversation. He stopped dead. One of them looked his way and caught his eye. As he stood and stared, the officer had a brief word with one of the others and then walked towards him.

'Ivan.'

'Jim.' He looked older, tougher. Not surprising.

'I thought you might be here. God knows there's enough of us. But I didn't expect to see you. I was hoping not to.'

'You're Captain then.'

'Yes, I am. We've lost too many officers. They know who we are: snipers pick us off.'

'You do know, don't you?'

'What about?'

'About Elsie.'

'About you and Elsie? Of course I do; you know that.'

There was no emotion in his voice. Not even anger.

'No, I mean …'

'That she's going to have a baby? Yes, I know that, too.'

He watched as his big brother paused, took out a cigarette, lit up, and took a long, hard drag, staring at the ground.

'Jim, I …'

'Did she write to you, to tell you?'

'No, she didn't.' He wished she had; she should have let him know.

'Well, that's something.'

'Jim, listen …'

'Ivan, if you're going to apologise, don't; it's too late. Don't do it.'

'No, it wasn't that. But I've got something … here … you should have it.'

He pulled the envelope from his tunic pocket; it was stained and a bit torn with all the handling.

'Here. It's yours.'

Jim frowned, but he took the envelope. He lifted the flap and drew out the photograph … Elsie standing in the garden, the sun on her hair. His eyes closed, briefly.

'You shouldn't have left without it, Jim.'

'And you shouldn't have taken it … or her.' He was still gazing at the image.

'Yeah, I know.'

'Thank you.'

Jim's hands were shaking as he put the photograph back in the envelope, then pushed it into his breast pocket, smoothing it down as if he was making sure it wouldn't disappear.

'Well, good luck.'

He wanted to touch him, put his hand on his shoulder, *anything*.

'Will you be coming back? To Bellingham, I mean?'

'No.'

'Good.'

What else did he expect him to say? But it still cut like a bayonet.

'Will you let me know when the child's born?'

'I don't know. Elsie might.'

'If you let her.'

'If I let her?' He was shaking his head with a pained half smile.

Over Jim's shoulder he saw one of the other officers walking towards them. Jim must be needed. He was nearly level with them. Time's up.

'Right Sir, I'll be off Sir, good luck Sir!' He saluted Jim then the other Captain, who looked from Jim to him expectantly.

'Off you go, Corporal.'

He turned and set off blindly, just wanting to get away. He touched his empty pocket; he already felt lost without the photograph. Why had he given it back? It had been his talisman, his good luck charm, always there, part of his uniform. Fuck it! Out of sight he stopped for breath; he wasn't ready to deal with horse or man just yet. It was right, though, to hand it over, because Elsie had always been Jim's, not his. Damn, that's what he should have said, he shouldn't have let himself be gagged. He turned and set off back, jogging now, but when he reached the place where they'd been standing the officers had gone. There were lines of men, all laden with full fighting kit, feet tramping towards the front line, but no Jim. It'd have to wait.

It was a grey dawn on the fifteenth. Their own guns had been going all night, knocking all hell out of the German front line was the idea. He'd tried to get some sleep but his meeting with Jim, even more than the bombardment, kept him wide awake with a rough, tense headache. He got up and went to where the horses were shifting and whinnying. They were safe for now. He walked slowly along the ranks, enjoying their familiar touch and smell, looking out for anything that would prevent the animals from doing their job when they were called forward.

'Hey, Sir, come'n have a look at this.'

He walked over to where he could see what the lad was looking at.

'What is it, Mikey?'

'It's one of them … it's a land ship.'

Mikey handed over his binoculars and he trained them on the front line over to his left.

He watched as whatever it was thundered slowly and heavily across the rough terrain in the distance. He'd heard about them, but seeing was believing. *Christ, it looked fearsome.*

'What d'ye reckon, Sir?'

'Well, I'd rather be this side of them than over there with the Boche, that's for sure.'

He gave Mikey his binoculars back and took his own out.

Whatever was going on, it was happening at a snail's pace. He lit a cigarette and watched, fascinated, as the metal giant trundled towards the line. He could see men around, officers presumably, gesticulating. This way, this way.

'They're dead slow, mind, eh?'

'Doesn't matter how slow they are if you can't stop them.'

'I could walk twice as fast!'

'I tell you, it doesn't matter.'

There'd been rumours about some secret weapon or another for months but this was the first time they'd actually seen one. The top brass had great hopes: the infantry can just walk behind them, finishing the job.

'Them fuckin' German machine guns won't hurt that lot!'

'Doesn't look as if anything could hurt them from where I'm standing.'

He scanned the line. There was another of the things to the right; presumably there'd be more – the front stretched for miles.

'This should change things, if there's enough of them.'

'Grand!' Mikey was grinning from ear to ear.

Because something needed to change. They'd been on the Somme for months now, but they were getting nowhere. They'd lost more than enough men and horses from day one, and it felt like they could be there for ever. The fifteenth was going to be a big day, and they were up to strength with drivers and shoe-smiths and the horses were fit for the job; he'd seen to that. They might end up taking munitions forward, as well as the gun tenders, but only if the troops advanced into German-held territory. Let's hope so.

****

At 6.20 the attack started. It wasn't long before the horses were being moved forward to shift guns and ammunition. As

257

the day wore on the news from the front was patchy: How's it going? Fucked if I know; could be worse. They'd smashed through the German line, taken their objectives. Best of all, they'd smashed the Hun's prized conker: they'd taken High Wood. But it'd been even tougher than expected, and there'd been a terrible cost in lives. The Boche were still at it though, pounding back with heavy artillery; all night the field guns kept going, an endless wailing. At his end the horses had taken a hammering and they'd done a lot of patching up work, all without their sergeant and one of the private smiths who'd been injured by a stray shell. He and the other corporal had taken on responsibility, working through the night to make the horses safe and as comfortable as they could manage.

* * * *

It went on for a week. They'd advanced, but not enough to make a difference. The hellish rain had started again and the Hun was still there fighting back, but with reinforcements. Had the ruddy great machines made a difference? Not much by the looks of it. Most of the buggers'd broken down or got stuck; you could see them dotted around, like stray boulders on a ploughed field. He'd take a closer look, when he could. For now he was doing a triage with the injured horses, trying to get as many as possible fit to work again. It took a good few days before he could make his way to the Fusiliers' HQ, in a small quarry about half a mile from his base.

'Sir, I'm trying to get in touch with my brother, Captain James Errington of the …'

'Not good timing, Corporal. Is it important?'

'Yes, Sir.' *Very important.*

'Well, you'll have to wait a while. Just sit there will you.'

'I'll wait outside Sir, if that's all right.'

He went outside and stood in the September sunshine.

It was blissfully quiet in the quarry apart from the noise of boots as men passed in and out of the hut. He lit a cigarette and looked over to the shattered remains of High Wood. It had never been high really, not compared with the flowing forests of the North Tyne Valley. And it wasn't even a wood, now: not a branch left, never mind foliage. Christ only knew what horrors would be lying in the undergrowth.

'Corporal?'

The adjutant was at the door, a sheaf of papers in his hand.

THIRTY THREE

Elsie

Archie insisted on a memorial service. She knew it was the proper thing to do, but it was all she could manage to get up in the mornings; the simplest act made her weary, and if it hadn't been for Grace and Mary she'd have sat in front of the fire all day, or stayed in bed. It was Grace who took her home after she read the telegram. She remembered smiling at customers and people on the street as Grace guided her out of the door and through the town. She must have looked mad, crazed, being led like a child, clutching the telegram. Mary came, knocking on the door in the mid-evening. She'd been told and she'd come to be with her, never saying, 'I know how it is', but she did know. Other people had called earlier in the day, but Grace had seen to them, making endless cups of tea; there was gingerbread on the table. When Mary arrived, she heard her voice down in the hall and dragged herself off her bed and along to the top of the stairs.

'Should I come down? Or will you come up?'

'Wait there.'

They laid their ghost, but it took a while: for her it meant a couple of hours in a painful spiral of honesty. Mary listened, mainly.

'He hated me, when he left. He didn't even want me to be at the station with him.'

'No, he wouldn't. I can see why, can't you? He was angry.

260

But he didn't hate you.'

'How do you know?'

'Because he loved you.'

'Yes, he did, before. But I ruined everything.'

'Not everything. And love doesn't just disappear when something bad happens.'

'His did. And it didn't just happen … I did it.'

'Not just you, remember. What about Ivan?'

'He tried not to, you know; for ages.

'Not hard enough. Not long enough.'

'And now Jim's dead.'

'But you didn't kill him. Elsie, listen to me: you didn't kill Jim.'

'I don't care who killed him; he should be alive. It's me that should be dead, not him.'

'Which do you think he'd choose? Of those two, which would he choose?'

'Well, he'd be wrong.'

'And your baby?'

That was the thing. That was where they kept ending up: with the baby. When Grace brought up some hot milk at ten o'clock, it was the child they were talking about, not its father, and Mary had agreed to come back to work.

The memorial service was grand, fitting. Archie and Edith took complete control, inviting all the right people: the Mayor was there, and some councillors, the ones still at home, too old to have been called up. A couple of officers came, to represent his regiment; they wore their swords. Where was his sword? Archie's sword, and his pistol? She needed to ask. Customers and friends packed the church behind her and some even stood outside in the rain. She was glad it was raining: it somehow felt right. Half way through there was a hymn, *O love that wilt not let me go* … It was Jim's

261

favourite and the only bit of the service she'd chosen herself, but as soon as she started to sing her lips began to tremble, and then the simple harmony took away what was left of her self-possession. She sat down in the pew, her body rigid with anguish as the congregation sang.

> *O joy that seekest me through pain,*
> *I cannot close my heart to thee;*
> *I trace the rainbow through the rain,*
> *and feel the promise is not vain*
> *that morn shall tearless be.*

More than anything, more than life itself, she hoped that this was how Jim had felt when he died: that he couldn't close his heart to her. Not Jesus ... *her*. And the child kicking inside her; he would have loved the child, wouldn't he?

Archie wore his medals on a dark suit. He spoke about Jim: what a fine man he'd been, what a courageous soldier and an inspirational officer. How he'd earned his MC. That he was a devoted husband, and would have been a loving father, if only he'd been spared. She could feel people staring at her when he said this, as if they'd only just realised the full implication of this death among other deaths. There was sobbing, not just hers. Then a soldier stood up at the back of the church to play The Last Post, and the haunting voice of the bugle echoed round the vaulted ceiling.

Afterwards they couldn't go and stand at the grave because there wasn't one, so she stood in the porch and shook hands with everyone, thanking them for coming. Actually there *was* a grave. She'd had a letter from his commanding officer telling her that they'd found his body the following day, during a pause in the butchery, and they'd carried him back behind the lines. The machine guns had been stopped by then. He'd been brave, done his duty, died a hero. He wasn't alone: thousands of men in his division had been killed or wounded that day. She wanted to make time go backwards and make him wounded in action, not dead. It was greedy to want him totally uninjured – she knew that – but let someone else have that bullet, the fatal one. At least he'd been buried, so she didn't have to imagine anything worse.

When she'd had a word with everyone she went back inside, to have a minute to herself before going over to Fairstead Hall. The Pumphries had laid lunch on, everyone welcome, but it was a couple of miles away so most of the congregation would be along at The Crown; Archie had seen the owner for her, left enough money at the bar to buy drinks for all the regulars.

There was a horse and trap waiting for her at the gate, and Grace and Mary were already up, waiting for her. It had stopped raining and weak October sunlight was filtering through the thinning clouds, onto the puddles.

'Elsie?' It was Lily.

Edith had sent personal notification to Lily and the other relations. There'd been cousins and an uncle from Newcastle in the church, but she didn't really know them. Lily had sat with them in the family pew, but they hadn't even exchanged a glance until now.

'Thank you for coming, Lily.'

'He was my brother.'

'Where's Frank?'

'He's gone.'

'Gone where?'

'To France. As a driver, in the Army Service Corps.'

'So his knee wasn't bad enough; to keep him at home?'
The limping hadn't worked, then.

'No. When's the baby due?'

'Soon. A few weeks.'

'And have you heard from Ivan?'

Ah, there it was: that way Lily had of twisting the knife, even here, even now.

'Yes. He wrote … after. He's left the horses – joined the infantry. He wants to be on the front line.'

'Why? Why would he do that? He's such a fool.'

Lily didn't understand. She probably wouldn't even if she'd read Ivan's letter. When they'd told him Jim was dead he'd gone straight away and asked to step down from shoe smithing: too safe, too far away from the action most of the time. And anyway, older men were coming over now, conscripted, people not as fit as him but well able to do his job. He'd been allocated to the Northumberland Fusiliers, Jim's regiment; he wasn't sure if it was deliberate. He'd kept his rank, not that he cared one way or another: he just wanted to kill Germans. The letter was angry, not like Ivan at all, but that's what guilt did: it made you angry.

'I think he wants to take Jim's place.'

'Again.'

'I mean, on the front line.'

'And after the war? Will he take Jim's place then, too?'

'No.'

'No?'

'Not even for the sake of the child?'

She'd heard enough. She turned away, went back through the porch and walked carefully down the slippery path to the trap. Will helped her up and she sat between Grace and Mary, a woolen blanket over her knees, as they clattered out of town. She wished she could just go straight home, locked away from all the sympathy.

* * * *

The parcel arrived only few days later. It was on the kitchen table when she came home in the middle of the afternoon. Grace was there, waiting for her.

'Sit down, pet. I'll make you a cup of tea.'

She turned the heavy package over and her heart lurched when she saw where it had been sent from: Cox's Bank in London.

'It's his things, isn't it?'

'I think so, yes.'

'Will you help me?'

'Of course I will. Or should I fetch Mary along from the shop? Would you like that?'

'Yes, please. If you don't mind going. I'll just wait here.'

She tried to undo the knots in the string, but her nails were brittle and she couldn't manage it, so she sat still at the table, one hand resting on the brown paper package, the other where she could feel the baby, restless inside her. Mary came as soon as she could, leaving Eleanor to close up. She was flushed with walking quickly, and she threw her shawl to one side as she came in.

'Oh heavens, Elsie ...'

'I'm all right. I just didn't want to do it on my own.' It was hard to talk, as if there were something stuck in her throat.

'Do you want me to open it? We could light the fire; you could sit in the parlour while Grace and I sort through it, and just ... we'll keep what you'd want of it. I'm sure we'll know.'

'No, I neeed to be here.'

She stood up, clinging to the edge of the table as Mary opened it up, cutting the string and carefully folding back the layers of paper. His uniform, or most of it, was there. It was neatly folded, but filthy, reeking of mud and death, the stench of the slaughterhouse. And his tunic was inked with his blood, stiff with it. Unspeakable. She retched and turned

265

away; Jim had always smelled wonderful. This was horrid.

'Just take it away, please. I don't want it. Why have they sent it? Mary, why? Who could possibly want to get foul stuff like this back?'

'It belongs to you, that's why.'

'Well I don't want it! Oh God … you can see the bullet hole, there in the top pocket. Please take it away!'

Mary took the tunic into the scullery out of sight. Then there was his soft cap, and his shirts, his breeches and quite a few of his other clothes, but all of them stinking. She felt panicky. *Please take them away … burn them or something.*

Other than that there was his wallet, his watch and a few books. And an envelope, dirty and blood-stained.

'What's that? What's in there?'

She reached over and picked it up. Someone had written in pencil, *found in Captain Errington's breast pocket (left)*. She folded back the flap. Inside was her letter, the one telling him about the baby. With it was a photograph, creased and faded: the bullet had nicked the edge and it was blotched with his blood, but she could still make out the sun shining on her hair. So she'd been there with him. When he died, she'd been with him.

The following morning her pains started. It might not have been: there were moments when she thought *no, this can't be it*; there wasn't a definite beginning. Her date was a couple of weeks ahead, so she waited. Then she grew sure that it would be soon, *today*. She stayed in the office, keeping the accounts up to date because that was all they'd let her do now, these women who'd become a family of sorts. Sitting among the invoices and receipts, stopping now and then to clutch her belly, her pains became regular, then shocking. She closed the ledger and put it away, as if she wasn't coming back.

'I think I need to go home.'

266

'When, now?'

'Yes, I think so. Yes, now. I think so.'

They took control, so all she had to do was walk with Mary, slowly, back to the house. Grace had prepared the room for her, Lily's old room newly painted, with fresh linen on the wide bed and a fire laid in the grate. It'd been ready for weeks now, long before the baby was. Grace went to tell Doctor Armstrong and Mary sat with her. In the mirror, on the dressing table Lily hadn't wanted to take with her, she could see her reflection: the huge belly, her eyes puffy, her skin damp with the all the effort.

Doctor Armstrong called in after his evening surgery. He patted her hand, told her she was doing well, not too long now. It was seven o'clock, and she was already exhausted and weepy, telling him she couldn't stand it for much longer. Even so, it was only as the first streaks of a pink dawn appeared, long hours after her courage had given way to exhausted sobbing, that the midwife finally eased the baby out and cut the cord.

'You have a son, Mrs Errington. A fine boy.'

'A son? Let me see ...'

Now he lay in her arms, swaddled, too worn out with being born to feed as they'd been urging him to; his pink mouth was slack on her nipple.

'Leave him be; he needs some sleep, poor mite.'

She kissed his head, with its dark hair still oily and matted. Her son: sleeping, beautiful James. She was too tired to doze, so she just lay and gazed at him. Later, when the square under her bedroom window came alive with passers-by, she stood with him in her arms, looking down, wondering how a world that had changed so completely since yesterday could carry on regardless.

She should write to Ivan.

THIRTY FOUR

Ivan

He was still having nightmares after weeks in hospital and a month's convalescence, and always the same horror: acres of barren, pitted mud and in every foul hole a wounded man crying for water, food, human contact … but the noise of the battle went on and on like Hareshaw Burn in spate, thundering over the Linn, and the pain and the utter loneliness went on with it, until there was silence worse than the noise and he woke up, sweating.

It was all because they hadn't been able to keep up, that was the problem: the ground had been a cratered morass and every yard took it out of you. Men had drowned. They'd fallen headfirst into stagnant, putrid water with so much kit they couldn't fight their way out and they'd drowned for fuck's sake.

His own lot had been on the left of the attack, and they'd been doing relatively well – nearly reached their final objective – but the bloody snipers were picking them off, one after another. If the shells didn't get you, they did, until they'd been ordered back to where they started. Twelve officers and over three hundred men killed or worse by nightfall, and for what? He'd been one of the 'or worse', caught by shrapnel and flung to the ground. He'd lain still until after dusk, then used his elbows and knees to drag himself to where there was a bit of cover. Some other poor bugger'd got there before him, except his bottom jaw was missing, and part of a shoulder; he'd been dead for a while and his eyes had gone: crows or rats. He'd closed his own eyes and waited for darkness so he couldn't see the hideous thing lying beside him.

It took a few hours before he'd found enough courage to work out the damage. His right arm had taken a hammering; he'd known that straight away. And he was bleeding from his side and his right leg; nothing seemed to be missing, but he'd lost a lot of blood and something was broken, perhaps the ankle. Definitely not the knee. Maybe he'd live then, if they found him before too long. What was too long? If he'd known it was going to be three days he'd probably have given up on the first night, when the pain set in. But he had drinking water and some emergency rations, and he took his dead companion's water as well. The nights were the worst, when he could hear the other wounded, some of them screaming like children in the darkness. On the third day – when there were fewer alive, or they were too weak to cry out – it was better.

By the time they found him he'd passed reason and was able to joke with the stretcher bearers, 'Six of you? What did you think was out here?' Six of them, because the mud was thick and treacherous as they trudged slowly back to the line where the medics would take over. They'd dumped his stretcher on the duckboards at the bottom of the trench and gone straight off, their faces white with tiredness … either that, or with what they were seeing out there. Hours later, the doctor looked him over, bandaged him up, gave him some morphine and then sent him further back again, first to a field hospital, then to the casualty clearing station at Bailleul.

Bailleul. What he remembered was the purity of it all: the startling white of the sheets and the nurses' uniforms after weeks and weeks of drab earth and grey skies. He'd been filthy when he arrived, ingrained with blood and battlefield muck; verminous too. Back there, in the line, it'd felt normal, but as the girl undressed him, with her scrubbed white hands and pale cheeks, he'd felt humiliated.

'I'm disgusting. Sorry.'

She'd just raised an eyebrow as she continued her expert clipping, stripping away the stained fabric of his uniform.

'If you were any cleaner I'd have to wonder where you'd been.'

Such a wise response. Had she been taught it? He wanted to be clean again, to be as immaculate as she was.

He'd lain back, relieved beyond expression to be in such capable hands, except that his own hand was a mess, so heavily bandaged that he didn't know much except that one, maybe two, fingers had been too mangled to keep. He closed his eyes as she went from head to toe, from one bandage to another, bathing sound flesh and gently cleaning raw wounds. As she started on his right leg, he watched her eyes and asked.

'When will I play football again, d'ye think?'

He wasn't going to mention being a blacksmith; he wasn't a fool.

'You've a broken tibia – that's your shin – and lacerations … deep ones. But it should mend, if we keep the leg clean. So if it's not too rough a game?' She had such a kind smile.

She moved on to his arm and hand:

'What about knitting?'

'Now, that may be a little more difficult.'

Oh Christ. He forced himself to watch as she peeled back the dressing. The pain was bad, but the sight of it was worse. He'd lost his little finger and the ring finger next to it, and the rest of the hand was discoloured and messy. It smelled foul. The nurse's face gave little away, but he wasn't surprised when the doctor came and told him that they were going to have to

270

take the rest of it.

'Won't it clean up?'

'We can't risk it; better to act now and save the rest of the arm, and your life, for that matter. Sorry, Corporal, but you know the score.'

That was back in late October, and since then he'd been slowly learning how to be healthy and safe again. He'd been sent to the base hospital at Rouen, spending Christmas with other men too damaged to go back to the front. Some of them were convalescent but hoping to re-join their battalions; others, like him, were glad to be out of it. Conscription had spread through England like a virus after 1916, so he was with men who'd never wanted to fight in the first place, or who'd been boys at school when it all kicked off in '14. The news wasn't good either, from the little they could wheedle out of the hospital staff. The Hun was doing well. They'd stood – those who could – round the battered old piano and sung carols, but peace on earth goodwill to all men had stuck in his craw and he'd dried up.

He was ready to go home, now. The impulse to kill had left him, if he'd ever really had it. Jim's death had tipped him into despair for a while, but he'd been on the edge anyway. He'd left the horses and joined the infantry with a pure intention – vengeance for the killing of his only brother. He'd been depraved, for a while. He'd heard men boasting about wiping out the enemy and he wanted to be like them; no conscience, no regret. He'd tried, but it hadn't worked, and he'd started almost immediately to find ways to *not* kill; for nearly a year he'd aimed and fired to miss, because once his anger dissipated, sorrow was what replaced it. Nothing else.

Half way through the last year he'd received a letter from Elsie, dated months before, to say he was a father. She didn't say that as such, but she'd written to tell him that she'd had

271

a son, James, born on the second of November. She hadn't mentioned the business, or Lily; just said he was a beautiful boy, a true Errington. They were both doing well. He'd written back, told her how happy he was to hear the news, that he'd be home soon on leave … or perhaps the endless war might end … but then he'd been wounded at Passchendaele.

So there he was, in Lincoln, in a hospital where people like him were being helped to feel better about having bits missing from their bodies, or being disfigured; unrecognizable even to themselves, some of them. He was better than most, really: his broken leg had mended. The slashes in his flesh where the shrapnel had torn into him had healed too, leaving proud welts on his chest, his arm, his neck. It was his hand that bothered him most, or the absence of it. He was learning to use his left hand for everything, but it was awkward and limited. They called him plucky, used him as an example – 'That's the spirit!' – but it was all show; he was sickened by the very sight of his stump and at a loss to know what he was going to do for the rest of his life if he couldn't be a smith, or a vet, or anything else useful.

Whatever he'd imagined about him and Elsie, about the future, it hadn't included him being a one-handed cripple. If she wanted him to be father to his son, would he even be able to pick him up? He'd be walking by now, probably. As soon as they let him out of here and gave him his discharge papers he'd be there. They'd told him he'd be away by the end of February.

THIRTY FIVE

February 1918

Elsie

'I've got you!'

She smiled as Mary plucked Jamie up as he tottered away from her, swinging him round to make him giggle, as he always did.

'That child is ruined!'

'I know.'

'He's got the whole lot of us exactly where he wants us.'

'And why not? Why not, the little precious!'

Mary handed him over to her, kissing his cheek on the way. It was true: he had them all in the chubby palm of his hand, customers included. What with his big brown eyes and lashes far too long for a lad, all he had to do was smile and your heart stopped. Even Archie, Godfather despite his age, couldn't keep away.

She carried him over to the door where he'd been heading, and opened it so that they could look outside. It was piercingly cold, even though there was a bright sun in the clear blue February sky. He pointed at this and that and watched some children race past, but the streets were quiet; the shop was quiet. It all looked a bit sparse, even though they'd moved things round, spread it out; German submarines were causing havoc so they were short of a lot of their usual stock, and rationing had started. Sugar was like gold dust. They were the lucky ones though; the poor folk in the cities were the ones with the problem, not country people. She'd taken on two ex-soldiers, unfit to fight again, to plant up half the Errington field: they had plenty of vegetables for the house and to sell; they could hold their own until things changed. God knew when that would be though: nobody had known in 1914 that they'd still be fighting four years later.

Jamie was wriggling to get down, wanting to explore.

'Wait a minute, little man.'

She closed the door and set him down, pulling over a basket of onions for him to empty and refill. He was deft, rarely dropping anything; he was going to be good with his hands. He glanced up at her and beamed, an onion in each palm as if he were going to juggle, then offered her one, holding it up as gift.

'Thank you, my angel.'

'Do I get one, too?'

Mary knelt down beside him and held out her hand. His brows furrowed as he sorted through the basket to find exactly the right onion, then placed it gently onto her palm with another wide smile.

'That's a lovely present. Thank you, Jamie.'

He was the lovely present. This time, since Jim died and Jamie was born, had been the worst and best of her life. Days passed when she didn't have time to grieve because she had a son to look after, but every now and then, especially during the winter nights, she couldn't shake off the longing, when being alone turned into feeling lonely. Little by little she'd been able to share this with Mary. In November, after Jamie's first birthday, Mary had stayed for supper one night and they'd sat together in the parlour, feet toasting against the brass rail. Jamie was long asleep and Grace was in the kitchen where she liked to sit with her sewing. Elsie had poured them each a glass of sherry, giggling as she told Mary about Lily's 'Just a small glass for me'.

'She used to have one "just a small glass" after another. Ivan used to offer her a tankard sometimes, just to see what she'd say. Their mother was the same.'

'And here we are, going in the same direction.'

'We've certainly earned it …'

They'd sat there, companionably. It *was* hard, trying to keep the shop going, even with three of them. Elsie was leaving Jamie with Grace for a few hours every morning so that she could concentrate on the paperwork and ordering, but Mary and Eleanor – Annie had left, gone to live with her brother and his wife in Haltwhistle – often needed her in the afternoon, so she'd take him with her. He was fine, with three of them to keep an eye on him, but it was exhausting. They didn't even have Will any more: he'd been called up months ago, so Eleanor had taken on the deliveries, although she wasn't so keen on Daisy. She'd started to think about buying a van, after the war. She'd need a man to drive it.

'D'you ever think about finding someone else?'

'Not really. I don't think I can imagine being with anyone except John.'

'But you're only twenty five. Surely you aren't just going to give up on life.'

'Is that what you think? That I've given up? It's not even three years, Elsie.'

'No, I don't mean *now*, I mean eventually, after the war, won't you?'

'I don't know. There won't be many men left. Not here, anyway. It's awful.'

'I miss him. In my bed, I mean. I hate it. I hate sleeping alone.' *There, she'd said it.*

'I rather gathered that.'

She'd looked at Mary, who'd continued to gaze at the flames, all innocence. There was still *that* between them, even though she'd come back and was like an aunty to James and was such a good friend, and they worked together all the time. There was still *that*.

'I mean Jim, I miss *Jim*.' And it was true.

'Well, of course you do.'

They'd changed the subject that evening, but over the months they'd begun to talk more freely, both of them, and with the talking she felt released somehow ... perhaps forgiven. It was a good feeling. Now, as she saw her with Jamie, it was hard to believe that there'd been months on end when Mary'd stayed away because of him, before he was born.

* * * *

'Could you watch him while I pop over to The Crown before it gets dark? They came across with an order earlier on; just a few bits and pieces.'

'Would you like me to go?'

'No, I'll do it, but don't let him charm his way into the sugar bag!'

She packed up the order and set off, wrapped up against the late afternoon chill. It was good to walk at her own pace now and then, stretching her legs and creating her own warmth; she could feel her cheeks beginning to glow with the exercise. And Mary loved having Jamie to herself: he'd be licking the sugar from his fat little fingers by now, no doubt. She passed some boys playing football in the street, yelling and laughing, barging into each other as they fought for the ball. It came skidding along the cobbles towards her and she put her basket down and kicked it back. Their surprised faces made her laugh out loud.

276

'Hey Missus, ye can be on wor team if yer like!'

'Well, I would, but I've got a delivery to do.'

'Wey, after that? Howay …'

'Sorry lads, another time.'

She walked on, wondering how many of the boys would still have a father, one that they recognized, by the end of the war. She knew that at least two of them already didn't; the town was scattered with children like that, and there'd be more as things got worse over there. She walked faster, dropped off the order in the kitchen of The Crown, refusing a cup of tea because she wanted to get back; the sky was beginning to close over and she needed to light the lamps. The boys were still larking about as she made her way back. A few of them waved at her, and she waved back. A few years' time and maybe Jamie would be out here, with scabby knees and a runny nose. They looked happy enough, in spite of everything.

There was a customer at the counter when she got back, standing with his back to the door. Another man home on leave, by the look of the uniform. Mary was serving him. The room was gloomy, she *must* light the lamps, but where was Jamie? She looked over to where his empty pram stood at the far side of the shop.

'Mary? Where's Jamie?'

There was a brief silence, and then the customer turned round. He was holding Jamie in front of him, in his arms, as if it were the most ordinary thing.

'Here he is. I've got him, don't worry.'

Ivan. It was Ivan, holding their son. Did Mary know who it was? Of course, or she wouldn't have let him hold Jamie.

'Ivan?' She was shaking. 'Why didn't you tell me you were coming? You look well.'

'I didn't know for sure until the day before yesterday, and

then I just thought I'd just come. I'm sorry.'

Jamie was squirming now and beginning to whimper; he held his arms out to her. She went over and took him, and he relaxed in her arms, thumb in his mouth.

'Are you here on leave, or what? They said you'd been hurt. I wrote to you …'

'I won't be going back.' His voice was quiet. Almost a whisper.

'Why? I mean, are you saying that you won't, or you *can't*?'

Without any warning his face twisted and he began to weep. He turned away in the half light, his shoulders heaving. She passed Jamie over to Mary, and then went to him and wrapped her arms round him. There was nothing to say; whatever had brought it on was beyond words. It was shocking, his grief; the loud sobbing of a man who hadn't wept for a long time; she could only imagine what horror had brought it on. She knew of a woman whose husband had come home on leave and it'd been a disaster … he couldn't talk about it, but there wasn't anything else he wanted to talk about either, not really. Maybe this was the same.

Once she felt she could, she pulled over the chair and gently pushed him onto it, then set about lighting the lamps so that they could do the last few jobs properly. It took a few minutes. Mary walked round with Jamie in her arms, singing silly songs to keep him occupied. Ivan was slumped on the chair, red eyed but calmer, his body still jerking involuntarily every now and then. On an impulse she opened a pack of cigarettes, lit one and handed it to him. He half-smiled briefly and took it with his left hand, keeping his right deep in his pocket. He was shaking now. She noticed a scar on his right cheek, just below his eye.

'Ivan?'

He face crumpled and then he was crying again, quietly

now.

'What is it? Ivan ... *dear*, what is it?' She kneeled down in front of him, tried to take his other hand.

He looked up at her, his eyes brimming, then slowly took his right arm out of his pocket.

'There.' He was looking for her reaction.

'Ivan, why didn't you tell me? Why?' She could hardly bear it – not the wound, but that he hadn't let her know about it.

'I couldn't tell you. What did you want me to write? Dear Elsie, they've just cut my right hand off, love Ivan?'

'Of course not ... but you could have warned me, at least. I wrote to you; why didn't you write back?'

'I don't know. Mind, even if I had written you wouldn't have been able to read it. If you thought my handwriting was bad before, you should see what it's like using my left hand. *Only* hand, that is.'

He spat the words out.

'Don't be like that.'

'Like what?'

'I don't know ... bitter ...angry.'

'Elsie, I *am* bitter and angry. Why shouldn't I be?'

'Because you're alive?'

This was Mary. She'd come over; she might as well, because she was there anyway, and she'd heard everything.

'Corporal Errington, I'm terribly sorry that you've been so badly hurt ... but at least you're here, alive.'

Ivan looked up at her, saw her clearly now that the light was better. He stood up; he looked awkward, but there was no need to shake hands because she was holding Jamie, rocking him gently.

'I've just realised: you're John's wife, aren't you?'

'No, I'm his widow.'

'I'm sorry … that's what I meant …'
'And that's what *I* meant.'

THIRTY SIX

Ivan

'He's my son.'

'Yes, but no-one else knows that.'

'Except you.'

'Yes, of course, me. And Mary. She knows.'

'Mary knows? Why did you tell her? If you wanted to keep it such a secret, why tell Mary?'

'It was Lily. She came into the shop and more or less announced it.'

'But no-one else was there?'

'Just me and Mary. She was being her usual self: it was just to make trouble.'

'Just to make trouble?'

'Just to make trouble. Why else would she do it?'

He nodded. Lily was Lily, nothing changes.

'Elsie, I …'

'You saw him, didn't you? In France …'

He wasn't expecting it, had no idea that she knew.

'Yes.'

'… and you gave him the photograph. The one he left and you took.'

'Yes.'

'Why?'

'Why what? Why did I take it? You know why.'

'Why did you give it to him?'

281

'I don't know. Because he never should have left it. Because I thought he'd want it.'

'And did he? Did he want it?'

'Yes. He took it anyway.'

'He was going to be a father to Jamie. It would have worked, you know.'

'For you it would, definitely, and probably for Jim. Not for me.'

'It's better for Jamie this way.'

'So's he can be proud of his hero father?'

'It's not that. Not *just* that, anyway.'

'Yes it is. You know it is. People say things. I'll be standing in the street and they come over and they say, "Bless the bairn, he'll never know his brave pa ..." They even say it to *me. Christ*, Elsie, can you imagine it? And I just have to stand there and agree with them.

'It's what it should be.'

'It's what it *isn't*, you mean! This is madness.'

'No, it's not. As his uncle you can stay here, being my brother-in-law and making us a family again. You can't be anything else, not now. It's too late.'

So Jamie's going to grow up believing his father's dead, when I'm here all the time? It's cruel, Elsie.'

'Not as cruel as making him a bastard, making me – us – have to move away, because of the disgrace. Don't you see? What good would it do? We have a home here, we have a business. Where on earth would we go?'

'Is it because of this as well?'

He held up his arm, with its leather cover over the stump. He'd expected ... no not expected, *hoped* ... that he and Elsie could be together; perhaps not straight away, but eventually. Why not? He hadn't wanted Jim to die, not at any point. In fact he would willingly have traded places with him for her sake, if that was what she wanted. But the truth was that he he'd been killed and now she was free to be his. Except that she didn't want him. Not now.

'You know me better than that.' She leaned over and touched him, just above where his hand would have been.

'Then why?'

'I've told you. Again and again I've explained. How many times, Ivan?'

'Well tell me again.'

'I let Jim down, badly. We both did. Whatever we felt, what we did was wrong. Wrong, wrong, wrong!'

Was she angry or just upset? Every time they talked it ended the same way: her in tears, him as close to tears as damn it. And it was always late at night because of Grace, so they had these quiet arguments in the kitchen when they were both too tired really, after she'd gone to bed at the other end of the house.

'How can love be wrong? I loved you. I still do.'

'But we had no right to that sort of love. Come on, Ivan; even you can't argue with that. And I'm not going to do it again.'

'So you regret it …us?'

He'd suggested this before, and she'd avoided answering him. When he was in France, when he heard about the baby he'd felt so full of guilt that he'd wanted to die for a while. But he'd never regretted it, not for a second.

'I'm going to bed. Will you lock up and do the lamps if I fill the stove?'

It was hard for him to manipulate the heavy scuttle with one hand; he could fill it out in the coal house using a small shovel, but when he went to lift it and shake the coals into the fire he ended up sending bits of coal skittering over the floor. Then he couldn't handle the brush very well to clear it

283

up, although he was getting better at it.

'Yes, of course. Off you go. And ... I'm sorry, Elsie.'

'For what?'

'For wanting what I can't have.'

'I'll not do anything to spoil Jim's memory.'

'I know.'

She clanged the fire door shut and put the scuttle back down, then washed her hands at the sink. He watched her. It was such a normal thing to do, but even that had become a trial for him: he kept dropping the soap and then it was awkward holding the towel against him with his useless arm to dry his other hand. Pathetic. She came over and wrapped her arms round him from behind, where he sat, so that his head rested back against her. He kept his own arms on the table, not wanting to respond in case she pulled away. She wasn't inviting him: it was what a sister would do, or a mother.

'Let's stop this.'

She left him and went up to her room; he heard her light tread on the stairs. She'd slip along to check on Jamie, then he'd hear the click of her door. Every night since he got back he'd forced himself to wait until she'd be in bed before going up in case he met her on the landing. He was back where he'd been a few years ago, except that now he couldn't escape as he used to. There was no Isabel waiting for him to pull himself together these days.

* * * *

He'd bumped into Isabel a few days after he got back. He'd come up behind her, walking faster than she did, but he didn't recognize her until she said his name as he passed her.

'Ivan?'

'Isabel. I didn't know. Congratulations.'

She was heavily pregnant, her face fuller than it had been.

284

Her long auburn hair was coiled up, hidden under her hat, but her smile hadn't changed a bit.

'Not really. I'm not married, like.'

'Who, then? Why hasn't he married you?'

'You mean, why hasn't me dad seen to 'im?'

'Yeah, I suppose I do.'

'It's Adam Baker, from High Lough. He was home on leave, wounded, then he had to go back.'

'Not badly wounded then?'

'He'd have been worse hurt if the lads had been haem.'

'I bet he would.'

'We're engaged though, he'd already asked us when … well, ye ken.'

He did know. She held up her hand, with its ring, to show him.

'And your brothers?'

'They've both been wounded. Joe's been in the hospital in France. But they're both back at the front just now. What about you, like? You on leave, or what?'

He'd turned his head to show her the scar on his neck, then pulled his arm out of his pocket where he'd kept it. Her eyes had widened, she'd looked at his face. *Don't you dare cry.* After what he'd done to her he didn't want any sympathy. He'd tried to joke about it.

'Not the man I used to be. Not as handy.'

'What about hor?'

'What about her?'

'She's had a bairn an all.'

'Yes, I'm an uncle. James, he's called; Jamie. He's a lovely boy.' What else could he say?

Me brothers guessed. About you and hor. A didn't say nowt til them, mind.'

Maybe, maybe not. They'd parted friends, and he'd

watched as she made her way slowly down the street. No white wedding after all, poor lass.

* * * *

The following morning he walked up to the forge for the first time. John Graham knew he was back of course, but he hadn't been able to face going up there. It was all he'd ever wanted to do, since he was lad and he used to watch the old smith: the way he calmed the horses; the smell of the forge. But there was no way he could take up where he left off, so he'd have to stop being such a lass about it. They needed to talk about what should happen next. If Graham would buy him out he could start thinking about it. What the hell do one-handed people do for a living? Elsie'd suggested he should think about coming into Erringtons. It was as if someone up there was laughing at him.

It was easier than he'd thought it would be. John was half expecting him, and seemed very glad to see him. After a second's hesitation he held out his left hand to shake Ivan's.

'It'll take a bit of getting used to, eh?'

'It will that.'

John showed him what he'd been doing. He'd made some changes, but not enough to make it feel strange to be there. It felt like home. He picked up one of his hammers; weighed it in his hand. He loved the heft of it.

'You'd made a canny business here.'

'It was good of you to take it on.'

'Good of you to ask, man. I lost a lot of work when the horses went, so you don't need to thank me. It's a grand forge.'

He spent well over an hour up there. They discussed figures, agreed on a price for the building and the forge and the tools. No use to him now. He stood to one side as John shoed a mare – not one he knew, but he'd worked for the farmer for years, so they talked while Graham worked. He was careful, steady; a sound man to take over the business. Did that make it better or worse? He wasn't sure.

Afterwards, when he strolled back down to Erringtons, there was a motor car outside, a beauty. He stopped to admire at it. It couldn't be Frank's could it? He hadn't seen Lily yet and he wasn't in any hurry to either. Inside the shop, Mary was serving and Elsie was standing with Jamie in her arms, talking to a man in uniform, an officer. Jamie was reaching out, trying to touch his shiny buttons as his mother talked to him. Who was it? No-one he knew. As he walked in Elsie saw him and turned towards him with a smile.

'Ivan, this is Major Lovage – Edward – Jim's friend from OTC. Do you remember? He spent Christmas at Edward's parents' home when he was down in Cambridge?'

'I do ... of course I do. How do you do, Sir.'

'It's Edward, please. I'm out of it for ten days' leave, so just ignore the uniform.'

'You're in the RAMC aren't you?'

'Yes, I'd qualified as a doctor before the Hun got uppity, so ... little choice.'

'What brings you to Northumberland?'

'Army medical business in Newcastle, then I'm on leave, so I'm having a few days' fishing. I'm staying with the Glantons in Rothbury, so I thought I'd come and say hello on my way there. I'd have known your sister-in-law anywhere, from Jim's description. And this is his boy, I see. Come here, little chap.'

He reached out to take Jamie, who allowed himself to be taken only because he was now in easy reach of the buttons.

'I have loads of nephews and nieces. Love them to bits. He's a fine boy.'

'We think so.'

'There's a strong family resemblance. He looks very like you, Ivan.'

'Yes, they say so.' *Not surprisingly.* 'But then, Jim and I were very similar in some ways.'

'Yes, I can see that. In fact ... if it weren't for the eyes Jamie could be yours.'

'The eyes?'

'Yes.'

THIRTY SEVEN

Elsie

What was he saying? What did he mean, 'If it weren't for the eyes'? She glanced at Ivan but he was looking at Jamie, not her; at his face. She wanted Edward to explain what he meant, but how should she ask without making too much of it?

'What were you saying, about the eyes?' She wasn't sure how her voice would sound until she opened her mouth.

'Well, Ivan has blue eyes, so have you. This little fellow's are brown.'

Jamie was bored with the buttons now and he leaned over towards Elsie, arms outstretched. She took him, then set him down in front of her, leaning slightly to hold both his hands. Edward was looking round the shop, smiling, unaware. Does he think we should understand now? She didn't. But she didn't want to ask again. She glanced at Ivan. He gave her a questioning look.

'Come again?'

'I'm so sorry ... I've become a bit of a genetics bore. All new stuff. Fascinating. Once this wretched war's over I'm hoping to go into it a lot more.'

'So what's this about blue and brown eyes?'

'Do you really want to know? I'm afraid it's a bit dull if you're not particularly interested.'

'No really, we're interested ... go on.' This was Ivan.

'Well, to put it very simply, we all carry these microscopic things called genes; they determine what we're like: tall, short, red-hair, big ears and so on. Are you with me so far? We inherit our genes from our parents, hence family likenesses.'

She nodded, unsure where he was going.

'Some genes are stronger than others. Blue-eye genes are weaker than brown-eye ones. So, when brown-eye meets blue-eye it dominates, usually making an offspring with brown eyes … unless there's a blue-eyed grandparent somewhere on the brown-eyed side, so there'd be a hidden blue gene in there. But two blue-eyed people don't have the brown gene at all so they have blue-eyed children … always. As far as they can tell.'

She was listening, but she couldn't take it in. She glanced at Ivan. He was looking down at Jamie, his expression unreadable.

'It's easier if you see a diagram. I could draw you one?'

'No, I think I've … you say *always*?'

'Well, that's what they say. Nature can always surprise us, but the boffins' papers are pretty definite about it. Height, hair colour and so on seem to be more variable, but the eye colour thing's being used to explain the whole principle. Not sure I've done a very good job though; teaching's not my forté.'

He was looking at them, eyebrows raised.

'No, I think I've understood … it's just so … interesting, isn't it, Ivan?

'It is.' He reached down and took one of Jamie's hands in his.

'Come on, let's you and me go and look at the pretty car.'

She let go of Jamie's other hand and watched as Ivan took him over to the counter. Mary would need to fasten his coat before he could go outside, and she was busy serving.

'I was tremendously fond of Jim. He made a fine officer as well as a good friend.'

'Yes.'

'I just wish I'd known him longer. The war does that. You meet a chap, learn to love him like a brother, then ...'

'I can imagine.'

Her eyes were stinging. There's so much to cry about, so much sorrow.

'Oh goodness, I'm so sorry. I didn't mean to make you upset. Here ...'

He handed her his handkerchief, a crisp white square of linen. It was far too perfect to use so she just clutched it as the tears dribbled down.

'No, *I'm* sorry. It doesn't take very much to make me weepy these days.' She tried to smile.

He took the handkerchief back from her and shook it out, then used it to dab her cheeks, holding her chin.

'You really are exactly as Jim described you.'

'I am?'

'Yes. Look, I'm going to have to get on my way before long. I only called in to pay my respects to you and the family. He'd have wanted me to. You know, my lot loved Jim; he was going to bring you down to stay, after the war.'

'Yes, he told me. I'd have liked that.'

She really would have liked it, but it was too late. They shook hands; he promised to call in again when he was in the North.

'Where's Ivan? I'll just say good bye, then I'll be off.'

Ivan was outside, holding Jamie, talking to a couple of lads on their way home for dinner. They'd crossed the street to admire the car. As the shop door opened he looked over at her with a weak smile, then away again. Edward went over and opened the driver's door, and one of the lads followed

291

him round, peered inside and gave a long slow whistle.

'Wey, Mister, that's a canny car, that, like.'

'Would you two like to climb in for a minute? Get the feel of her?'

'Would wer? Howay!'

He held the door wide to let the pair of them clamber inside. They touched the steering wheel, took the controls, grinning at each other. They couldn't believe their luck.

'You'll never get them out of there.'

'Yes I will: I'll use my best Major's voice; you'll see. Always works.'

In the end he didn't need to. The boys knew when they were onto a good thing and were quick to climb out as soon as they were asked. 'Thanks, Mister', then they dashed off, late for dinner.

Edward started the motor and they waved him away, standing apart on the street. As soon as he was out of sight, Ivan turned to her.

'Where'd he say he was going?'

'Rothbury.'

'I wish he hadn't bloody come.'

'Here, let me have Jamie. It's too cold out here for him.'

'He'll be back.'

Why was he looking at her like that? She took Jamie and went back into the shop, leaving the door open for him to follow her, but he didn't. Mary was stacking packets of tea, but she stopped as soon as she walked in.

'He was rather grand, wasn't he.'

'He certainly was.'

'Don't get many like that round here.'

She took Jamie's coat off and handed him a biscuit to chew on.

'He's a doctor, a friend of Jim's ... *was* his friend, I mean.'

'So he came to … what? Say hello?'

'Yes. But he said more than that. Let's have a cup of tea while it's quiet. I'll tell you.'

She wasn't sure she'd got all the details right, but she managed to explain to Mary what Edward had told them. It helped her to talk about it, but she was worried, now, about Ivan.

'So … how do you feel about it?'

'It's … what I wanted from the beginning. But I can't believe it. It must have been when he came home, the last time.' Her stomach churned at the memory of that last weekend with Jim.

'Ivan's upset, I think. He's gone off.'

'Yes.'

'Where'll he have gone? Do you know?'

'He always used to work his way through things – hammer it out up at the forge – but obviously not now. He can't. So … no, I don't know. He might have gone home, I suppose. I hope.'

'You know you're free now?'

'How d'you mean, "free"?'

'Well, you. From Ivan. And he is, for that matter.'

'He doesn't want to be free, that's the problem.'

'Give him time.'

'Do you think so?'

'I do.'

The shop began to fill again and Jamie finished his biscuit and tottered over to her, arms raised. She lifted him up, regarding his crumb covered face as if she'd never really seen him properly before. Jim's boy. Their son.

Ivan reappeared in the late afternoon looking worn out. It was nearly dark outside, and the rain was turning to sleet. They were both busy serving when he came in, but she mouthed, 'Are you all right?' He nodded briefly, but he didn't look all right: his face was ruddied by the sharp wind but he looked grey and drawn underneath. His hair was windswept, flopping over his forehead, and his boots were caked in mud and ice. *He'd been walking, then.* He went over to the pram where Jamie lay asleep on his back, arms outstretched above his head. He stayed there, his one hand resting on the handle, gazing down at his sleeping nephew.

When she could, Mary ducked under the hinged counter and went over to talk to him. He looked surprised, shook his head, but she persisted. Elsie stayed where she was at the counter, keeping out of earshot, putting up an order. If they needed her, she would know.

Ivan was listening now, head bent forwards to hear what Mary was saying, nodding briefly every now and then. He smiled ... said something, and Mary put her hand on his arm. What had she said earlier, about Ivan? Give him time? She smiled to herself as she measured out some sugar for Dorothy Charlton. You mean, give *me* time, Mary. After a while he came over to her as she packed Dorothy's parcels into a box.

'I'll take Jamie back to the house with me, if you like.'

'Good idea. Grace'll be there to help, if you need her. Don't let him sleep too long, mind.'

'That's fine with me.'

He manoeuvred the heavy pram out of the door. Even though Mary held the door open for him it was still a struggle, but neither of them went to help. He can manage. He would need to learn to manage more than a pram.

She was bone weary by the end of the day, her mind and her body both needed some rest. As they packed away, the telephone rang in the office; Mary was closer, so she nipped through and answered it. Please let it not be something urgent, to deliver tonight; I'm too tired, I want to go home.

'Elsie?'

'Yes?' *Damn!*

'It's Edward Lovage, to speak to you.'

What? Why? Why would he be ringing her?

'Hello? This is Elsie.'

'Hello again. I'm sorry to trouble you. I expect you were just about to go home.'

'Yes, I was. But it doesn't matter.'

'I'm at the Glantons'.'

'Yes.' Why would he ring her just to say that?

'Yes … in Rothbury. It's not so far away, really. Not in the motor.'

'I've never been.'

'No. I suppose not. Look …'

'Yes?'

'I was wondering … might I come over and take you out to lunch?'

'Lunch?'

'Could you get away for an hour? Could someone look after Jamie?'

'When?'

'Whenever you can. I go back south on Friday, then I'm over the channel, back to the show.'

'Well, I'll have to ask …'

She glanced up at Mary; she was standing in the doorway, nodding her head and smiling broadly at her.

'Just a minute please, Edward …'

Mary whispered over to her, still grinning. 'Yes, you can go out for lunch. Yes we can look after Jamie. Say "Yes".'

'Hello? Edward?'

'Yes, I'm here …'

'Would Wednesday be a good day?'

Half day closing.

THIRTY EIGHT

August 1926

A well-dressed couple are taking breakfast in the dining room of the Hotel de la Gare in the town of Albert in Northern France. With them are their two children: a boy aged nearly ten and a girl aged six. The mother seems a little pensive. She's asked for tea, but she doesn't appear to be touching it. She's eaten nothing. The father is in good spirits, talking to the children, answering their questions. He helps his daughter to some jam from the small glass dish on the table. She's very taken with croissants.

'Papa, may we have hot chocolate in bowls when we get home, like this? I like it very much.'

'I don't see why not. You should ask Mama.'

"May we please, Mama?'

The mother looks up; her thoughts are elsewhere.

'May we what, Alice?'

'Mama, you aren't *listening*!'

'Sorry, my darling.'

Her husband takes her hand, across the table. He smiles at her, she smiles back. They're relaxed together, and loving, but even so she's distracted.

'What time is the taxi coming? Did he say?'

'Ten o'clock. We have half an hour. Come on children, upstairs, teeth cleaned, at the double.'

Alice goes with her father, but her son hangs back, waiting

for her. He takes her hand, smiling at her.

'Don't worry, Mama, you have me with you.'

She ruffles his hair, touches his cheek with her fingers.

'I know that, and I'm very lucky.'

The taxi is punctual. They leave the windows wide open as they travel the six or seven miles of their journey. Alice sits on her father's knee, pointing at things ... *what's that in French? What's that?* He answers correctly when he can, makes up silly words when he doesn't know. She realises this, but repeats the words anyway; it's their joke.

Mother and son watch as they pass rusted vehicles idling outside broken-down farms, long abandoned. Shutters hang from blank windows. They see goats and one or two dairy cows grazing fields of lush grass.

'Will they build them again, Mama?'

'The farms? I'm sure they will, in time.'

When they arrive, there's someone there to meet them; her husband has arranged it. He's in uniform; smart, polite. He nods and salutes.

'This way Major, Madam.'

They follow him up a central path, past row upon row of headstones, glaring white in the morning sun. Ahead of them is a monumental cross, striking against the solid blue of the summer sky.

'Here it is, Sir.' He indicates one of the massed headstones, salutes again, then walks away to stand at a discreet distance.

When she sees the grave, the wife puts her hand to her mouth and tears well into her eyes. Her husband – he looks moved, too – puts his arm around her shoulder and they stand, just looking. Alice wanders along the row, touching the flowers planted there, their colours rich against the stone. It's very warm.

The boy kneels down in front of the headstone. With his

finger, he begins to trace the letters inscribed there:

CAPTAIN JAMES GEORGE ERRINGTON MC.

He looks up.

'He was very brave, my father, wasn't he, Papa?'

'He was, Jamie. He was a brave officer for his country. But he was also a loving husband to Mama and a good friend to me. And he would have been a wonderful father to you.'

'I know.'

His mother crouches down beside him. Underneath the name is *Aged 30*, and at the bottom:

GREATER LOVE HATH
NO MAN THAN THIS.

She isn't sure about it, whether it's true, but the words had seemed fitting.

'When you're ready, Jamie, stand beside the grave. We said we'd take a photograph for Uncle Ivan and Auntie Mary.'

'Wait … wait a minute.' The mother opens her bag and takes out a small box. Inside it, wrapped in velvet, is a metal cross on a purple and white ribbon.

'Here.' Her son stands with his arms straight by his sides as she pins it to the breast of his light summer jacket. It pulls the linen a bit so she smooths it flat again, then brushes his fringe back from his forehead.

'There, you're ready now.'

And so the boy stands, one hand resting on his father's headstone, his brown eyes squinting into the bright French sun.